BLOOD WORK

BLOOD WORK

MARK PEARSON

ISIS
LARGE PRINT
Oxford

First published in Great Britain 2009
by
Arrow Books
A Random House Group company

Published in Large Print 2010 by ISIS Publishing Ltd.,
7 Centremead, Osney Mead, Oxford OX2 0ES
by arrangement with
The Random House Group Limited

British Library Cataloguing in Publication Data
Pearson, Mark.
  Blood work.
  1. Police - - England - - London - - Fiction.
  2. Murder - - Investigation - - England - - London
  - - Fiction.
  3. Detective and mystery stories.
  4. Large type books.   LP
  I. Title
  823.9'2–dc22

ISBN 978–0–7531–8600–8 (hb)
ISBN 978–0–7531–8601–5 (pb)

Printed and bound in Great Britain by
T. J. International Ltd., Padstow, Cornwall

For Mum and Dad

Acknowledgements

This is a work of fiction and although all of the characters are indeed fictional some of the places mentioned within are real — so firstly a big apology to London! One of the most diverse, exhilarating and dynamic cities on the planet, and yet in these pages it comes across as rather a bleak place, to say the least; but all cities are viewed through different eyes and Jack Delaney's are a little more bloodshot and jaundiced than most. Some of the places mentioned in the book, however, are not real. Delaney works out of an entirely fictional police station and The Pig and Whistle is a pub that, sadly, does not exist; likewise a curious tourist would struggle to find South Hampstead Common or South Hampstead Tube or the Royal South Hampstead Hospital, but they would be well rewarded indeed, however, if they decided to check if the Holly Bush pub really did add a dash of wine to their Bloody Marys!

A lot of people should be thanked for the hard work they have put into bringing *Blood Work* to the bookshelf. And so, many thanks to James Nightingale, Tess Callaway and the lovely Caroline Gascoigne for their incredible help and support, the sales and marketing team from Hutchinson who did so much to get Jack Delaney out amongst the public, Justine for her eagle eye, Anna Hughes who handled the baton like an Olympiad and Robert Caskie for his continual encouragement and advice. Lucie Birnie of Lucy's Cafe for making me big in the Runtons and especially Lynn Butler for keeping my spirits high and the decanter full!

But the biggest thanks to you the reader, without whom Jack Delaney would just be a sad and bitter man, mumbling incoherently to himself in the corner of an empty bar as he sips his solitary pint.

The woman's muscles spasmed and as she floated towards consciousness she heard a man's voice, and what she heard made her want to scream and kick and thrash her arms. But she couldn't move. She had been drugged, she knew that. And the drugs held her paralysed. She could barely open her eyes a millimetre but it was enough to see what the man held in his hand and if she had been able to scream she would have ripped her lungs apart doing so.

The blade in the man's hands dipped and she could feel the flesh and muscles of her stomach parting. No pain. But she could feel it. She could see his head bending lower, his other hand reaching forth, reaching into her. Violating her. Then he stood back, holding a mass of tissue in his hand, blood dripping from it as if he was squeezing what he held. And she closed her eyes, willing it to stop. Suddenly she could feel the cool air, feel it lift the heat from her skin. As she sank deeper inside herself, she could picture that heat like a fine cloud of particles swirling up into the black inkiness of the night sky, separating, dissolving and lost to the universe.

And then she didn't feel anything at all.

MP

Prologue

A group of noisy, enthusiastic young men gathered around one corner of the bar of the Unicorn, a mock-Tudor pub. A large-screen TV was commanding their attention. England was playing South Africa in a friendly and the atmosphere in the pub was rowdy, but not aggressive.

Detective Inspector Jack Delaney stood at the other end of the bar and waited patiently for the young man, with short cropped hair and arms like strings of rope and the word "WRATH" tattooed in big, black letters along the length of one forearm, to get around to serving him. Any other day he would have been simmering with barely contained fury as the barman flirted with a couple of South African girls with hair as yellow as corn and strong, bright teeth. But Jack Delaney had other things to occupy his mind that night.

All things coalesce somewhere. All things come together in a pattern. He couldn't see it yet, but he knew it was there. Finding patterns was his job, after all, seeking what linked seemingly disassociated events. What Delaney did know just then, as he waited at the bar, with dark images flashing through his memory, was that he had a focus again. Something to help concentrate all the hurt and pain and anger he had lived with for four years into a single point of energy and use that to move forward out of the wreckage of his past, annihilating anything that got in his way. Jack Delaney didn't do standing still very well.

The barman's casual smile died as he approached Delaney.

"Help you?"

"Pint of Guinness and a pint of lager."

Delaney threaded his way back through the crowd, smiling almost imperceptibly at the pair of blonde women, who were straining quite noticeably the yellow and green fabric of their "Boks" rugby shirts, happy to draw attention to themselves. He put the drinks down on the table in front of his erstwhile boss who held a cigarette, as ever, in one hand and a lighter in the other.

Chief Inspector Diane Campbell looked up at him, a devil-may-care smile dancing in her puppy-brown eyes. "Fifty-pound fine, it's almost worth lighting the bastard up."

She held the cigarette aloft as if there may have been some doubt as to the identity of the illegitimate object.

Delaney pulled out a chair and sat down. "True."

"Meanwhile the fat cats of Westminster can smoke in their bar at the Houses of Parliament. Never mind their bleeding expenses, that's the real problem."

"Not going political on me, are you, Diane?"

Campbell whipped her neck, flicking her bobbed hair left and right. "Not in this lifetime."

2

"Good to hear."

Campbell looked at him for a moment, the mischief still in her eyes. "I saw Kate Walker talking with you at the cemetery."

"And?"

"Anything you want to tell me about that?"

Delaney took a long pull on his pint of Guinness and thought about it. Thought about Kate and her dark hair, her haunted eyes, her beauty. Her fragility. Remembering the hurt in her eyes as he had stood beneath the naked sky of a west London cemetery and told her that they had no future. He knew the damage that had been done to her as a child by her uncle, his ex-boss Superintendent Walker, knew that damage had scarred her as an adult, knew that that same uncle had tried to kill her because she was helping Delaney rescue his own child, Siobhan, from his clutches. Kate Walker had suffered enough, but he had made her suffer more. He'd already buried one wife, had carried the guilt of it for four years, and when it came to making a choice between the living and the dead . . .

He had chosen the dead.

He took another swallow of Guinness before putting the glass down and looking Campbell in the eye. "Not a thing."

"Wouldn't blame you if there was. She's got a fine figure on her for a brunette."

Delaney didn't smile. "We're about to put her uncle away for a long, long time, Diane. That's all I care about." He leaned across the table and gripped his ex-boss's hand. His grip was firm, uncompromising, but she neither flinched nor sought to release herself from his hold. "Just tell me what you've heard about my wife's death."

She nodded, and Delaney released his grip. She resisted the temptation to rub her hand but held Delaney's gaze as he took another long pull on his pint of Guinness.

"Kevin Norrell."

Delaney put his glass down, his voice arctic. "What about him?"

The water fell like hard rain. The kind of powerful, punching rain you get in a tropical downpour. Kevin Norrell put his hand against the cool white tiles of the prison shower and felt it pound his body, the jets of water like needles. He bared his teeth. If he had his way the man who had put him in this prison was very shortly going to get him out. The water sounded like rain too as it spattered and puddled around his feet. He'd never liked the sound. It reminded him of his father, Sean Norrell. The memory, as ever, making his hand form involuntarily into a hamlike fist as his mind wandered back to his childhood, the summer of 1977 and the first time he was ever incarcerated.

The Hunter's Moon was a spit-and-sawdust pub halfway between West Harrow and Harrow on the Hill, set in a concrete housing development built in the sixties, complete with a small, built-in shopping precinct. The pub was at the end of a row of shops including a laundromat, a convenience store, an

4

off-licence and a chemist. Three floors of council flats rose above the shops and pub, and were echoed on the opposite side of the street by four floors of similarly grey, utilitarian boxes. The Labour government's vision of utopian, urban living on the architect's drawing board may well have looked like a sunny vision of an ideal future; but whereas his green ink had imagined trees and benches and contented people, the stark concrete reality was inked in far more abrasive colours. The graffiti, though distinctly urban, certainly wasn't art, and couldn't be considered political, unless "Jane fucks Ted" counted. You could lay money on the fact that the romantic dauber wasn't referring to Edward Heath and Jane Fonda.

It was raining. The kind of constant, wind-blown, swirling, miserable rain that clogged up drains and sewers, and it went with the soulless, plastic signboards above chain-link shutters, the sick, yellow light that leaked from the street lamps, and the garbage that floated on the street like rats go with sewage, or pigeons go with shit.

Half past eight on a cold November's night and the reality of the place was as far removed from the architect's sunny vision as Sean "The Coat" Norrell was from a working grasp of quantum physics.

Inside the Hunter's Moon, the smoke hung heavy in the air, like a pale cloud. The lino on the floor was colourless and faded, but had once been red, presumably to hide bloodstains. The lights behind the bar were bright, though, as were the coloured lights in the jukebox that was pumping "Float On" through crackling speakers that, like the rumpled person standing at the bar, had long since seen better days. He was a long-haired, fifty-year-old man with a knee-length, black leather coat. He scowled as he ran filthy, dirt-stained fingers through his greasy locks of hair and winked at the barmaid as he sang along with the record. He cupped his crotch with the other hand and bucked his hips forward in a crude, suggestive motion.

The barmaid had been in the job for well over thirty years and hadn't been impressed by much in the last twenty-nine years of it. Her low-cut top revealed a chest as smooth as corrugated cardboard, and her rasping voice held as much affection as a wheel clamp. "I wouldn't touch your fucking cock, Sean, if I was wearing asbestos gloves."

Norrell leered at her and gave a final thrust. "Your loss, darling."

"Sit down, and shut the fuck up, Norrell," came a voice beside him.

Sean Norrell turned to say something but, when he saw who was standing next to him, the words died on his lips. He nodded a deferential smile and sat back on his stool, fumbling a cigarette nervously from a stained packet. He took a sip of his lager and scowled. Harp, thirty-two pence a pint now and it still tasted like cat's piss.

The man stood next to him was dressed in denim jeans, with a denim jacket, short blond hair and piercing, blue eyes. Mickey Ryan, thirty years old with a heart as cold as a Norwegian whore working al fresco. He looked at Norrell now with the kind of approval usually reserved for faecal matter discovered on footwear.

"You got my money?"

"It's in hand."

Ryan's voice was level, dispassionate as he leaned down and glared in his eyes. "Your dick will be in my left hand and I'll cut your fucking balls off with a rusty knife you haven't got it by Friday." The barmaid smiled, approvingly.

"You take my gear you pay me for it."

"I'm good for it, Mickey. You know that," Norrell muttered.

But Mickey had already turned back to the barmaid. "Double vodka."

She fluttered her spider-leg eyelashes at him and smiled seductively. "On the house."

Ryan looked back at Norrell, his eyes like flint. "You still here?"

Norrell hastily swallowed his lager as Mickey Ryan picked up his drink and headed back to the pool table where a couple of nineteen-year-olds, in skintight hot pants and platform shoes, waited for the territorial pat of his hand on their young backsides, marking ownership. He'd have liked to pick up a pool cue and smash it across Ryan's smug face. But as the blue-eyed man turned back to look at him pointedly, Norrell put his empty glass on the counter and scurried for the door. You didn't mess with Mickey Ryan. Not ever. Sean Norrell knew where to pick his fights and it wasn't at the Hunter's Moon.

He stepped out from the pub, blinking as the driving rain lashed his face and made his way across the street to the block of flats where he lived. He stumbled into the stairwell and held his hand against a concrete pillar to steady himself, and shake water rain from his long hair. He grunted and walked up the steps to his flat and fumbled his key into the lock of the faded red door of 13 Paradise Villas. They got that about right. Paradise in neon and street lamp. Nirvana by substance abuse. Heaven and hell in a fucking handcart.

He fumbled the door open and stumbled inside to domestic bliss. The theme tune to *The Good Life* was playing on the television, his runt of a son curled up on the stained, brown velour sofa watching it, his eyes fixed, not even glancing at him. Norrell's nose wrinkled at the smell of charred food.

"For fuck's sake, Linda. How fucking hard is it to cook a sausage?"

His wife, Linda Norrell, glared at him from the kitchen set off the small lounge. She was thirty-two but looked fifty, a sick fifty at that. Rail-thin, with straggly mousy hair that had, at some time, been dyed blonde, she was wearing a pair of tight, drainpipe jeans that made her legs look like sticks, a mauve shirt and a white tank top. The make-up on her face was applied with the delicacy of roadworks and did little to hide the bruising, or the emptiness, around her eyes. A cigarette dangled from tightly pursed lips as she flipped some sausages in a smoking pan, she looked across at her husband, expressionless for a moment, and then a light flickered somewhere in her eyes. "Fuck you, Sean."

On the sofa Kevin Norrell tensed. He knew what was about to happen next. On the television screen Barbara Good was telling her husband off for not wiping his wellies before coming into her kitchen. In his kitchen his father was slapping his wife open-handed across the mouth, opening up her lip to bleed afresh. Her screams of abuse mingled with his father shouting back at her, slapping the side of her head like a contrapuntal melody. And suddenly Kevin Norrell had had enough. Tom and Barbara Good might not have a television, but he did, and all he wanted to do was watch it.

The thin boy uncurled himself and stood up from the sofa. At school they called him Pencil Norrell. A gangly boy, tall for his age, his head disproportionately large, a head his neck seemed to struggle to hold up. Once of the older boys had stuck a condom over his head, and laughed as he almost suffocated. Pencil Norrell with a rubber top!

Kevin walked over to the kitchen table and picked up the almost empty bottle of cheap vodka that was stood on it. Lipstick marks smeared the spiralled glass at the top. He held it for a moment listening to the sound of his parents' invective mixing with the cutting bray of Tom Good's laugh. Then he smashed it against the wall. His parents stopped, and looked back at him astonished, their mouths agape like cartoon characters.

Sean Norrell was the first to find voice. "What the fuck you think you're doing?"

And Kevin Norrell punched the jagged, broken bottle forward, as hard as he could, stabbing it into his father's thigh. Sean Norrell squealed like a snared

9

rabbit and dropped to his knees, his hands cupping the wound, watching horrified as blood spilled through his spread fingers.

Thirty-two years later on and Norrell held up his own hand, letting the shower water run through his fingers, shaking his head as if to clear the memories.

His father hadn't died that night. The damage to his thigh was excruciating but treatable, an inch higher and it would have been his groin, the surgeon had pointed out, and that would have been a lot more serious. Sent home from hospital he managed to sell the remaining lump of cannabis resin he had left and pay Mickey Ryan most of what he owed him, not enough to save himself from a beating, mind, and the boys who gave him it laughed as they remembered that he had been nearly bottled in the nuts by his own son. They made sure to give him a kick or two in the groin before they were done. The kicking reopened the wound and Sean Norrell, rather than seeking medical attention, simply self-medicated with cheap whisky and strong lager and the wound became infected. He died some weeks later from septicaemia.

Norrell turned the shower off and wrapped his towel around himself. He had been in juvenile detention when he had heard the news of his father's death, and if he had shed a tear at the time it was certainly not through grief. As he left the shower block he nodded at a thickset man who occupied the cell next door to his. The man didn't meet his eye and Norrell knew it meant something. But he was ready. The time was long past when Kevin Norrell was going to be anybody's bitch. That interfering, bastard Irish copper was going to make sure of that.

Jack Delaney shrugged. "So he's not happy where he is. Why should we give a monkey's toss?"

"He claims he knew nothing about Walker's paedophile activities. He fears for his safety at Bayfield."

"The sooner that shite is put down like a rabid dog the better, you ask me."

"Not too soon. Norrell claims to know something about your wife's death. That's his bargaining chip. He says he'll only speak to you."

"And you'll let me do it?"

"I will if you're back on the force." Diane dug into her pocket and pulled out an unopened letter. "I never processed your resignation, Jack. Far as anyone knows you've been on extended leave these last weeks." She smiled once more. "Emotional problems."

"You must have been pretty sure about me."

Diane held the smile like a sniper cradles a rifle. "Men might not be to my taste, Jack. Doesn't stop me understanding them pretty damn well."

Delaney finished his pint and stood up.

"Where are you going?"

"I'm going to talk to him."

Campbell shook her head. "Not today. I've arranged the interview for tomorrow morning. Come on, cowboy. Sit down, I'll get you another pint."

Diane Campbell picked up his empty glass and headed for the bar, threading her way through the group of young men who had now started singing, "Get 'em down you Zulu warrior, get 'em down you Zulu chief." She had never understood what the song was about, and the prospect of seeing a naked man, however young and fit, held as much attraction for her as a Cherry Cola held for Jack Delaney. She waited at the bar for the drinks and looked back at him. She had put her career on the line keeping him in his job. Bringing down Superintendent Walker, however guilty he might have been, had not enamoured Delaney to the senior brass. In fact she had to outright lie to the powers that be to keep him out of jail, let alone keep his warrant card. Possession of an unlicensed firearm was not looked upon with favour, not to mention the little matter of nearly killing one of her sergeants. That the sergeant in question, Eddie Bonner, helped to cover up Walker's activities was neither here nor there. Sergeant Bonner was dead and, whatever forensic pathologist Kate Walker might think, the dead did not make good witnesses. Diane handed the barmaid the correct change, flashed her a flirty smile then walked back to Delaney carrying the drinks carefully through the packed bar. It might very well come back and bite her on her bony arse, but she reckoned she had done the right thing. Delaney was a good man to have in her camp, she knew that much about him if little else.

Diane handed the Irishman his pint, spying the barely contained violence in brown eyes and figured Norrell better not be yanking on the cowboy's lariat.

★ ★ ★

Kevin lay on the top bunk in his cell squeezing an exercise ball, the tendons of his hand standing out like ropes of wire as he contracted it. The man below him fidgeted nervously. Norrell didn't blame him. Like the man in the shower, he wouldn't meet his eyes. Something was in the air. He could almost taste the tension. Norrell smiled humorously as he squeezed the ball again. Whatever it was he would be ready to meet it, or die trying. One way or another he was getting out of prison.

Diane Campbell glanced across at the pub windows, noticing that the rain had eased up a little. She sipped on her third glass of mineral water and looked across at Delaney. There was a glassy look in his eyes now, less anger and a softer focus. Not surprising since he had moved on to drinking Scotch with his Guinness, for some reason insisting on Glenmorangie rather than his favoured Bushmills, and had had six or seven doubles. She wasn't sure that he hadn't slipped in a quick one or two when she had gone to the Ladies. Never mind about the ban on smoking in pubs, what about putting enough cubicles in and banning women from using the place like a lounge for gossip? She didn't envy a man his penis, that was for sure, but she did admire its functional practicality. She swallowed her drink. She was desperate for a cigarette. Diane looked at Delaney pointedly. "Come on, cowboy, drink up. I'm taking you home."

Delaney looked at her steadily, the very faintest of slurs in his voice. "I've got my car outside."

"Yeah, and that's where it's staying. You're not causing anyone else's death this month. Not on my watch."

Delaney laughed. "Did you really just say 'not on my watch', Diane?"

"You heard it, partner. The mule is staying parked right where you left it, and I'm taking you back to the High Chaparral."

Delaney shook his head as he stood up. "Just drop me off at a Tube station."

"Which one?"

"Northern Line." He drained his pint of Guinness, coaxed the last drop of whisky from his glass into his mouth and walked with her to the door. He was almost balanced.

Kate Walker didn't normally take the Tube. It wasn't so much that she was a snob, she just didn't like the crammed-in, close proximity of people. It wasn't just the look of them or the smell of them — which was bad enough with their wet, rain-sodden clothes — but she knew what people were capable of, the extent of their random cruelties. As a forensic pathologist she knew that far better than most. If she had learned the hard way that you couldn't trust the people you were related to or worked with . . . then you sure as hell couldn't trust strangers. She wouldn't be taking the Tube at all, in fact, but her car was booked in at the garage for a service and an MOT, and her mechanic wouldn't be dropping it back at her house until the early evening. So she had gone by train and taxi to the cemetery for

14

the funeral earlier that afternoon of the caretaker who had been murdered in the course of Delaney's last case. She was pleased she had been able to take flowers for the grave, but in all other ways the journey had been wasted. She had hoped to be able to speak to Jack, discuss what happened with them, but she might as well have been speaking to the dead caretaker for the amount of emotional response she got from Delaney. The prospect of going straight home to an empty house had depressed her even more and so she had spent the rest of the afternoon shopping and buying nothing. Nothing fitted. Nothing was right. Nothing shifted the black cloud of her mood. And so here she was now, stuck on the Tube with a bunch of people she neither knew nor felt any inclination to know.

She looked down at her court shoes. Expensive, chic, sexy, she thought. Black suited her colouring. The shoes were now spattered with mud and rain and the shine had come off them, just like the shine had come off her day.

The train juddered to a halt, mid-tunnel, and the lights in the carriage flickered and dimmed before coming back up. She positioned her heel in one of the grooves that ran along the floor and swivelled her foot, wondering when they were going to update the trains. It took just over a couple of hours to get from Paris to St Pancras on the Eurostar fast link nowadays, but it could take an age just to go a few stops on this damned service. The lights dimmed again; low and yellow. Kate looked along the length of the carriage. There was something curiously Gothic about the Northern Line,

15

she thought. Other lines, other stations had a late-Victorian sensibility to them, she knew that, but the Northern Line in places had a quintessentially spooky feel to it. Wood and brass and strange lamps, transportation by Hammer House of Horror.

The train shuddered and clanked as the wheels started turning again. She looked out of the window as the train flashed noisily through the tunnel once more and pulled her coat tight about her. It was early evening and the train was full, its motion, as it rocked from side to side, throwing the overweight man next to her against her body every time the train rounded a corner. He didn't seem too keen to move away, either, perfectly happy to invade her personal space. She sighed and gritted her teeth.

She was in a foul mood. Jack Delaney, the son of a bitch. She didn't know why she let him get to her, but he did. Kate Walker, in her own opinion, was, if anything, a woman born of logic, of reason. She was clinical, sharp; her judgement a precision instrument. Only that instrument was letting her down lately, and she didn't know how to fix it. She looked out of the window again, seeing her reflection smudgy and blurred, and that was exactly how she felt. Smudgy and blurred. She wasn't sure quite who she was any more. She leaned against the side of the train, putting as much space between her and the fat man as possible and felt a shiver run up her spine. Somebody was walking on her grave. Dancing on it. She looked around expecting to see someone watching her, but, if they were, they had looked away. Looking away was the

English virtue after all. Never get involved, never show your emotions, never get off the boat. Maybe Jack Delaney was more English than he would have liked to admit. There was a man who was never going to get off the boat.

Delaney stood in the carriageway, swaying with the rhythm of the train, holding on to a strap hanger and keeping his balance, just about, as the train bucked and shifted under his feet as it rattled noisily through the underground tunnels.

He should have let Diane Campbell take him home, back to his sterile new house in Belsize Park. He should have left the pub after just one drink and then made a start on the decorating, making the place a home and not just a house. Somewhere where his daughter Siobhan would want to visit, would want to stay a few days with him. But Delaney didn't do one quick drink, and he hadn't wanted to go home, it didn't feel like home to him, nowhere had for a long time. Those dark thoughts hadn't been turned off yet and he didn't think they would. Not tonight. Tonight he needed more than alcohol to fight his demons.

He wished he had never visited the cemetery. He'd told Kate Walker that he'd only gone because he owed it to the old man who had taken a bullet for him. But it wasn't true. He'd gone to see her and now he wished he hadn't. It wasn't a time for complications. He had a focus now and he needed to keep that focus, but Kate had set a fire burning, created a physical thirst that he needed to quench.

17

A man leaned against him as the train turned a corner and Delaney looked back at him and the man quickly moved away, half muttering an apology and avoiding eye contact.

Delaney watched the man move through the crowded train, keen to put distance between them and Delaney didn't blame him. Tomorrow he was going to take steps. People were going to pay for what happened four years ago and pay in blood. But tonight he could taste the iron and copper in his mouth, could feel the murmurs in his blood like the low thrumming of a bass string. Tonight Delaney had another agenda.

He looked ahead, past the crowded-together commuters who were packed into the carriageway with the resigned look of cattle being herded to slaughter and as some stood up to disembark he saw the dark-haired woman. She was looking at her own reflection in the window as the train jolted and the lights dipped, yellow and sulphurous, so that Delaney's brown eyes smouldered in the low light like a hunting wolf's.

He came to a decision and reached into his pocket as the train clattered to a standstill.

Kate walked out of the Tube station scowling as the wind came howling up Hampstead High Street sweeping the rain into her face. She stepped back into the entrance and waited for the weather to abate. She looked at her watch, still not relishing the idea of going back to her empty house, but she had a film on DVD to watch and three-quarters of a bottle of Cloudy Bay chilling in her fridge. Damn Delaney, she thought for the hundredth time that day, wishing again, also for the hundredth time, that she'd never gone to the funeral. She tried to persuade herself that she'd gone for the old man, not on the off chance of seeing that ungrateful Irish bastard. She'd nearly put her life on the line to save his miserable skin, not to mention that of his daughter's, and what thanks did she get? Used and discarded. He made her feel like the cheap kind of whore he obviously felt comfortable with. She strode angrily out into the rain, sod the man, her life had been on hold for long enough. Time to push the play button, and not on the DVD machine. She hurried up the street towards the Holly Bush. Physician, heal thyself, that's what they said, didn't they? Well, she was going to write out a large prescription in her own name: vodka-based, repeat as required.

She crossed the street and, as she did, she felt that familiar tingle in her spine again, but, as she blinked the rainwater from her eyes and looked back, she couldn't see anyone following her. She hurried on up the slight hill, keeping her face down and angled away from the rain. Within minutes she was pulling the old, heavy door behind her, closing out the wind and the weather, the rainwater dripping from her black overcoat on to the rough wooden floor of the pub as she shook her hair and wiped a hand across her eyes, hoping her waterproof mascara was holding up and hearing the sweet, soulful tones of Madeleine Peyroux cutting across the chatter in the room. They didn't always have music playing; the manager said that the hubbub of

19

conversation was the real music of the place and she agreed with him. It was just part of what made the pub special. Tonight though she was grateful for the music, it shielded her from other people's thoughts.

As she knew it would be, even this early, the pub was busy. She walked up to the right-hand bar where luckily there was a vacant stool. She pulled it forward, sat on it and smiled briefly at the young, Australian barman behind the counter. "Large one please, Stuart."

The barman nodded back at her, lifted up a jug of ready-made Bloody Mary and poured Kate a glass. Kate took a long pull, the sharp kick of vodka mingling with the bite of the pepper and the tang of the celery salt. She took another sip and sighed. Time to heal.

Janet Barnes had never had to work hard at soliciting admiring glances from men; her ex-boyfriend, a failed stand-up comic, said that she had the kind of body that pouted if it didn't get attention. Usually she enjoyed that attention, but tonight there was one man in particular who was looking at her from across half the length of the train carriage, and her skin crawled. She pulled her raincoat tight around her, but if anything it just accentuated her lush, curvy figure. She looked out of the window, the featureless rush of Victorian brick wall flickering past scant inches away. There was talk of London flooding in the news again. Steps being made to improve the Thames Barrier. She remembered the flooding of last year. Whole areas, families, homes, lives ruined in the North of England. She couldn't help wondering what would happen here if the Thames were to ever break its banks. The Underground system would be flooded. Thousands of tonnes of water would pour into the network. Would the passengers all be drowned or electrocuted? All those electric rails running everywhere. Another problem for that Eton-educated, class clown Boris Johnson to sort out. Not a problem for her, mind. Any luck and she'd be out of the miserable city long before that happened, if it ever did. Just a few more quid saved up, a few more months, get the winter over with and she'd be out of the capital, out of the country and over the mountains she'd fly to sunny bloody Spain. Put this miserable, sodding, rain-drenched country behind her once and for bloody good. Just because she dressed like a goth didn't mean she had to live like a bloody vampire, time for a change of image she reckoned.

Her double reflection in the windows, hovering over the flashing bricks, was smeared and bleary, a ghostly dull orange from the flickering lights in the tube carriage. She was sure, though, she could still make out the dark-haired man watching her. Good-looking, she supposed, but definitely something creepy about him, the way he stared at her when he thought she wasn't watching. She wouldn't be surprised if he was having a crafty hand shandy under the dark coat he was wearing. If she had a five-euro note for every time some man had accidentally brushed up against her in the crowded tube with a hard-on in his pants and a glassy look to his eyes she could have retired and moved to Spain years ago. She could have papered the road there and back with them.

The lights in the Northern Line tunnel brightened, and the train shuddered into Camden Town Tube station like a mechanical climax. She stood up and tightened the belt on her shiny, black, mid-thigh-length raincoat. She knew it did little to distract attention away from herself but didn't care. She was a living Betty Boop. People could look all they like. If they wanted to touch, however, that was a whole separate matter. A whole different negotiation.

She stood on the right of the escalator, some people packed around her and others rushing up the stairs to her left. God only knew what they were in such a hurry for, she thought. At the top of the stairs Janet flashed her Oyster card at the bored-looking Rastafarian who had opened the barrier, which had broken down again, and walked towards the left-hand exit, scowling as the wind blew the rain into her face. She turned back, certain she could feel the eyes of the dark-haired man, now lost in the steady throng of commuters, watching her still. Shaking off the thought she opened up her umbrella and walked out on to the pavement.

It was half past six and the streets were busy, people hustling to the warmth of pubs and restaurants, or pouring like a stream of wet ants into the shelter of the Underground. Janet walked away from the noise and the bustle of the main high street, and the clack of her sharp-heeled footsteps rang out as she walked along Kentish Town Road, fighting to keep control of her umbrella in the swirling wind. After a couple of hundred metres she was grateful to see the welcoming glow of light spilling from the windows of the

Devonshire Arms. She folded her umbrella down, opened the door to the pub and stepped inside.

Since the closing of the Intrepid Fox in Wardour Street the Devonshire Arms was now regarded as London's Goth Central. Janet's jet-black hair, black skirt, leggings, T-shirt and make-up were about as unusual there as a pair of chinos and a striped shirt in All Bar One. In fact, some nights, if you weren't dressed all in black, you couldn't get in, and quite right too, Janet thought. There were plenty of places for the squares and the geeks and the city slickers to go to, places that would turn people dressed like her away. That was the thing about London: a place for every prejudice.

The lighting was low, and the pub was already busy. Janet had chosen it for the meet, for just that purpose. It was like a blind date, after all, and it was best to be prepared; in addition to the pack of condoms and the tube of lubricant that she carried in her handbag, she also had a small can of mace. She had smuggled it back illegally from a long weekend trip she had made to New York some months ago.

Music was playing, muting the buzz of chatter that filled the air. The Velvet Underground. She ordered a bourbon from a bald-headed woman with multicoloured tattoos snaking either side of her neck, and sat in the corner of the bar sipping it and watching people as she listened to the music. John Cale's viola screeched discordantly against the slow, hypnotic beat of the drums while Lou Reed sang about a woman not unlike herself. A girlchild dressed in black wearing boots of shiny leather.

The music stopped and Janet looked up as a dark-haired man approached. Hunger in his brown eyes and an amused smile playing on his soft red lips. She looked down at his snakeskin boots that had Cuban heels almost higher than hers, then looked back up at him and smiled herself, her painted lips opening to reveal white, perfect teeth.

"Hello, cowboy."

Kate finished her second Bloody Mary. The two drinks had done little to lift her dark mood, but she was feeling just a little bit more numb. The edge had been taken off, and she was certainly warmer. She looked over at the rain lashing against the windowpanes and then looked at her watch, debating. It was only a short walk home, but she didn't want to go out in the filthy weather again. She held her glass out to the barman, who went to refill it, and slipped her jacket off, hanging it on a hook in the bar in front of her.

"You tried Nigella's?"

She turned round to see that a tall curly dark-haired man in his late thirties with brown eyes was talking to her.

"I'm sorry?"

"Nigella Lawson. Her recipe for Bloody Marys. It's very good."

The barman handed Kate her drink and went off to add the charge to her tab.

24

"No, I don't think I have." Kate turned back to her drink.

"Got to love a woman who puts Bloody Marys in the breakfast section of a cookbook."

"I guess," Kate said without looking at the stranger and sipped her drink. She wasn't in the mood for chit-chat.

Despite her blatant disinterest the man was not put off. He pulled out the recently vacated stool next to hers. "Do you mind?"

Kate shrugged indifferently.

The man chuckled. "Half a pint glass with half as much vodka as tomato juice. For breakfast! Like I say, you've got to admire the woman."

Kate thought that if the woman cut down on her breakfasts a little it might not do her any harm. But maybe that's what men wanted. Meat on the bones. Well, she wasn't going to put on weight to imitate some quasi-Italian domestic goddess, however gorgeous she was. She realised the man had spoken to her again, but didn't have a clue what he had said.

"I'm sorry?"

"I asked . . . do you know what her secret is?"

Yes, she thought. She knew what her secret was all right. She looked like a woman of appetite. What was it you were supposed to be? A lady in the supermarket and a whore in the bedroom. Well, Nigella Lawson looked like Sophia Loren with a voice that oozed sex and sophistication in equally unfair measures. And could cook to boot. Bitch.

"I don't," she said simply.

25

The man smiled. He had quite a nice smile. "It's to add a dash of dry sherry."

Kate nodded. "They put a drop of red wine in them here."

He smiled again. "My name's Paul. Paul Archer."

"Nice to meet you, Mr Archer." Kate's voice was cordial, but cool.

The man held out his hand. "Actually, it's Dr Archer."

Kate hesitated then shook his hand. He had a firm confident grip, and his hand was dry and warm. She smiled and it didn't take much of an effort now. "Kate Walker."

"Well, Kate. Can I buy you a drink?"

Kate looked down at her glass, swirling the drink for a moment then downing it and placing the glass firmly back on the bar. Why not? she thought to herself. Why the bloody hell not?

Janet Barnes felt consciousness returning. Not suddenly, it was a struggle like crawling through treacle. Like waking from a long coma. Or nearly waking, that is. Flashes of memory fought to come through as she fell back into the nightmare she was struggling to escape. A train swaying off balance as it rattled along the spine of ancient rails that lay deep beneath an even more ancient city. She felt the eyes of men upon her. Eyes that peeled her clothes from her body. Sweating eyes. Hot, dry, hungry eyes. The sick yellow light of the train carriage wrapped itself around her again as she tried to raise herself to consciousness once more.

26

She had no idea where she was or how long she had been there. She moaned softly, the sigh escaping her lips like the last breath of a dying man. Her eyelids fluttered briefly, the orbs beneath darting back and forth under the fragile pink membrane, as images flashed through her cerebral cortex like the sparking of a badly wired circuit, and, as she drifted towards unconsciousness once more, she thought she heard snatches of conversation, a voice she almost recognised. She tried to latch on to the thought, but it was like a butterfly dancing out of her hands and high out of reach. Then her eyes stilled and the half-formed thought, and all others with it, floated away entirely as she fell back into oblivion.

Day One

Six thirty and fog hung in the morning air like lowlying cloud.

Arnold Fraser shambled through the wet undergrowth on South Hampstead Common. He had spent the previous night huddled in the entrance to the local Tube station. In a different life he once had been a sergeant in the Royal Green Rifles, but he had come back from the first Gulf war with a shattered right femur and a broken mind. In a country that treats its old war heroes with pomp and ceremony every November and its returning soldiers rather less well, he ended up, like many of his comrades lucky enough to make it home, as an alcoholic, mentally ill and living on the cold and comfortless streets of London. Early commuters had disturbed his lager-fuelled sleep and he was setting out across the common to a homeless shelter where he could get a hot cup of tea and a moderately warm bacon sandwich.

His bladder full, he stopped to relieve himself against a tree, but even as he fumbled with his trouser zipper, hidden deep under many layers of shirts, jumpers and coats, he saw the body lying in the undergrowth near

28

his feet, saw the unnatural pallor of her skin, alabaster against the black shine of her hair, and knew it for what it was. He had seen enough corpses in his days of service. He turned away and shuffled off. He'd learned that in the army as well. Never volunteer. Never get involved. He'd done that once for Queen and Country and what had he got for his troubles? Royally fucked over, that's what. He spat and limped onwards. Let the citizens deal with it.

Seven o'clock. Kevin Norrell was back in the communal shower room of Bayfield Prison. He took the towel from his waist, put it to one side and twisted the dial set into the wall, standing beneath the jets of water as he let them pummel his massive, chemically enhanced body and groaned in satisfaction. He had spent the last hour lifting weights in the prison gym. Being on remand had not affected his workout routines at all and he intended to leave in better physical condition than he entered. Having an office right across the road from a burger bar had helped put a layer of fat over the hard muscles of his stomach. But that fat was being quickly burned away, and with every bench press he had but a single thought in his mind. Kevin Norrell didn't intend spending much more time inside prison walls and to escape he needed to be moved to another, lower security facility. He grunted as he turned the heat up on the shower. He'd already made a start towards the road to freedom and this morning he'd take another step and it wouldn't be long before he was moved to the prison of his choice. He could practically guarantee it.

He poured some shower gel in his hand, his eyes flicking back and forth watchfully as he did so. It was a reflex you needed to develop in prison, if you wanted to survive, and if Kevin Norrell had learned one thing in all his time over the years in institutions and prisons it was that you never dropped your guard. Put it in the bank. You dropped your guard and you'd be fucked ten ways by Sunday. Especially in the shower. He continued soaping his body and let the powerful jets pummel the suds away, but he kept the shampoo from his hair, keeping his eyes clear. As he reached up to turn the shower off he felt, rather than saw, the three men who approached, moving on him fast now. He flailed out instinctively, slamming his ham-like fist sideways, crushing one man's throat and knocking him down before the others held his arm and two more came into the shower room. He felt himself being pushed to the floor, and charging foward he fell; landing on one knee in a toilet stall, he reached out, putting his arms around the stainless-steel base of the lidless toilet and gripping hard. One of the men pummelled his head with a heavy fist as the other kicked him viciously in the ribs, trying to dislodge him. He felt a rib crack. Norrell grunted with pain and anger and wrenched upward, tearing the bowl clear from the floor as his steroid-enhanced, brute strength ripped the screws free. He roared up, red-faced, furious with effort and smashed the bowl full into the face of the first man, the second slipping on the water that was now gushing from the exposed plumbing. He smashed the bowl again, turning the fallen man's head into a shapeless mass of blood and hair, and swung the bowl at the head of another man who was trying to escape, the man screamed like a frightened pig as the lavatory bowl smashed into his jaw, pulverising it. There were just two of his attackers left now but they backed off as he turned and snarled at them, holding the steel toilet bowl like the weapon of a demented, lavatorial gladiator. Norrell moved towards them but his right foot slipped on the wet floor and he dropped to his knee again, wincing with pain as his cracked rib flexed. One of the men jumped forward at him, a blade flashing in the brightness of the overhead lights, and a thin shaft of steel was punched hard into his ribcage. His other knee buckled and he dropped to the floor barely registering the shouts and cries of uniformed guards running into the room. His vision blurred and he struggled to draw air, his breath a painful, wet wheeze. He tried to raise himself up but those muscles that defined him in more senses than one, those muscles that had been built over years of dedicated and painful exercise, failed him at last. He slumped back on to the cold tiles like an exhausted walrus and as the blood pumped from his body, the room seemed to darken and the light, very slowly, faded from his eyes.

A muffled knocking sound brought Delaney groaning to consciousness. He half opened a gummed-up eye and cursed as a bright, white light stabbed into his sore optic nerves. He held an arm across his face and groaned again. As far he could tell, he was lying, fully dressed, on a cold concrete floor, but he had absolutely no idea where. A sharp pain lanced through the back of his skull as he tried to move, and he gasped out loud. He crinkled his eyes again to open them a merest crack. He was in a white room. Bare white walls, white ceiling and a painted concrete floor. A light bulb dangled overhead and there was a low, mechanical, murmuring hum coming from somewhere close by. Delaney's head felt like he had been hit by a heavy, blunt object, but he had no memory of it. He rolled to one side, wincing with pain, and slowly opened one eye again. As his vision blurred into near focus he could make out a chest freezer against the opposite wall from where he was lying. He realised that was where the humming was coming from. The knocking resumed and Delaney suddenly realised where he was. He had made it home, but only as far as his garage. He rolled over again, covering his eyes, and tried to ignore the knocking which was becoming more urgent now, snatches of memory coming back to him of the night that had just passed.

But the knocking persisted. Delaney stood up, wincing as the blood flowed through the sore and swollen areas of his brain and lurched to the garage door. He opened it, shielding his face against the sudden lash of wind and rain that spiralled in, and looked angrily over at the attractive young woman, dressed in a smart black suit, who was standing on his front doorstep.

"What the hell are you doing here, Sally?"

DC Sally Cartwright smiled at him, enthusiasm and energy radiating from her like a Ready Brek advert.

"The chief inspector thought —"

"She thought what?" Delaney barked. And regretted it immediately.

"She thought that you might like someone to drive you for your meeting with Norrell. She mentioned dropping you off at the Tube station last night."

"Did she?"

Sally smiled again, innocently. "She suspected you might not have gone straight home, sir."

Delaney flapped his hand and gestured her in. "'Meeting', you make it sound like a bloody sales conference, and for God's sake, come in, Constable."

Sally walked into the built-in garage, gratefully shutting the door on the wind and rain behind her.

"What the hell happened to summer?"

"Don't know, sir."

"Come through."

Delaney led her through the garage up a couple of small steps and into the kitchen that lay off it. It was almost as bare as the garage. White modern units, but nothing personal, no pictures or furniture. A kettle on the countertop. A couple of mugs. A whisky tumbler. Delaney opened some cupboards, scowled and shut them again. "Have you got any Nurofen on you, Sally?"

She shook her head. "Sorry, sir."

"Co-codamol? Paracetamol? Aspirin? Anadin? Ibuprofen? Panadol?"

"Don't use them, sir."

Delaney slammed a drawer shut, frustrated, and again regretted it. "You'll learn," he said, wincing.

"I've got a line of coke."

Delaney looked across at her, half hopeful, and Sally laughed. "Joking, sir."

Delaney nodded. "Not funny, Constable." There was a time when Delaney had used the stuff, and not that long ago. Only a little dab now and again, mind, a wet tip of a finger's worth, to keep him sharp. But the business with Walker and Bonner had made him more circumspect. He'd never been a user. Whiskey was his drug of choice, even using the Scottish variety lately. And cigarettes of course. The day they made them illegal was the day he resigned for good. He fumbled in his pockets and pulled out a packet. "You got a lighter, Sally?"

"You shouldn't smoke in the house, sir."

"It's my goddamn house."

"Exactly. And you want to keep it nice, sir." She smiled, taking the edge of her words. "For your daughter's sake."

Delaney cursed and stuffed the packet back in his jacket pocket then sketched a hand in the air. "What do you think of it?"

Sally smiled politely. "Very minimalist."

Delaney opened another cupboard and found a jar of coffee. "Not got round to sorting it out yet."

"How long have you been here?"

"A week."

"Just a suggestion, but maybe some furniture."

"You any idea what this cost?"

34

Sally shrugged. "Three-bedroomed house, integral garage, Belsize Park? Way out of my league."

"An arm and a fucking leg that's what it cost me. You want to investigate serious fraud, look into the price of property."

"You don't have to tell me."

Delaney found a couple of mugs and poured some coffee into them. "Karl Marx had the right of the matter, I reckon." He opened the integrated fridge and cursed. "No frigging milk."

Sally smiled. "I'm all right anyway, sir."

"Well, you bloody would be. We'll get one on the way. Just have a seat and look shiny. I won't be a minute."

Delaney opened the door to the lounge. Sally went through to the lounge as Delaney headed upstairs. It was a large room with French windows leading on to a small courtyard garden. Like the kitchen the lounge was noticeably devoid of furniture, but there were some packing cases, one of which had a small television sitting on top of it. The walls were bare. The house, unlike its owner, was a blank canvas.

Sally sat on one of the packing cases and felt a spark of jealousy. A three-bedroomed house spitting distance from the station. Like she had said it was far more than her salary could afford, could ever afford looking at the way house prices had gone, never mind the recent fall. Ten per cent or twenty per cent off bleeding expensive was still way out of her league. She hoped Delaney got round to buying some furniture and making it a proper home soon, though. Criminal waste otherwise. Delaney had only bought the house, she knew, so that his young daughter, Siobhan, could visit him sometimes. After the death of his wife, Delaney's life had been such a train wreck that he didn't even have to think about it when his sister-in-law, Wendy, offered to look after his young girl. That was four years ago, though, his daughter was now seven years old, and the fact that Delaney had wanted to make a home for her with him, at least for some of the time, was a mark of how much he had changed, even in the little time she had known him. The poor girl had been through a lot recently, her aunt stabbed in her own home while Siobhan was held captive upstairs by his deranged ex-boss Superintendent Walker. Delaney and Kate Walker had arrived just in time to save them both; she shuddered at the thought of what might have happened if they hadn't. But Wendy had survived, though she had needed several weeks' recuperation in a private hospital and would be discharged soon. Perhaps Siobhan could get some stability back in her young life. Sally decided she would do her bit, she'd get Delaney to furnish his house properly if she had to drag him down to Ikea herself!

A short while later and Delaney was back downstairs. He'd had a shave, changed his shirt and put some eye drops in. He didn't look a million dollars she thought, but it was a vast improvement to the raw-eyed man who had greeted her at the garage door. A couple of hundred euros maybe.

"Come on, then." Delaney led her back through the garage and out into the rain. He scowled up at the sky.

"What's the deal? We don't get autumn any more, it just goes straight from summer to winter."

"Global warming, sir."

"Global warming my arse. In the seventies they reckoned it was the Russians fucking about with the weather. But do you know what it's really down to, Detective Constable?"

"Sir?"

"England, Sally. That's what it's down to. God's punishing us, each and every one of us. And He's doing it by making us live in this shitehole of a country."

Sally followed him out the door, not replying. She guessed some people just weren't morning persons.

The window was slightly open and the wind whistling outside knocked the blind against the wooden frame with an inconsistent rhythm. Kate woke slowly. Lifting one eyelid, she winced a little and closed it again. She murmured softly and turned on to her side. She reached out a hand and snaked her fingers through the man's curly hair and smiled. "Jack, wake up."

She slid her hand down over his shoulder to tangle her fingers in his chest hair, only his skin was completely smooth. She frowned, puzzled for a moment, then her smile faded, her eyes shot open with realisation and she looked, horrified, at the naked man sleeping beside her in her bed.

"Shit!"

She turned over again and looked at the clock radio on her bedside cabinet. It was half past seven. She cursed again and tried to remember what had happened the night before. And couldn't.

"Shit."

Quarter to eight and the rain was still falling, although lighter than it had been. Detective Inspector Jack Delaney and Detective Constable Sally Cartwright were stamping their feet as they stood outside "Bab's Kebabs" burger van round the corner from the police station. Roy, the corpulent owner and chef, was flipping bacon on the hot griddle plate as Delaney and Sally sheltered from the persistent drizzle as much as they could under the awning.

"Point in case . . ." He pointed his egg slice at Delaney. "What did you reckon of Madonna's 'American Pie', Inspector?"

Delaney shrugged. "I liked it."

"Yeah, well, you would. My point exactly. Every man and his dog in the rest of the world thinks it's a piece of shit, but you like it."

"It's a song, not a sacred cow. People should be more tolerant."

Roy laughed. "Ever heard of the pot and the kettle?" He fixed Delaney with a puzzled expression. "I heard you'd quit the job anyway."

"I did."

"What happened then?"

"Shit happened, Roy. You ought to know about that. And they needed me to clean it up. Only man for the job."

Roy winked at Sally. "And I bet you're right glad to have this little ray of bog-trotting sunshine back."

Sally laughed. "We're all glad."

Roy shook his head. "Yeah, well, I wouldn't be betting any large change on that."

Delaney stirred some sugar in his coffee. "You got that right."

Sally took a sip of her herbal tea. "Why?"

"He put down some of your own, Detective Constable. Never very popular thing to do."

Delaney scowled at Roy. "I didn't sign up for the police force to win popularity contests."

Roy handed a bacon sandwich over the counter to him. "Just watch your back is all I'm saying, cowboy. You put the Pied Piper away, doesn't mean there isn't more of the vermin that were on his payroll still on the job, scratching their feet and sniffing their noses in the air." He looked pointedly across as a couple of uniforms approached.

Delaney took a bite out of his sandwich. "I'll bear it in mind." He turned back to Sally. "Come on, let's get out of here."

Roy called after him. "Madonna? My doughnut more like!"

Delaney walked off, Sally took a couple of gulps of her tea and threw the cup in the black plastic dustbin at the side of the van. "Cheers, Roy."

"De nada. And you watch your back too, Detective Constable. That man is a disaster area in size ten brogues."

Sally winked at him. "At least you know where you are with him."

Roy nodded. "In fucking trouble most like." Roy turned to the two uniformed constables who had arrived and were watching Sally hurry after Delaney with undisguised appreciation. Roy grunted at them. "Out of your league, boys. Out of your league."

"Just give us a couple of bacon rolls, Roy."

Roy leaned forward confidentially. "Can I interest you lads in some pirate DVDs?"

The older uniform sighed patiently. "Go on?"

"I've got *Treasure Island*, *The Black Hawk*, and of course *Pirates of the Caribbean*, the complete boxed set."

Neither of the uniforms laughed.

Kate stood for a long while in the bathroom. The clothes she had been wearing last night were in a heap in the corner. She pulled the belt tight around the towelling robe she had on and looked at herself in the mirror. Her waterproof mascara had lived up to its name, but her eyeshadow and lipstick were smeared and her face looked pale against the almost black of her tangled and disarrayed curls. Whatever slight tan she might have picked up in the summer months seemed to have disappeared overnight. She walked across to the shower unit and put her hand on the tap. She held it there for a moment or two, the metal chill on her hand. And then she took it away again. She wouldn't shower that morning. She took the towelling robe off and carefully folded it, then picked up her clothing from the night before and dressed herself.

In 1903 Holloway Prison became a purely women-only facility. Coupled with the ending of transportation and the closing of Newgate, it meant a new prison for male offenders had to be built, a place to house those prisoners who were to be evicted to accommodate the fairer sex. The site chosen in the last, dying breaths of the Victorian era was a bit of undeveloped park and scrubland some two miles or so south of Hampstead Heath and a mile or so west of Delaney's new house in Belsize Park. Bayfield Prison was an all-categories facility that held up to six hundred prisoners. As the urban wealth of Hampstead and Belsize Park spread further out, the building was an incongruous intruder, a social blot on an increasingly upmarket landscape. But it lay hidden in its own ten acres of land, tall trees sheltering the place from view on the main road; it was still a lot closer, in many ways, to Kilburn than it was to Hampstead.

Sally pulled up at the iron gates that stood at the end of the long driveway and waited for the uniformed guard to check her identification. She wound her window down, flinching as the rain lashed at her face, and held her warrant card out. The guard grunted, monosyllabically, then waved her forward and signalled to the guard house. Electric motors whirred and the heavy iron gates swung open. Sally slipped the car in first gear and drove down through the gates and along the quarter-mile or so of private road that led up to the prison.

"What's Norrell got to say do you think, guv?"

Sally's question pulled Delaney out of his reverie. He had been thinking along the same lines. "I've no idea."

"You reckon he was involved in the petrol station hold-up?"

Delaney shook his head. "Maybe, but who knows? If he was involved he'll have lived to regret it."

Bayfield Prison, finished late in 1902, was three storeys high and had four wings on four sides, forming a central exercise area which could be monitored from observation posts on each corner. There were no windows on the exterior walls, which gave the brick building an imposing, severely functional look.

Sally pulled the car up to the parking area and they walked over to the visitors' entrance and, after the usual security checks, were shown through to a waiting area in the front of the prison. Delaney sat on an orange plastic chair bolted to a wall underneath a window, then stood up again and paced impatiently, looking out of the window and wishing he could fire up a cigarette. He kicked his shoe against the wall and looked at his watch. Ten past eight and way past time they should have seen Norrell.

He paced around the room for a minute more and had just decided to go and have a hard word with somebody when he heard the door open and looked across to see the warden walk in. Ron Cornwell was a tall man, six foot five but thin. He had pale blond hair and an apologetic smile on his face. "Sorry, Inspector, I tried to get hold of you on your mobile earlier. And I've been held up on the telephone."

Delaney walked over to him. "What's going on?"

"You've had a wasted journey, I'm afraid."

"What are you talking about?"

"Kevin Norrell was assaulted this morning. By some of his fellow prisoners. It was a very serious incident."

"He's dead?"

The warden shook his head slightly. "He's in intensive care in the South Hampstead up the road. He hasn't recovered consciousness."

Sally joined Delaney. "Comatose?"

The warden shrugged. "Unconscious is all I know."

"What's the prognosis?"

The warden spread his hands. "I don't know; you'll have to talk to the hospital but it's probably too early to say."

Delaney nodded. "Who did it?"

"We're not exactly sure."

Delaney glared at him. "What the hell do you mean, you're not exactly sure?"

"All right, Inspector. Just calm it down, will you? Five men attacked him in the showers early this morning. He was knifed, hit his head badly. He lost a lot of blood."

"Who were they?"

"We don't know who all of them were. Two of them got away."

"How?" Delaney couldn't believe what he was hearing. "This is supposed to be a secure prison for God's sake."

"Three of the men were badly hurt by Norrell. Two of them are dead, the other is in intensive care."

"And you've got no security footage?"

"The camera was taken out. That's why the two officers were dispatched. If they hadn't got there in time, Norrell would definitely be dead."

"And they just let two of them walk away from it?"

"They were prioritised on dealing with the injured people."

"Convenient." Delaney couldn't keep the sarcasm from his voice.

"What exactly are you implying, Inspector?"

"What motivated the assault?"

"You know as well as I do, there could be any number of reasons. I have it on good authority that Norrell was involved in the manufacture and distribution of child pornography. Particularly nasty child pornography at that. You know what happens to people like that in prison if they're not in a segregated unit."

"And why wasn't he in a segregated unit?"

"Because he wasn't charged with paedophile activities, Inspector, as you very well know. He was charged with murder and conspiracy to commit murder. He was a category-A prisoner and treated as such."

"I want to talk to the guards who broke up the fight."

"I'm afraid that won't be possible right away."

"Why not? There's been a death, a serious assault. This is a police matter now."

44

"And an investigation is under way. Your involvement will need to be officially sanctioned." He shrugged, apologetically. "At this moment it is out of both our hands."

Delaney looked at him steadily. "You know why I was due to speak to him?"

"I do. And I'm sorry."

"Then you also know why I'm not going to just let this go?"

"Of course I do. And I want you to know that I will do everything in my power to help you, Inspector Delaney. Work with me on this."

Delaney turned to Sally. "Come on, Constable."

"Sir."

Delaney held the door open and turned back to the governor pointedly as Sally walked out. "I'll be coming back. And in the meantime, you have my mobile number. You call me night or day you hear anything."

"I *am* on your side, Inspector."

Delaney held his gaze a moment longer and then left. The governor took off his glasses, running his hand over his brow, damp suddenly in the airconditioned room.

Kate Walker shrugged out of her raincoat as she entered the suite of rooms and nodded distractedly to Lorraine Simons, her recently graduated assistant, who was still in the early days of training to become a forensic pathologist. She hung up the coat on an old wooden hatstand and walked past the trainee's desk, straight to her own office. She heard the young woman say something but had absolutely no idea what it was. She closed the door behind her, sat at her desk and, holding her head in her hands, cursed herself in a low whisper as she tried to put together a picture from the jigsaw pieces of memory from the night before.

She remembered travelling on the Tube, she remembered deciding to go to the Holly Bush rather than returning straight home, although now she wished to God she hadn't, she remembered having the first couple of Bloody Marys, and then she remembered chatting to the tall, handsome man in his late thirties, with dark curly hair and the kind of dark, come-to-bed eyes that were lately proving to be her undoing; but after that she had absolutely no memory whatsoever. It was a complete blank. She couldn't remember a damn thing from about eight thirty last night to waking up with a complete and total stranger in her bed at seven thirty that morning. And that wasn't something Kate Walker did. Ever.

She had shown the man, Paul Archer, out in the morning but had barely said ten words to him. Just hurried him out before closing the door on him, feeling the heat burn her face then as it was now as she shamefully tried to recall the previous night's events. Tried desperately hard, but failed absolutely.

The door to her office opened and Lorraine stuck her head round the corner. She was twenty-five, with strawberry-blonde hair, a body trim from cycling, a heart-shaped face, innocent eyes and the kind of optimism only found in the unworldly young or the terminally stupid.

"I was asking if you wanted any coffee, Dr Walker? I'm just about to make a trip to Starbucks."

Kate found a smile from somewhere. "Thanks, Lorraine, get us a hot chocolate and a croissant. And, please, it's Kate, not Dr Walker."

Lorraine nodded. "It's the weather for it. Don't know what happened to the summer."

Kate smiled again, ironically. "In our job you get to learn pretty fast that all things pass, Lorraine. All things end."

Lorraine grimaced. "Cheery thought."

Kate flapped a dismissive hand at her. "Go on, get the drinks."

Lorraine closed the door behind her and as it did Kate's smile headed south faster than a penguin on a promise. She made a small fist of her right hand and put the nail of her thumb between her teeth. She deliberated for a second or two, then picked up the phone and rapidly tapped in some numbers. After a moment her call was answered. "It's Kate," she said quickly, needing to spill the words out. "I think I've done something really stupid."

She listened to the response, looking up at the ceiling. "It's nothing like that. But I need to see you." She looked through the glass window of her office to see Lorraine, bundled up against the cold, heading out the door and sighed. "I need you to do some tests on me, Jane."

"What kind of tests?" Jane Harrington's voice boomed, shocked, from the earpiece of her phone. Kate held it away from her ear then put it back and spoke into it, her voice a hoarse whisper. "I think I might have been raped."

South Hampstead Hospital was built, like many similar institutional buildings throughout the country, in the mid-Victorian era. In the year 1860 to be exact. It started life as a hospital for consumption and other diseases of the chest and much of the old Victorian architecture was still present, although new buildings had been attached over the years, most notably the teaching wing of the hospital which was inaugurated in 1904. The majority of the property was Grade II listed, now, which meant a lot of the offices and consulting rooms were poorly heated, relying on old, cast-iron radiators that the administration hadn't yet managed to justify the expense of replacing. What the rooms lost in terms of heat, however, was more than made up for in terms of ambience and in architectural charm.

Jane Harrington's office was a testament to clutter. The shelves lining her walls were jammed with books, with papers, with articles clipped from medical journals, with videos and DVDs and with a poorly tended ivy or two in inappropriate pots. Her equally cluttered desk sat beneath a bay window that looked out over a small quadrangle, at the far end of which stood the towered east wing of the original hospital. The windows were leaded lights, the desk was old oak and a visitor might be forgiven for imagining they were in the study of a don from one of the older colleges of Oxford or Cambridge.

Jane hung up her telephone, shocked at what she had heard. Kate Walker was more than just a dear friend, she was like a younger sister to her.

She drummed her fingers on her desk for a moment, then snatched up her telephone and pushed the button to connect with her administrative assistant. "Adrian, it's Jane. Can you cancel my tutorials for this morning and rearrange as best you can? Thank you."

She hung up again and looked out of the window at a group of nurses who were walking across the quad, their traditional black cloaks flapping in the wind like a storytelling of ravens. She always thought the collective noun rather odd. Less sinister, she supposed, than a murder of crows. The cloaks were originally coloured blue with the founding of the hospital, but with the death of Prince Albert they had been changed to black. Like the ties of Harrow schoolboys, the colour was originally only to last for a hundred years as a memorial to the German father of nine, but like the school, again, South Hampstead Hospital had stuck with it. Jane watched them thoughtfully as they walked out of sight, hurrying out of the persistent rain into the main part of the hospital. She came to a decision and picked up the telephone once more and punched in a number. "I'd like to speak to Dr Caroline Akunin please."

She waited for a moment while the call was put through. "Caroline. It's Jane Harrington. Have you left for the frozen steppes yet or are you still on call as a police surgeon?" She listened and nodded tersely. "Good, I need a favour."

49

* * *

The sight of a man's penis would not normally have alarmed Valerie Manners. She was a nurse after all and nearing retirement. She had seen more examples of the male reproductive organ than most women of her generation, even including those who had lived through the free love era of the sixties and the wife-swapping fad of the seventies. This one, however, was attached to a raggedy man, and although not impressive, was unpleasantly semi-priapic and being wagged in her general direction as she cut though the lower part of South Hampstead Common on her way home after a late shift at the hospital. Caught off guard, she ran off the path and through some trees and bushes into open grassland, running uphill and not looking back. She ran for three and a half minutes and then stopped, realising that she wasn't being followed. Panting for breath she leaned against a tree and willed her wildly beating heart to calm down. She berated herself for a fool, flashers weren't rapists. They might develop into rapists but at the flasher stage of their development they were usually harmless. She knew that much from reading American crime novels. She put her panicking down to tiredness and being too wired after far too may cups of coffee to get her though the night shift. She was getting too old to work nights, she told herself. Her breathing slowed eventually and as she smoothed down her rumpled uniform, a bird fluttered noisily up through the branches of a tree nearby, startling her again. She looked across at the undergrowth beneath the tree and something caught her eye. She moved a little nearer, tentatively, and bent down to have a closer look. When she saw what it was, Valerie Manners, who had been a nurse for more years than she remembered, who had always despised those trainees who fainted or screamed at the sight of blood and injury, screamed, backed against the tree, all colour drained from her face, and fainted.

Sally Cartwright spun the wheel, kicking up loose bits of gravel, and parked her car next door to a brand-new Land Rover Discovery. She turned to Delaney. "You got any coins, sir?"

Delaney looked across at her puzzled. "What for?"

"The parking meter."

Delaney shook his head in disbelief and opened her glovebox and pulled out an *on police business* sign, which he put on the dashboard.

"Anybody clamps this car, Constable, and they'll have their bollocks as Adam's apples."

"Yes, sir."

Sally smiled and opened the door, looking up at the neo-Gothic splendour of the grand entrance to the South Hampstead Hospital. Delaney followed her glance, taking in the familiar sight. One thing the Victorians were good at. Hospitals and cemeteries.

They walked in through the main reception and headed towards the intensive care unit, or ICU; just like the acronyms with the Met, Delaney had trouble keeping up. Why they couldn't just stick with what people knew and what made sense, was a puzzle beyond the capabilities of his detective brain. Too many middle managers in unnecessary jobs, he suspected.

Sally followed him as he walked up the long sweeping staircase at the end of the corridor. The floor was cool, tiled and clean, but the smell of the place was just as every bit unpleasant to Delaney as it always had been. Even as a kid he had hated the smell of hospitals, the particular ethyl odours hanging in the air like an anaesthetist's gas. As a child it had reminded him of boring hours at sick relatives' bedsides, and of operations he had had, once for a broken wrist and another when a kidney was removed. But as an adult the smell reminded him of just one thing: the death of his wife. He strode forward purposefully as he reached the top of the staircase and turned left to the intensive care unit. At least now, maybe, if Norris survived, he could learn something about why his wife had had to die four years ago on that cold station forecourt in Pinner Green. He could finally learn who did it. And, more importantly, with that knowledge he could visit retribution on those responsible. It wouldn't ease the guilt he still felt over her death, nothing would do that, but the need to root out and hurt the people who had cut short her life was as powerful in him as the need for his lungs to draw breath and his heart to pump blood.

Since his mid-teens Kevin Norrell had been a larger-than-life character. Now, however, as Delaney looked down at his massive frame he looked as harmless as a beached and rotting whale. He nodded at the armed and uniformed police officer who stood on guard outside the intensive care room and turned to the young doctor who was adjusting a drip that protruded,

52

like a number of others, from the comatose Norrell's arm. "What's the prognosis?"

The junior doctor shrugged. "He lost a lot of blood from the stabbing. He had to be resuscitated on the way into hospital and again on the operating table."

Sally looked down at the grotesque figure on the bed. "What does that mean?"

Delaney answered. "It means his brain was deprived of oxygen for a while, he could be braindamaged." He turned back to the young doctor. "How bad is it?"

The junior doctor shrugged again. "We'll wait and see. If he doesn't come round we'll do some more tests. Check his brain activity."

"When will you know?"

"Check back later in the day."

Delaney nodded. "Can I see the other guy?"

"He's in surgery now. When he comes out you can see him. You won't be able to talk to him though, not for a while."

Delaney and Sally walked back down the corridor, outside and across the car park to a small canteen that was run by volunteers to provide refreshment to the hospital visitors. It was a wooden A-frame and built like an alpine ski lodge, as incongruent in the rain-slashed English morning as a palm tree in Piccadilly.

Sally went inside while Delaney held back, taking advantage of a lull in the rain to spark up a cigarette. He drew deep on it, ignoring the disapproving glances from passers-by as he let out a stream of smoke. He felt conflicted. Ordinarily, seeing Norrell in intensive care would have brightened his mood. But the steroid-enhanced, bonehead muscle for hire had information stored somewhere within his Neolithic brain that Delaney needed. The thought that the man might die was almost too much for him to bear. Not when he was this close, not after so long.

He ground his cigarette under heel and went inside to join Sally who had brought a couple of teas over to a small table by the window. Inside the cafe was more like a scout hut, or the village hall from *Dad's Army*. Delaney sat down half expecting to see "Dig for Victory" posters on the wall or "Eat less Bread". He took a sip of his tea, scowled and poured some sugar into it from a glass dispenser.

Sally looked at him for a moment. "Do you want to talk about it?"

"Talk about what?"

"What happened that night?"

"No."

Sally didn't answer him for a second. "We were due to interview Norrell this morning, right?"

"Operative word being due."

"In connection with the murder of your wife?"

"That's right."

Sally seemed to steel herself. "Well, the last time I looked, and with all due respect, sir, I'm a police detective. Not a waitress. Not a chauffeur. Not a dogsbody."

Delaney waved a hand, a little amused by her angry tone. "And the point would be?"

"That this is a police investigation, as you told the governor. And as far as I know I'm on your team, aren't I?"

Delaney looked at her for a moment then sighed. "I'm sure you know it all anyway."

"Go on."

"About four years ago. I was off duty. I stopped to fill up in a petrol station when it was being raided. They were armed with shotguns. My wife was in the car with me."

"What happened?"

"One of them fired his sawn-off, shattering the plate window. I jumped in the car and attempted to follow them. They shot back at us. Disabling the car. Killing my wife."

"I'm sorry."

Delaney nodded. "As I said, you've heard it all before. We were never able to trace the van, we never found out the identity of the raiders. It was a closed book. A cold case. And then Norrell started talking about it."

"You think he was genuine? You really think he knew something?"

Delaney shrugged his shoulders. "I hope so. I hope he lives long enough for us to find out."

He looked out of the window; the wind had picked up again and with it the rain. Fat beads of water were splashing repeatedly and loudly against the glass of the window, running quickly down the pane now. Delaney turned back to Sally Cartwright.

"I'm going outside for another smoke."

★ ★ ★

Kate walked across the quadrangle. Her head was angled down, her eyes squinting against the rain. She looked at her shoes, getting more spattered and besmirched by the minute, but she barely registered the fact. Still numb, her mind still reeling, she walked in a daze, not noticing her friend waving to her through the window of her office or the man at the far end of the quadrangle who was watching her.

She crossed the quad and walked into the entrance, shaking her hair as she hurried up the stone steps to the first floor. Jane Harrington ushered her into her office, making sympathetic noises about being wet through and helping her out of her coat as she shut the door behind her. "Sit down, Kate. I'll make some tea. Are you hungry? Can I get you anything?"

Kate shook her head. "Just tea would be great." She smiled gratefully, pleased that her friend was letting her take her time and hadn't demanded to know what had happened straight away. If she could have answered that question she wouldn't be here in the first place. Jane had been her friend for many years. In her forties she was older than her and wiser than most. She had been pestering her for years to join her in private practice at the teaching hospital and clinic attached to the university, but Kate had always had different ambitions, a different agenda. Now, as she sat cocooned in an armchair behind mullioned windows, she was not sure she had made the right choices. But what she did know was that she didn't know anyone she would rather turn to if she ever needed help. And if she ever needed help, it was certainly now.

A short while later Jane handed her a mug of strong, sweet tea and sat opposite her.

"Ready to talk about it?"

"I don't know what happened, Jane." Her voice was strained, she felt on the verge of tears.

"Then tell me what you do know."

"I was at the Holly Bush. Taking a swim in a bottle of vodka."

"That's not like you."

"I met Jack yesterday."

Jane nodded understanding. "It didn't go well?"

Kate shook her head. "I decided to drown my sorrows. Bad enough to get dumped by the man. Now I'm turning into him."

Jane smiled sympathetically. "Go on."

"I got chatting to a man at the bar. He'd started talking to me. I didn't think he was trying to pick me up."

Jane Harrington frowned.

"Yeah, I know, you don't have to say it. His name is Archer. He's a doctor so I thought I could trust him for goodness' sake."

Jane reacted at the name. "Paul Archer?"

Kate looked up, surprised. "Do you know him?"

Jane jerked her thumb at the window. "He works here. He's a paediatrician."

"What do you know about him?"

"I know he has a reputation."

"Reputation for what?"

"As a ladies' man. He's married but it doesn't stop him apparently."

Kate put her head in her hands. "Shit."

"Or didn't stop him, I should say. His wife's divorcing him."

"What am I going to do, Jane?"

"Tell me exactly what happened."

Kate stood up angrily. "That's just it, I don't know what happened. I don't remember leaving the pub, I don't remember going home. I remember being in the pub, listening to Madeleine Peyroux, drinking Bloody Marys, talking to Paul Archer and the next thing I remember is waking up in my bed at seven thirty this morning, bare as a jaybird with a stark bollock naked man lying beside me."

"Dr Archer?"

"Yes, Dr bloody Archer." She sat down again and looked at her friend with sore, bloodshot and devastated eyes. "I think he raped me, Jane. I think he slipped some Rohypnol, or something like it, in my drink and he raped me."

Jane took her friend's hand and held it as tears ran down her cheek. "It's going to be okay, Kate. We're going to find out what happened and if he has done what you say, then we are going to make him pay for it."

"But if I can't remember . . .?"

"The first thing we are going to do is take a blood test. See if there is anything in your system."

"And then what?"

"I've asked Dr Caroline Akunin to come over here."

Kate looked up agitated. "No, Jane. I don't want that."

58

"You haven't showered, have you?"

Kate shook her head.

"So you must have had it in mind."

"I don't want to go to the police. I can't."

"That's why I asked her to come here."

Kate held her head in her hands again. "I've performed the procedures often enough in the past. Feeling sorry for the women. Pitying them. Christ, Jane, I never thought I'd be in their shoes."

Jane took her hand again. "You're not at fault here, Kate."

"Aren't I? I went out and got smashed. Maybe I did want to act like Jack. Wash my problems away in a lake of alcohol, have meaningless, emotionless sex."

Jane shook her head. "Are you saying this is what you wanted?"

"If it's what I wanted, I would have remembered, wouldn't I?"

Dr Caroline Akunin was a stunningly beautiful, black woman in her late thirties. She was tall, elegant, shaved her hair and was seven months pregnant. She looked sympathetically at Kate as Jane Harrington closed the door behind her office, leaving the two women alone.

Kate nodded at the doctor's swollen belly. "Nearly due then?"

Caroline ran her hand instinctively across her bump. "How can you tell? A couple of months to go."

"And how's your gorgeous husband?"

"My gorgeous husband is being a pain in the butt right now."

"Why?"

"He wants this little one to be born back in his own country."

"Russia?"

"Yup. Moscow, just where I want to be in the middle of winter."

"Will you go?"

Caroline smiled, the brilliance of it lighting the room. "I don't mind really. Quite looking forward to it. Never let him know though. You have to keep your man on his toes, don't you?"

Kate looked away. "I guess."

"I'm sorry, Kate."

Kate put her hand on her arm. "That's okay. Let's just get on with this."

Caroline nodded sympathetically. "We should really do this back at the station."

"White City?"

"Yes."

"You can't be serious?"

"Any evidence I collect here won't be admissible in court, you do know that?"

"I know, Caroline. But I can't go there. Not with this."

"You wouldn't be the first."

"I just want to know what happened. After that . . ." Kate shrugged. She had absolutely no idea what she would do if her fears were confirmed.

Dr Akunin opened up her medical bag, took out some plastic bags and a pair of latex gloves. She pulled the gloves on, snapping the latex tight to her fingers. "You'd better get undressed then."

PC Bob Wilkinson scowled as he looked down at the body that lay barely hidden in the undergrowth. He sighed, unclipped his police radio from its holster and he shared a look with his colleague, a young, black constable called Danny Vine. The boy was ashen, he looked down at what lay on the ground and then dashed off to the bushes to be violently sick.

"Foxtrot Alpha from thirty-two."

His police radio crackled. "Go ahead, Bob."

Wilkinson looked over at his colleague who had stood up and was now wiping the blue serge of his uniformed arm across his mouth. He felt sorry for him, you never got used to it, though, even after nearly thirty years. "We have an IC1 female. Somewhere in her twenties." He paused. "It's not an accidental death."

Kate stood in the centre of the white cotton sheet that Caroline had spread on the floor. The doctor was on her knees in front of Kate with a comb in her hand. Kate looked away as she worked, carefully placing the combed hairs in a small, clear plastic bag.

"When was the last time you had consensual sex, Kate?"

Her memory flashed back to around three weeks ago. She had no trouble recalling that.

Jack Delaney.

"Tell me, Jack. Talk to me." Low, breathless, husky.

"Dig your nails in. I want to taste blood."

"Pleasure and pain, Detective Inspector. Very Catholic."

Delaney laughed, looking into her eyes, at the mischief sparking within them. "I want to remember the moment."

And Kate dug her nails into his buttocks, pulling him deeper into her. "Oh, you'll remember. I'll make sure of that."

She remembered the savagery of their lovemaking. Remembered him on top of her, penetrating her almost painfully, his powerful arms clutching her tight to his muscular body like a life raft as he rode the waves of their passion. She remembered his soft eyes wet with emotion as he shuddered to a climax, taking her with him. She remembered the absolute nakedness of his emotions as he held on too long afterwards, kissing her salty shoulder and whispering her name like a prayer.

And she remembered the love she felt for him.

She looked over at the curtained window and felt tears running down her cheeks again.

Caroline Akunin looked up at her. Misunderstanding her tears. "I'm sorry. I have to ask."

"That's okay, Caroline. It was three weeks ago."

Caroline nodded. "I am going to take some swabs, is that okay?"

Kate nodded. Her body was already feeling like it was something apart from her once more. Distancing herself from her feelings, something she had learned at a young age. Something she had lived with for years until Delaney had made her feel connected with her body again. Now she felt violated and ashamed and wretched. But most of all, she felt angry.

A buzzing sound then a sharp ring. Kate looked across at her mobile phone that was vibrating on Jane Harrington's desk. "You better pass that to me, Caroline. I told the office to call me only if it was really urgent."

Delaney looked at the bloodshot eyes of Martin Quigley. Eyes that darted nervously back and forth. Eyes that squirmed under his scrutiny with pain and with fear. His right arm was suspended in a sling and covered with plaster. His fingers, that were visible, flexed nervously. His lower jaw was covered with wire and metal and held immobile. He grunted through the metal but quite clearly couldn't speak. He was a large man, somewhere in his forties. His nose had been broken many times in the past, and the home-made tattoos on his neck would quickly dispel any lingering suspicions that this man was employed in white-collar work.

Delaney didn't know the man, but he knew the type. Bruisers who communicated with their knuckles. Strong-arm men for cleverer criminals. A foot soldier, cannon fodder, a gorilla just like Kevin Norrell. He moved around the side of the bed, closer to him. "You attacked Kevin Norrell, and I want to know why." The man grunted again, an animal in pain. Delaney couldn't make out what he was saying.

Sally Cartwright took out a pad and a pen and held it out to Quigley's good hand. He flicked his broken-veined eyeballs to the left, where she stood, then back at Delaney and grunted again, but made no move to take the pen or notebook.

Delaney smiled at him. "You taking what our American cousins would call the fifth, Quigley?"

Quigley glared at him with defiance in his eyes and didn't move.

Delaney glanced over at Sally. "Give him the pen, Sally."

Sally put the pen in his left hand but he made no move to hold it. Delaney reached over, put his own hand over Quigley's broken one and pulled it. Quigley grunted, loudly, his face red with pain and tears starting in his eyes. Delaney released his grip. "He'll take the pen now."

This time Quigley held the pen. Sally put her notebook under it so that he could write.

"Why'd you attack him, Quigley?"

Quigley wrote one word. The scrawl was nearly undecipherable but Sally could just make it out. "He's written 'Nonce', sir."

Delaney looked at Quigley. "You saying you attacked Norrell because he was a paedophile?"

Quigley grunted an affirmative.

"Who put you up to it?"

Quigley grunted again and wrote some more. Sally read it out again. "He says no one."

"Just doing your civic duty, were you?"

Quigley grunted again, trying to keep his head as still as possible. Sally looked over at her boss. "Do you believe him?"

"I don't know." Delaney smiled at her then tugged on Quigley's hand again. Quigley's breath hissed through the metal mask of his teeth and he gurgled in pain. Delaney let go of his hand. "You telling me the truth, Martin?"

Quigley's eyes pleaded with Delaney, his gurgling incoherent but comprehensible as Delaney reached towards his plastered arm once more.

Quigley pleaded with his eyes as Delaney's mobile phone rang. He grabbed it out of his jacket pocket and flipped it open.

"Delaney."

"Jack, it's Diane."

"I'm at the South Hampstead, interviewing someone."

"It'll have to wait. I heard about Norrell and I'm sorry, but something's come up."

"What?"

"We've got a dead body in the woods, South Hampstead Common. A young female."

"We know who she is?"

"Not a damn thing. Uniform are securing the site, but given the weather we want it processed as soon as possible. Paddington Green should be handling it but they've got some big anti-terrorist initiative tying up their manpower."

"Lucky us."

Delaney looked across at the rain-speckled window and through it at the grey clouds overhead. "Give me the details." Delaney listened for a moment or two then closed his phone. He put his mobile back in his pocket and gestured to Sally. "We're out of here."

The sigh of relief from Quigley was audible. Delaney turned back to him. "I'll talk to you later. Meanwhile, you better pray Norrell makes it. Because if he doesn't I'm going to come back here and finish the job he started. And I'm a professional."

Quigley glared at his back as they left his field of vision then closed his eyes nervously, snaked a tongue around his dry lips and swallowed with evident pain.

Kate Walker flicked the end of her long, multicoloured scarf over one shoulder and walked quickly across the quadrangle and around the corner, passing the main entrance to the South Hampstead Hospital as she started for the car park. Her head was down and although the rain, for the moment at least, had stopped, the north-east wind still had a chill edge to it. She fumbled in her pocket for her keys when a voice called out to her.

"Kate."

She looked round, her heart thudding in her chest, to see Paul Archer.

He smiled at her, his voice friendly. "Kate, what are you doing here? Were you looking for me?"

Kate couldn't speak, she couldn't breathe, she leaned back against her car, fighting to control the panic.

Archer smiled at her. "Is everything all right?"

She found her voice. "Get away from me."

Archer looked puzzled. "What are you talking about?"

"I know what you did. So just stay away from me."

"I've got no idea what you're talking about. I haven't done anything."

"Last night . . ."

"Last night was your idea. You invited me back to your place, remember."

Kate shook her head angrily. "You're not going to get away with this."

"Get away with what? I didn't do anything."

"You're lying."

"Nothing happened, Kate. We both got drunk, you suggested I stay over. We slept together, but nothing happened, if that's what you're worried about."

Kate desperately wanted to believe him, but knew that something was wrong, something was definitely wrong. She knew her own body, didn't she? "Then why can't I remember?"

Archer smiled at her, genuinely amused. "You were absolutely paralytic, Kate. It's not unusual."

Kate stepped closer to him, she wanted to knock the arrogant smirk off his cocky face. She wanted to hurt him, really hurt him. "You're not going to get away with it, you sick pervert!" Archer grabbed both of her arms and she struggled furiously but his grip was like a vice. She looked up at him with livid eyes, her face contorted in fury. "Let me go now, or I swear you will regret it!"

He pushed her away, the thin veneer of urbanity stripped from his face now as he sneered, "What makes you think I'd want something like you?"

67

Kate slapped him hard across his face and went to slap him again but he caught her hand. "Let go of my hand!" she yelled at him, red-faced with fury.

"You heard the lady."

Archer released his grip on her and turned round to see a man looking at him impassively, scant inches away, a young woman standing behind him. The man was easily Archer's height, but had a few years on him and Archer was in far better physical shape. He poked the stranger in the chest. "Back off, sunshine, and take your little friend with you. This is none of your business."

Delaney punched him in the face. A hard straight punch to the bridge of his nose. So fast Archer didn't even see it coming. He gasped out in pain and dropped to his knees, completely taken aback. "You've broken my fucking nose." Blood was spilling from his nose on to his hands.

Delaney turned back round to speak to Kate but she was already striding towards her car, her scarf of many colours flapping behind her long, curly hair like a sexy Doctor Who. Roy, from the burger van, would have approved, Delaney reckoned. He walked up to her as Kate got in her car, slammed the door shut and kicked over the engine.

"Kate!"

But she was gone, her wheels spinning, throwing up gravel like tiny shrapnel as she accelerated to the exit.

Archer was still whimpering, incredulous. "You broke my fucking nose."

Delaney ignored him, "Come on, Sally." He walked across the car park to their car.

DC Cartwright looked down at Archer who was staring at the blood on his hands in shock and utter disbelief. "I'd get a plaster for that if I were you. They should have one in there."

She jerked her thumb towards the hospital entrance and walked after Delaney.

Sally Cartwright adjusted the rear-view mirror watching the man Delaney had decked as he hobbled, clearly in pain, to the hospital entrance, a bloody handkerchief held to his nose. She turned the ignition key and looked across at Delaney, a slight frown creasing her neatly shaped eyebrows. "Seat belt, sir."

Delaney rolled his eyes and pulled his seat belt across, snapping it into place. "Just drive, will you, Constable?"

"Sir."

She slipped the clutch out and pulled the car smoothly out of the exit; no gravel flew behind them as she indicated left and headed towards the south part of Hampstead Heath.

After driving in silence for a couple of minutes she flicked a glance at her boss. "What was all that about, do you reckon, sir?"

"I have absolutely no idea, Sally."

"She seemed pretty upset."

"Yup."

"Do you think he'll make a complaint against you?"

69

"He doesn't know who I am." Delaney shrugged and went back to staring out the window. Sally raised an eyebrow again and concentrated on the road ahead.

When he was sure the detective constable wasn't looking, Delaney rubbed his left hand over his right knuckles and winced. He had no idea what was going on with the man he had punched, or what he had to do with Kate. He had probably broken the man's nose who, after all, was right, it had been none of his business. It had felt good though, for all the wrong reasons. It had been a morning of frustrations, getting so close to discovering the identity of his wife's killers, only to be thwarted at the final hurdle. And he wasn't so unaware as to not realise he still had issues with Kate Walker. He had punched the man half out of anger, half out of a desire to impress her. He had told Kate that he didn't have room in his life for her, and it was true. He had too many unresolved matters to set straight. But if he had no room in his life for her, then why was there such a great hole in it?

Kate Walker's hands were still shaking as she slipped the gear into fourth and stepped on the accelerator pedal. Shaking, she realised, with shock and anger. Of all the people in the world she didn't want knowing about last night and what had happened to her, it was Jack Delaney. What on earth was the man doing there, for God's sake? It was bad enough that he had humiliated her yesterday, broke her heart and made her so depressed that she went to chase her blues away with vodka. If it hadn't been for him she would never have gone to the Holly Bush, would never have let a complete stranger chat her up at the bar. She wasn't a student, she wasn't a silly young girl who didn't know any better and didn't realise the dangers. In fact, she knew the dangers better than most, but had still let the man under her guard. Just like she had let Delaney under her guard, and look what had happened there. And, of course, he just had to be there when she confronted Paul Archer, making a fool of herself. She slammed the palm of her hand down hard on her horn, the hooter blaring out loudly and causing the cyclist she was overtaking to wobble dangerously to the side of the road.

She fought to calm her anger, steady the adrenalin coursing through her veins. But the truth was she was getting angrier by the minute. She had seen it in Paul Archer's eyes. He was amused. He was mocking her. There was a cold chill in those eyes. He had raped her. She absolutely believed it now. Believed it with a cold certainty in the heart of her soul. But she had absolutely no idea what she was going to do about it.

Paul Archer held a water-soaked handkerchief to his throbbing nose and wiped away the last vestiges of blood. The pain was like a thin spike driven into his forehead. He looked at his face in the mirror and turned left and right to look at each profile. As far as he could tell, and he was pretty qualified to tell, his nose wasn't broken. He put his hands under the cold water, watching as the deep red blood became thinner and paler as it swirled away. He scooped some of the cold water into the palm of his hand and held it against his forehead for a moment or two, waiting for the pain to ease.

Stepping away he snatched a paper towel and rubbed his hands dry as he walked across to the window, fumbling open a pack of Demerol and swallowing a couple. He looked out at the car park below and beyond. Puddles of rainwater, like irregular-shaped, murky mirrors, reflected the dark clouds, scudding in the skies above. There was nothing reflected in Paul Archer's eyes though. They stared ahead with a blank, cold certainty.

When he was nine years old, a couple of older boys at school, brothers, had bullied him. Making him drop his packed lunch of cheese and piccalilli sandwiches on to the rain-soaked tarmac of the playground. Kids didn't like other kids who were different and these two reckoned Paul Archer fancied himself as better than them because he didn't have to eat school lunches. As Paul watched his sandwiches soak up the muddy rain he didn't fight back, he didn't say a word, just picked up his Tupperware box and walked away, not even hearing the laughs and insults that were shouted after him. Paul was too intent listening to the cool voice of reason inside his head. The one that said no slight should go unpunished. And if he wasn't big enough or strong enough or old enough to make them suffer then he would hurt the thing they loved. He waited three weeks and then very early one Saturday morning he climbed over the fence of their back garden, rolled a lawn-mower against the door of the kennel where their pet dog, a Staffordshire bull terrier, slept, poured petrol he had taken from his dad's shed all over it and set it alight.

The adult Paul Archer held a hand to his throbbing nose again; there were many things he knew now that he hadn't as a child, but one thing that hadn't changed was that certain knowledge of the joy of retribution. He knew it as surely as night follows day. As death follows life. As pleasure follows pain.

Someone was going to pay.

In the front part of the head, in the roof of each nostril, lies a group of mucous-covered sacs. The olfactory epithelium. About five square centimetres in size and containing about ten million receptor cells. Using these receptors the human nose can differentiate, it has been claimed, between four thousand and ten thousand different odours. Odour is at the very genesis and denouement of human existence. A smell receptor has been identified in human sperm — the sperm literally smells its way to the egg. And death, as any policeman or mortician knows, is certainly no friend of the olfactory organ. However, the unmistakable smell of a deceased and decaying body had had no time to develop that morning and PC Bob Wilkinson reckoned his young colleague was as glad of that fact as anyone.

PC Danny Vine had already thrown up twice within the space of half an hour and Wilkinson, taking pity on him, had sent him to the front of the path to prevent anyone from disturbing the crime scene. Move along

73

please. Nothing to see here. Only, of course, there was. There was plenty to see. But none of it pleasant.

The mechanics of investigation had already been set in motion. A large section of the surrounding area had been cordoned off with yellow tape stretching from tree to tree in a rough diamond shape, covering about a quarter of an acre. The yellow tape with *"police do not cross"* written upon it, the yellow tape that unfailingly attracted the prurient attention of the scandal-hungry public, just as the scent of another dog's waste always attracted canine interest. The sort of thrill-seeking interest the public had in other people's misfortune and pain, feeding off it like some kind of sick parasites. Road crash syndrome.

Police vans had been parked outside the cordoned area and uniformed police and white-suited scene-of-crime officers, SOCOs, went about containing the integrity of the site. Aluminium telescopic poles had been snapped open and joined together to form a skeletal framework which was positioned over the area immediately surrounding the body. Plastic sheets had been run over the frame so that the structure took on the appearance of a wedding marquee. Only within the frame, there was no cheery fiddle music, there was no three-tiered cake on a stand, no punchbowl, no laughing guests, no nervous best man and certainly no blushing bride with a blue garter on her stocking and a hungry husband by her side. Inside was the dead body of a woman in her mid-twenties, with black hair, black lipstick and black blood crusting the edges of the deep slash wounds to her chest, throat and abdomen.

Delaney and Sally Cartwright nodded at PC Danny Vine as they ducked under the tape and headed towards the murder scene. Danny responded with a half-hearted smile.

"You all right, Danny?" Sally asked.

The constable nodded again, unconvincingly. "Something I ate."

"You still on for tonight?"

The constable smiled again, more warmly this time. "Yeah, I'll be there. Bells on."

Sally flashed him a quick smile and hurried to join Delaney.

"Something I should know about?" he asked.

"Sir?"

"Poster boy back there. You and he sharing handcuffs?"

Sally coloured lightly but laughed out loud. "A few of us are meeting up for drinks, that's all."

Delaney nodded, not entirely convinced. "Right."

"You're welcome to join us."

Delaney nodded again. "If you say so."

"Anyway. It wouldn't be a crime, would it?"

"Not in my world." Delaney's brief moment of good humour curled up and died as he walked forward and saw the dark-haired woman standing outside the scene-of-crime tent.

"Dr Walker. Nice scarf."

Kate turned and looked at him, and cursed inwardly, as she took her scarf off and pulled the protective coverings over the work boots she had changed into. She should have known Delaney would turn up. He was, after all, less than a mile away, just like her, when the call had come in.

"Inspector." She was surprised at how calm her voice sounded, how cool.

"Have you got anything for us?"

"Like you I've only just arrived. From what I've seen from here, a young woman, I'm guessing mid-twenties."

"No ID?"

PC Wilkinson stepped forward. "Nothing yet, sir. We're going to finger-search the area but there was nothing on her person. She had a handbag but it was empty apart from some condoms and a tube of KY jelly."

"Nothing else?"

"She had a Tube ticket."

Delaney nodded. South Hampstead Tube station was a stone's throw from the edge of that part of the heath.

"Who found her?"

Wilkinson nodded over to the path where the nurse, Valerie Manners, stood, sipping shakily from a cup of tea as a female PC talked to her.

"I'll want to speak to her next. Make sure she stays here, Bob."

"Boss."

Delaney moved to the entrance of the tent. "Let's have a look."

Kate Walker followed him in. The small space was already bustling. SOCO had cleared the overhanging undergrowth, carefully cutting away the branches and shrubbery that had partially hidden the body. A

76

video-camera operator was filming the scene, while a photographer, blond-haired and in his twenties, was doing the same. The bright flashes poked needles in Delaney's sore eyes.

Kate looked down at the woman. She had black boots on her feet, calf-length and high-heeled, black leggings, a short black, leather skirt with an ornate, silver buckled belt. She was naked from the waist up. Her long hair was dyed deep black, and she was wearing black eyeshadow and lipstick. A goth. Kate felt the irony of it. A subculture that had death as part of its make-up, no pun intended. She would have laughed if it wasn't so pitifully sad. The woman was beautiful, in a painted-doll kind of way, with a full, voluptuous figure. Kate had to blink tears away as she looked at what had been done to her.

A bruise ran along the lower part of the dead woman's jaw on the right side of the face. The purple mottling even more obscene against the deathly white of her skin.

On the opposite side her neck had been slashed from ear to the larynx. Below her neck, a knife had opened up a circular hole, ripping down and exposing the bones of her spinal column. The large blood vessels on either side of the neck had been slashed, and blood had run down her semi-naked body in jagged sheets. The heart had been pumping when the wounds were made, spraying the blood outward with considerable pressure and telling her that the cuts had been made pre-mortem.

Kate turned to Delaney who was standing beside her and, thankfully, holding his counsel for once. "Whoever did it, I'd guess, used a large, relatively sharp blade, wielded with great force. He was full of rage, out of control I'd say. There are no defence wounds on her hands or arms so I would surmise the woman may have known her attacker."

"Was she killed here?"

Kate nodded. "Going by the arterial spray on the ground and undergrowth around her."

She looked down at the young woman's body again. Was she right? Had she known the man who had done this to her? Or was it a random attack? Kate's gaze ran across the woman's mutilated body, past the slashes on her neck and down to her lower abdomen where a jagged cut ran across it. As if the man had held the knife down in a grip and had sawed through, like a huntsman gutting a deer. That could have been her, she realised, last night. Drugged, raped, she could have been mutilated too and dumped in the woods. Suddenly, the pinpricks in her eyes started in earnest and she could no longer hold back the tears. She felt her stomach lurch and knew she had to get out of there. She turned, pushed past Delaney, and ran through the opening of the tent. Ducking under the tape cordon she staggered into a wooded area away from the shocked looks of the police, fell to her knees and threw up. She bent her head low, holding her long dark hair away from her face, and threw up again. She put one hand on the wet ground to balance herself, weak with despair, and retched again painfully. She gulped in some ragged breaths of air, her throat cramping, and ran her hand over her forehead, now damp with perspiration. Her voice was a rough whisper as she swore through her panted breath.

It wasn't the Hippocratic oath.

Back in the scene-of-crime tent Delaney turned to Sally Cartwright. She had offered to go after the doctor but had been told her to stay where she was. "I guess a lot of people ate something dodgy this morning," Delaney had said.

Sally looked down at the dead goth's mutilated body and felt queasy herself. "I can't say I blame her."

But Delaney was puzzled. Kate Walker was a consummate professional, had seen more dead bodies than even he had. Something was clearly up with her and he couldn't help wondering if it had something to do with the confrontation he had witnessed in the car park of the South Hampstead Hospital just a short while ago.

Kate Walker stood up. She took the bottle of Evian water she always kept in her handbag and took a swallow, rinsing the water around her mouth a few times and then spitting it out. She did it once more and then took a long swallow of the cold water. She poured a little more on a handkerchief and wiped her brow and lips and took a couple of deep breaths, willing her heart to slow down. She placed a hand against the damp bark of a tree and forced herself to breathe evenly.

79

Since an early age ambition had been Kate Walker's middle name. At school she had come top of her year seven years running. Unlike many of her peers she hadn't been distracted by boys or music or become fanatical about sports, she wasn't obsessive about ponies and didn't have a crush on her French teacher, she didn't spend hours shopping for outfits, had no fascination with shoes or handbags or jewellery or make-up, she didn't take an interest in anything, in fact, that wasn't going to further her academic career. As a young girl in prep school she hadn't been like that, she was a bit of a tomboy. She was as interested in climbing trees or playing cricket as any of her boy cousins. Her favourite novel was Arthur Ransome's *Swallows and Amazons* and a day cooped up inside on a fine summer's day was torture to her. All that had changed, however, one summer when she was eleven years old and her outer life became driven inward. It was a solemn-faced and earnest girl who went to St Angela's for Girls, keeping her dark thoughts behind her dark lashes. If the eyes were the window to the soul, Kate Walker's were tinted glass. St Angela's was for the wealthy and gifted children of the south London suburbs whose parents couldn't bear to send their daughters further south to Roedean or west to St Helen's. Kate's studies became her life, and she quite literally lost herself in books. She might not have lost her love for Arthur Ransome but the adventures took place in her imagination now. As a fresher at university she ignored all entreaties to join societies that were about fun and not study. Most people went to university to play hard and work hard, a few went to party. Kate went to work hard and that was it. She got a first and went on to become an exemplary medical student. As a qualified doctor she wasn't content with the prospect of general practice. She took courses and the extra work as a police surgeon. It was while doing that, and working closely with the police, that she became fascinated with forensic anthropological science and the work of pathologists. One dealt with bones, the other with soft tissue. She had gone back to medical school, qualified and became a forensic pathologist. Overall it had taken over twelve years and it was all she ever wanted. And she was good at it, already targeted for the head of her department and beyond. Her future was as plotted out for her and as detailed as an Ordnance Survey map.

Today, though, as she looked across at the blue lights that were flashing through the trees and undergrowth ahead like a carnival for lost souls, she put a hand on her sore stomach, aching with the cramps of throwing up, and thought about the ravaged body of a woman just starting out in life, an unfinished symphony cut tragically short, about the horrible waste and the madness of it all, and she realised suddenly that she was sick of being a pathologist. She was sick of the blood and the pain and the daily reminder of the absolute evil that mankind was capable of. She was sick of dealing with the hard-headed cynicism of people like Jack Delaney and his ilk. Sick of death, in fact.

Sick to her stomach.

As she walked back to the crime scene she realised she had already come to a decision. She was going to phone Jane Harrington to see if the general practice position in her clinic attached to the hospital was still available. She had been offered the post a few weeks before and this time she would take her friend up on the offer. She'd have her resignation in to her boss by the end of the day. She had one last case to deal with first, though. She didn't know who the young girl in the woods was. She didn't know how she had died. But she would give her all finding out how and why she had died. She gave the unknown woman her oath on that much.

A blood oath.

Delaney tried to look sympathetic as the nurse, Valerie Manners, recounted the morning's events. "I'm sure it was all very traumatic for you."

"Traumatic isn't the word. I'm used to traumatic. You work enough shifts on the accident and emergency unit at a large hospital and you get used to trauma."

Bob Wilkinson spoke out. "What would you call it then?"

Delaney threw a "leave it out" look to the constable who was standing by Sally as she took notes.

Valerie Manners was a bit taken aback by the question and had to think a little, giving up after a few moments of struggle. "Well, *very* traumatic I would say."

Delaney nodded, again with sympathy. The trouble all too often with the public when they were caught up

82

in a crime, was to make too much of everything. The answers to solving a crime were all too often in the everyday, mundane, prosaic details, not in the dramatic and the astounding. Many of the witnesses he had interviewed over the years had a tendency to vicariously sensationalise their own drab lives by way of someone else's tragedy. Memories became embellished with imagined detail. But Delaney was a seasoned enough copper to know how to winnow the wheat from the chaff. At least he hoped he was. "Go back to the beginning, Mrs Manners."

"It's Ms Manners."

"Back to the beginning then please, Ms Manners."

"I had stopped to catch my breath, leant on the tree over there —"

Delaney interrupted her. "Before then?"

"When I saw the flasher?"

"Before that."

"Back to leaving hospital?"

"Yes."

The nurse looked at him perplexed, like he was an idiot. "Is it relevant?"

Delaney sighed and looked at her, any sympathy he had for her draining fast. "I'll tell you what, Ms Manners, let's make a deal. I won't tell you how to dress a wound or change a bedpan, and you let me decide what details are important or not in a particularly brutal murder case."

"All right, no need to get snitty. I can get that kind of attitude any day of the week, if I want it, from the consultants who think they're better than good God Himself."

Delaney ignored her. "What time did you leave work this morning?"

"I left the hospital about eight o'clock."

"And you always cut through this part of the heath?"

"Yes. It takes me about fifteen minutes to walk home. And a bit of fresh air never hurt anyone. I've learned that much in my job."

Tell that to the woman in the scene of crime tent, thought Delaney, but didn't say it. "And you didn't see anything out of the ordinary?"

"I saw a man wagging his penis at me! I'd count that as a pretty unusual event, wouldn't you?"

"Can you describe it?"

"The penis, or the event?"

Delaney sighed and Sally Cartwright and Bob Wilkinson had to try hard not to smile. "Just tell us what happened?"

"I was walking on to the heath —"

Delaney interrupted her. "You hadn't seen anybody earlier, somebody coming off the heath perhaps?"

The woman shook her head. "Not a single soul. Weather like this tends to keep people at home or in their cars, doesn't it?"

Sally looked up from her notebook. "And the man who exposed himself to you . . .?"

"He was in his late twenties I'd say, maybe thirties. Semi-priapic."

"I'm sorry?" Sally asked.

Wilkinson smiled. "He had a hard-on, Sally."

84

"Yeah, thanks, Bob," said Delaney.

"Well, partly so, enough I guess for him to waggle," added the nurse. "It was early, and it was pretty cold, mind you."

Delaney held up his hand. "Can we concentrate on the man, not just the member?"

"He was about five ten, wearing a fawn-coloured overcoat, he might have had a suit on under his coat, he had dark trousers anyway."

Sally flicked back through her notebook. "You called him a raggedy man earlier."

Valerie Manners nodded. "Yes, it was his hair."

Delaney waited patiently, but when there was nothing forthcoming, said, "And? What about his hair?"

"It was raggedy, you know?"

"No?"

"Sort of wild, curly. A bit like yours." She pointed to Delaney. "Only longer and it hadn't been combed, it was sticking out."

"Like his cock," said Bob Wilkinson, his smile suddenly dying on his lips as Delaney glared at him, the detective inspector's already thin patience finally worn through.

At the mortuary Kate Walker scrubbed her hands, holding them under the hot water and rubbing the brush as if to scratch away the touch of Paul Archer. She felt like dipping them in acid.

"Are you all right, Dr Walker?" Lorraine Simons had come into the room and was watching her, concern evident in her eyes.

"I'm fine." Kate finished her hands, drying them and slipping on a pair of latex gloves.

"You had a phone call earlier. Dr Jane Harrington. She didn't leave a message."

Kate nodded. "It can wait. She can't." She walked across to the mortuary table where the body of the murdered girl was laid out in cold, clinical repose. Her naked skin pearlescent white under the bright lights, like a dead snow queen.

Kate watched as her assistant joined her at the table, wheeling across the stack of instruments with which they would try and ascertain the manner of the young woman's death. Quantify it. Render a human life into its constituent parts. Why was she doing this? she thought to herself. Working with the dead? Maybe her friend Jane was right, she had always been so sure of herself. But suddenly everything was shifting for her, nothing was fixed. Her career had always been a focus, a constant. Now? Now she didn't even know who she was any more.

She glanced across at her young assistant. "What made you want to do this job?" she asked.

Lorraine looked at her a little puzzled. "Don't you remember asking me that in my interview?"

Kate smiled apologetically. "There were a lot of interviews. A lot of interviewees, all of them saying the same thing. I just wondered what it really was for you?"

Lorraine picked up a scalpel and ran her thumb along the blunt part of it. "All through medical school I wanted to be a surgeon."

"What changed?"

"It was a gradual thing, really. But one night, I was an intern on surgical rotation and a couple of children were brought in. A ten-year-old boy and a six-year-old girl. They had both been repeatedly stabbed. By their father."

"Go on."

"He was a manic-depressive. On a cocktail of antidepressants, booze and marijuana. He had an argument with his wife, picked up a carving knife and stabbed both his kids to punish her."

"Nice."

"The boy lasted an hour. We did what we could but he had lost a lot of blood. We worked on the girl through the night. There were multiple complications, she had been stabbed nine times. We brought her out of surgery and had to take her back in as she arrested in recovery. She arrested again on the table." She put the scalpel down and looked steadily at Kate. "When she arrested again we had to let her go. Even had she survived she would have been brain-dead. There was nothing we could do. We had to tell the mother she had lost both her children. Some hours later the mother jumped in front of a train on the Northern Line at Chalk Farm."

Kate shook her head sympathetically. "It wasn't your fault. You did what you could."

Lorraine nodded. "I don't blame myself. There's only one person responsible for their deaths. But I couldn't deal with it any more. I couldn't deal with the fact that whatever you do, however much you try, eventually someone will die. And if you are going to be a surgeon you have to be able to deal with that. You have to be able to detach emotionally. And I couldn't. And I didn't want to go into general practice." She looked down on the cold body of the dead woman. "At least in here you can't fail. Nobody pays a price for your mistakes."

"That's true . . ." Kate looked at the dead woman's face, at her neck, at the start of the first incision, but knew that she was lying to her young assistant. ". . . and at least you didn't say you had a crush on Amanda Burton."

"Who?"

"Good answer."

Kate looked back at the dead woman's neck again and then bent down to get a closer look. "What do you make of this?"

Lorraine moved around the table to see what Kate was looking at. "It appears to be some kind of puncture wound."

"Get the camera. Let's take some close-up shots."

Jack Delaney took a big bite out of his second bacon sandwich that day and grunted with approval. "You're an irritating bastard at the best of times, Roy, but you make a halfway decent sandwich."

"From anyone else I'd tell them to stick their head in a pig, but coming from you, Inspector Delaney, I'll take that as a big fucking compliment." Roy smiled broadly, his teeth like an old piano with half the keys missing, and turned back to the book he was reading. A new science-fiction blockbuster by Peter F. Hamilton from whom he had nicked the name for his burger van.

Delaney walked across to Sally Cartwright who was delicately eating a bean burger as she leaned against the bonnet of her car. Her small teeth made precise, uniform bites. Delaney leaned beside her on the bonnet finishing his sandwich and considered matters. Now that the body of the young goth woman had been removed to the morgue, the SOCOs and uniforms were conducting a fingertip search and dusting any suitable surface. Given the overnight rain Delaney doubted there would be any chance of lifting any prints. Kate Walker had barely said three words to him since returning to the scene-of-crime tent. He hadn't expected her to be sweetness and light to him but he had hoped she could keep a professional neutrality, at least. He knew he had hurt her, but they had only slept together once after all, and that hardly constituted a relationship. And the fact of the matter was he had only ended their affair because he didn't want to see her getting hurt. He knew his own failings better than anybody and he knew he wasn't in a place right now to be of any use in her life. He couldn't remember who said it but he remembered the quote about the eleventh commandment. "Never sleep with anybody who has got more problems than you have." He reckoned that between Kate Walker and himself that would be a close run thing. One thing was sure, though, she was certainly taking the case this morning a whole lot more personally than he had ever seen her take one before. Kate Walker had always been practically a byword for

89

icy efficiency, but the dead goth had certainly got to her in some way, that much was painfully obvious.

"Sir?"

Delaney blinked out of his thoughts and looked at Sally. "Sorry, what?"

"I was asking about the raggedy-haired man. You think he's connected with the dead girl?"

Delaney finished his sandwich. "I don't know. I think we should find him, though."

"Do you think there is a sexual connection with the murder?"

Delaney wiped his hands and stood up. "We'll find out soon enough if there is. But she was naked from the waist up which suggests a sexual element. And the psychiatrists tell us often enough that in these sort of crimes the knife becomes a phallic substitute."

"Boys and their toys, eh, Inspector?"

"Something like that. Come on, Constable. Or are you going to take all day eating that burger?"

Delaney walked off, crossing over the road and headed towards White City police station, purpose in his stride.

Diane Campbell looked up from her desk as Delaney came into her office. She gestured to him as she took out a packet of cigarettes and walked to the window. "Keep an eye out. The new super has a bug up his arse about smoking. Anyone would think it's against the law."

"It is, Diane."

She smiled and fired up a cigarette and opened her window slightly. "So, what have you got for me, cowboy?"

Delaney shrugged. "Nothing new. The body is at the morgue."

"What's your instinct? Sexual predator? First date gone wrong? Homicidal maniac?"

"I don't know, boss. A lot of anger there, that much is clear."

"Killed in the woods, or dumped there?"

"The doc reckons she was killed where we found her. The blood-spatter patterns seem pretty conclusive."

"Did she give a time of death?"

"Last night." He shrugged. "Hopefully we'll know more after the post."

Diane took a drag on her cigarette and looked at him. "And what did you get up to after I dropped you off?"

"I went home and tucked myself straight up in bed like a good boy."

"Yeah, right."

He smiled, but his eyes were flat. Remembering.

Delaney hunched the collar of his jacket around his neck and leaned back, shielding himself from the wind as he lit the cigarette that was his excuse for getting off the train. The dark-haired woman in the carriage had reminded him of Kate. It wasn't her. Wasn't remotely like her, apart from the hair. But he couldn't keep her out of his mind and, suddenly claustrophobic with his thoughts, he had hurried through the closing doors, shouldered through the crowds, up the escalator and out into the fresh, cool air.

Eight o'clock at night and it was already dark. The black clouds overhead were pregnant with rain, a real burst of it looked imminent, but the pavement was bright from the street lamps and the wash of light that spilled from the broad windows of WH Smith which Delaney was leaning against. He stood there for a moment or two, watching people hurry across the road and into the safety of the station. He watched a woman in her forties with dyed, ill-kempt, blonde hair and a red vinyl jacket walk near the phone boxes, scanning the eyes of approaching men, looking to make a deal, needing another fix and not caring about the weather.

Delaney finished his cigarette and walked back to the station entrance. A couple of stops up the Northern Line and he'd be in Belsize Park. Back home. Only it didn't feel like home to him and he was not sure it ever would. He paused at the entrance. Maybe he should do as his boss suggested. He'd had quite a few drinks already but he was a very long way from being rat-arsed. He shook another cigarette out of a packet and lit it, feeling his heart pound in his chest, and came to a decision. He blew out a stream of smoke and started walking. Away from the station towards the British Library. He crossed over the road, running to dodge the traffic, and walked a couple of hundred yards up Pentonville Road towards Judd Street and went into a pub on the corner of the two roads. An Irish bar, a proper one, not a diddly shamrock theme pub. The warmth and the noise wrapped around him as he entered, the light was bright but, for a change, Delaney didn't mind that. He walked across the scuffed wooden floor to the long, scruffy bar and ordered a large whiskey and a pint of Guinness from the freckled woman in her thirties who was stood behind it. He had downed the whiskey before the Guinness had settled and ordered another one. He was sipping it a little bit more slowly when a soft, hot, moist voice whispered in his ear.

"Hello, stranger."

He turned round and took another sip of the whiskey, looking into the cool, green eyes of the woman who had sat on the stool next to him. Her hip rubbing against his thigh. She was dressed in skintight jeans, a cream-coloured wool jumper and a brown suede jacket. Delaney smiled at her and raised his glass. "Stella Trant."

"In the flesh." Stella leaned against the bar putting her shoulders back in a feline manner, stretching the jumper across her braless chest.

Delaney smiled again and looked again into her deep, green eyes, seeing the playfulness sparking in them now. "Buy you a drink?"

Stella smiled, nodding, and rubbed her arm, wincing a little.

"You hurt yourself?"

"Tennis elbow. Professional injury."

"You play tennis?"

"Swinging a whip. Toy one, made of suede. Some guy had me manacle him to a wall in his cellar and pretend to whip him heavily for an hour." She rubbed her arm again. "The novelty soon wears off." She looked at him pointedly and smiled. "Reminds me a lot of you by the way. Same hair, same dress sense."

Delaney shook his head, a smile on the edge of his lips. "Not me. I don't play at things."

"Is that a fact?"

Delaney looked at her steadily as he finished his second whiskey. "Not unless I win."

"Maybe next time I'll let you."

Superintendent George Napier did little to hide his dislike of the man standing in front of his desk. The man's eyes were bloodshot, his hair was too long, too curly, too far from neatly combed. Altogether there was a sense of looseness to his appearance. Jack Delaney. Slack Delaney more like! Too cocky, too casual, too damned indifferent. George Napier was not a man who did casual and had little time for those that did. He didn't much care for the Irish either. He didn't trust them. He still remembered hundreds of Irish men and women lining the streets of Kilburn to mark the funeral of one of their IRA heroes. Once a criminal always a criminal in his book, and he recognised the status of the IRA as a legitimate political operation about as much as he recognised the legitimacy of the claim Argentina had on the Falklands. Mainly he didn't like the man's sullen, mute insolence. No respect for authority. That was obvious. Like many of his generation he would have benefited from National Service.

George Napier was too young himself to have gone through National Service, but he had joined the Territorial Army while at university and when he graduated it had been a toss-up between the armed forces and the police. The police had won by a narrow margin. The man in front of him wouldn't last a weekend with the TA he decided, let alone the proper army.

As far as he was concerned the police force should be like a domestic army. Anybody who didn't realise they were fighting a war nowadays hadn't read the papers or listened to the news. Never mind the war on terror; the amount of guns and knives on the streets made the boroughs of London every bit as dangerous a place to live as Beirut in his opinion. And to fight that, to bring law and order back to the country, took vision, it took backbone and it took discipline, by God. And although he knew that the man standing in front of him had been responsible for bringing down a couple of bad apples within the department, he was far from convinced that Delaney wasn't a bruised fruit himself. He put the report he had been reading into a folder and shook his head.

"I'm sorry, but that won't be possible. It wouldn't be appropriate, I'm afraid, Inspector."

"I was responsible for the man's arrest, and he has vital information on another case, sir."

The superintendent picked up the folder again and waved it at Delaney. "As I recall it, after his arrest he had to spend time in accident and emergency with a suspected fractured skull. And the other case is the incident in which your wife died?"

"That's right."

"Given your involvement in that incident, and the fact that it was your wife who was killed, I don't think it is appropriate for you to take the lead on this investigation. Which is why I have instructed Detective

Inspector Skinner to coordinate with the prison authorities and their internal investigation."

"With respect, sir, Norrell said he would only speak to me."

The superintendent frowned. "I don't think he is in any condition to speak to anyone just now."

"Convenient timing."

Superintendent Napier sighed. "Concentrate on this dead woman on the common, Delaney. Any movement on identifying her?"

"Nothing yet, but we're working on it. She doesn't match anyone on the missing persons' register."

"I want a tight lid, Delaney. I've already had the press wanting details."

"Maybe it would help, sir. Someone probably knows her."

"We speak to the press when I say. We clear on that, Inspector?"

"Sir."

Delaney turned to leave, pausing at the door as the superintendent called him back.

"One more thing, Delaney."

"Sir?"

"I am well aware what happened between you and my predecessor. Diane Campbell argued very strongly for bringing you back into the fold. I think you should know that I had grave misgivings but allowed myself to be persuaded by her. I hope you are not going to let me down."

"Just let me do my job, sir. That's all I ask."

The superintendent stood and picked up the file, nodding a dismissal to Delaney. "Go and do it then."

Delaney shut the door behind him. Napier walked across to a filing cabinet and put the folder in the top drawer. He looked at himself in the mirror and smoothed his hair with the flat of his hand. He kept himself in very good condition. A punishing fitness schedule, good bone structure and clear, ebony skin made him look younger than his fifty-two years, but the white hair above his ears told the true story. As he looked at his temples critically, he considered, yet again, dyeing his hair, but then discounted it, as he always did. Gravitas was far more becoming in a career policeman than vanity. And George Napier was nothing if not ambitious.

He sat back behind his desk and thought about the surly policeman who had just left his office. He wasn't sure there was a place for people like him in the force any more, but time would tell: Jack Delaney could be a help or a hindrance to him. And most of the people who had spoken to the superintendent said Delaney was a first-rate detective with good instincts and a great success rate. If his foot danced a little outside the touchline now and again that was fine by him, as long as he didn't drop the ball. But if he did lose it in the tackle, if he became more of a liability than an asset, then George Napier was going to come down on him like an All Blacks front line. Guaranteed.

Delaney paused at the drinks cooler filling a cup as DI Jimmy Skinner approached. Delaney was still considered tall, at six feet, but Jimmy Skinner had a good few inches on him. He was a lot thinner, though, and pale-faced from too many nights playing Internet poker. His wife had left him the previous January because he had refused to walk away from an online game at midnight to hear Big Ben chime the New Year in and kiss her on the final bong. He had felt quite justified, however, as he was holding two aces with a third on the flop. But his wife didn't see it that way, and now he had even more time on his hands. "You've simply got to know when to hold them, know when to fold them," he had told his divorce lawyer, who had told him that it was his balls his wife was holding, fiscally speaking, and that she was going to cut them off. Which she proceeded to do, leaving Skinner a fiscal soprano.

Skinner helped himself to a cup of water and looked at Delaney. "You spoke to the new big cheese then?"

Delaney drank his water in a long gulp almost feeling the liquid rehydrating his veins. "Yup."

"What do you make of him?"

"Remember the old joke about how to become a policeman?"

"Grow a tit on your head and paint it blue?"

Delaney threw his cup in the bin. "You're looking into the Norrell thing, I hear."

"You tag along any time you want to, Jack."

Delaney nodded. "Appreciate it, Jimmy."

"You were due to see him this morning?"

"First thing, yeah."

"Seems like a hell of a coincidence he was taken out before you got there then."

Delaney grunted. "I don't believe in coincidences."

"You think he genuinely knew something about your wife's death?"

"Nothing in it for him if he was making it up."

"Kevin Norrell was never a grass."

"Yeah, well, your perspectives change when you're standing naked in a shower surrounded by hardened criminals. No pun intended."

"True."

"Or when there's a contract out on you."

Skinner looked at him, a little surprised. "You think that was the case?"

"I think as soon as he started offering to sing like a canary, someone wanted to snap off his beak and clip his wings. Permanently."

"He was meant to go down hard. That's for certain. But if they thought he was dealing kiddie porn . . .?" He shrugged. "Could just be that, cowboy."

"It's too neat. Someone in there wanted him shut up and quickly."

Delaney and Skinner walked back towards the CID offices. "You saw one of the guys who attacked him?"

"Martin Quigley. But he isn't saying anything. Norrell smashed him up pretty good with a lavatory bowl. Fractured his jaw in three places."

"Helpful."

"But he can write. He claims they took Norrell out as a matter of course, like they would any other kiddie fiddler, given half the chance. No other agenda."

99

"You believe him?"

"I don't know. He might have been roped in. He's just as much an ape for hire as Norrell himself. Paid to hurt not to think. And Norrell was involved with Walker who was involved big time in kiddie porn. It's a good cover story if you have another reason for wanting him dead."

Delaney said goodbye to Skinner, stuck his head round the CID office door and beckoned to Sally Cartwright. "Come on, Constable, you're with me."

Sally stood up from her desk, a little flushed, quickly closing down the report she had been reading on her computer. She picked up her jacket from the back of her chair and joined Delaney.

He looked back at her computer as her screensaver came on. "What are you working on?"

"Just catching up with some paperwork." She avoided his eyes and headed briskly out to the corridor. "Where are we going?"

"South Hampstead Tube."

"Sir?"

Delaney walked beside her and held out a photofit picture that the computer artist had generated from Valerie Manners' description of the flasher on the common. "Our man might have been wearing a suit, she said?"

"Apparently. Under his mac," Sally confirmed.

"So what does that tell us?"

"That flashing isn't just a blue-collar crime and he's probably not a student."

100

"Exactly, he's up too early in the morning for a start. Maybe he was giving his John Thomas a quick airing before putting in a hard day at the office . . ." He looked at Sally and smiled. "As it were."

"Which do you reckon came first, sir? The book or the expression? I've often wondered."

"What are you on about?" Delaney asked, puzzled.

"John Thomas and Lady Jane. *Lady Chatterley's Lover.*"

Delaney threw her a look. "I know you've got a degree and all that shite, Detective Constable, but do you think you could save the book-club chit-chat for your weekend dinner parties and concentrate on the case?"

"You reckon he was heading for the Tube?"

"He lives or works near here. And given the timing it is more likely he was on his way to work somewhere out of the locality."

"So you think he lives somewhere near the heath?"

"Sexual predators like to operate within a comfort zone. Somewhere they know well. So if something happens they know where to run to."

"And the murdered girl. Does she live locally, do you think?"

The desk sergeant called out as they headed to the front entrance. "Good to see you back, Jack."

"Cheers, Dave." He opened the front door for Sally. "I don't know about the girl. It depends if it was an opportunistic or planned killing. Time of death will help."

"Not going to be wandering on the heath in the dead of night you mean."

Delaney nodded as they walked over to Sally's car. "It's unlikely."

"Mind you, it was a full moon last night."

"Meaning?"

Sally fished out her car keys and opened the driver's door to her car. "Well, it brings out the crazies. And her being a goth. Maybe there's a connection. The mystic power of the moon and all that."

Delaney got into the car next to her and stretched his legs forward. "The moon might play a part in paganism. Witchcraft, Wicca, that kind of thing. Not sure it applies to goths."

"No. But the belt buckle. I've been thinking about it."

"What about it?"

"Looking at the photos more closely both sides had a representation of the Green Man. Big pagan symbol."

Delaney nodded thoughtfully. "Maybe, and there may have been a full moon last night, but you'd never have been able to see it. Not with all that cloud cover and rain."

"I suppose not. So, it looks like the body was dumped there. She could have come from anywhere."

"'Ill met by moonlight, proud Titania.'"

Sally looked across at him, frowning as she fired up the engine. "Sir?"

"What? You surprised I know a little Shakespeare? They do have schools in Ireland, you know."

"Yeah, I do know that. Put your seat belt on."

102

Delaney sighed and pulled the strap across. "And it's cockney rhyming slang."

"What is?"

"John Thomas. So the expression came first."

"Oh." Sally smiled. "So what does it rhyme with?"

Delaney considered for a moment, then sighed and flapped his hand. "Just drive the car, Constable."

"On average two and a half million people use the tube system every day and I'm guessing something like bloody plenty of them use South Hampstead station," Delaney said as he stood up from the computer, rubbed his sore eyes and yawned.

Sally paused the CCTV footage and looked up at him, amusement quirking the corners of her mouth. "Must have been some night."

Delaney yawned again, putting his hand in front of his mouth. "You have no idea."

Sally gestured at the computer screen. "We're up to twelve o'clock."

Delaney nodded and stretched his eyes. "Let's get these photos in front of the nurse, see if she recognises any of them."

Sally collected three photos that had been printed out of some possible men that matched the description of the flasher they had been given by Valerie Manners and stood up.

Kate Walker was sitting at her computer typing up her notes for the post-mortem on the mystery woman. She pushed the print icon and some moments later picked up a ten by eight, black-and-white close-up of the woman's neck. Someone had slashed her hard enough to slice the flesh clear to the bone. What kind of anger could have fuelled such brutality? Even if the attack was sexually motivated it still came down to anger. Impotent rage, maybe, as it was clear the woman had not been sexually assaulted. No evidence of it at least. The irony of the thought was not lost on her and she shivered again, thinking about the possibility that it could have been her dead body being examined by one of her colleagues. How close a tightrope to death we walk in life, she thought. How fragile the human body is. How soft and defenceless against true purpose, true will to hurt. And yet we dance on the tightrope blindfolded, and laugh while we do it. Only Kate didn't feel like laughing today. She wasn't sure she ever would again. The telephone rang suddenly, shrilly. She started, her heart thumping in her chest, and snatched the phone up, taking a moment or two to steady her shattered nerves before answering. "Kate Walker."

"Kate, it's Caroline Akunin."

Kate took in a deep breath. "Go on."

"I haven't got the blood work back . . ." She paused.

"But?" asked Kate.

"But, I ran a check on Paul Archer."

"And?"

"He's out on police bail at the moment, Kate. Pending trial. He's already been charged with rape."

Kate was puzzled for a moment. "What do you mean?"

"His estranged wife. She's charged him with rape. The court case is coming up this week. He's a rapist, Kate."

Kate nodded, taking it in, she couldn't speak for a moment. "I'm coming in to White City now for a briefing, I'll come and see you while I'm there."

She hung up the phone and collected the photographs and her printed out notes. She stood up and winced, holding a hand to her stomach and had to fight the urge to throw up again.

Valerie Manners looked impatiently at her watch and scowled at Danny Vine, the uniformed constable who was stood by the door of the interview room at the front part of White City police station. It was a featureless, plain room, with a rectangular table, six plastic chairs and a couple of windows looking out to the car park. Not a particularly pleasant place to spend any length of time. She looked at her watch again. "How much longer are they going to be?" she snapped.

The newly qualified constable shrugged. "They're on their way. Hard to tell."

"Well, it's not good enough. I'm due back on shift in a few hours and I've hardly had time to catch forty winks, let alone have a proper sleep."

"You could always call in. You have had a traumatic day."

The nurse shook her head angrily. "You see, that's what's wrong with this generation. The slightest thing and people can just call in. Where would we be if the RAF had just *called in* in 1940?"

"I don't know, ma'am."

"Well, I tell you where we'd be. We'd be right here," she said, realising that wasn't quite what she meant. "Only we wouldn't be speaking English, would we? We'd be speaking German."

"I've got an A level in German."

Valerie glared at him. "Is that supposed to be funny?"

"No. I was just saying."

"And that's another wrong. People are always 'just saying'. In my day, young man, people *did*. They didn't say. They got on with it. They got the job done."

Danny Vine sighed inwardly with relief as the handle on the door turned and DI Jack Delaney and DC Sally Cartwright came into the room.

"Sorry to keep you waiting, Ms Manners."

Valerie smiled sweetly at Delaney. "That's quite all right, Detective Inspector. As I was just explaining to the young officer . . ." she gestured unimpressed at Danny Vine, "I am only too happy to do my civic duty. Only too happy."

"We're very grateful."

The nurse held her hand up. "No gratitude necessary. I am from a generation that steps up to the line when the call comes."

Delaney pulled out a chair and sat opposite her. He opened a folder and put the photographs of the men they had pulled from the security footage from South Hampstead Tube station.

"I'd like you to look at these photos, Ms Manners. See if you recognise any of the men as the gentleman you encountered this morning."

106

"The pervert, you mean. He was certainly no gentleman."

She pulled out a pair of glasses from her handbag and perched them on the end of her nose as she looked at the photographs Delaney had handed her across the table. She studied each one for a long time before looking up and taking her glasses off. "They all look possible."

"But you can't be sure."

The nurse shrugged apologetically. "Well, if I'm honest my eyes weren't exactly drawn to his face, if you see what I mean."

Sally Cartwright stepped forward. "Could you look again, Ms Manners?"

Valerie Manners picked up the photos and looked at them again, then shook her head and handed the photos back to Sally. "Sorry, but any one of them could be him. Is it possible to see photos of the area of exposure, as it were?"

Sally blinked, not quite sure she had heard correctly. "I beg your pardon?"

"I am a nurse after all. And it might help."

Danny Vine couldn't hold back a short laugh and Delaney glared at him. "Wait outside, Constable."

"Sir." Danny hurried out of the room, shutting the door behind him.

Delaney turned back to Valerie Manners. "I'm sorry, ma'am. But that won't be possible. It would be a procedural irregularity, I'm afraid."

"It's just the injury. Very unlikely two people would have the same."

Delaney took the photos off Sally and flicked through them quickly. "What do you mean, the injury?"

"To his penis. Quite extensive scarring, and some deformation I would say."

"What?" Delaney couldn't believe what he was hearing.

"It was quite noticeable." She looked up at Delaney's surprised expression. "I'm sorry. Didn't I mention that?"

"No, ma'am. You didn't."

"Do you think it might be important?"

DI Jimmy Skinner was well aware that the chatter beneath him had stopped as soon as the clang of his hard leather shoes on the metal walkway echoed around the large building. He looked over the railing, down at the many prisoners who were scattered about the recreation area, their faces turned up to his momentarily and then back to what they had been doing. Noise filled the building again. The sound of caged men resigned to their fate. The truth was Jimmy Skinner felt a lot of empathy for them. They were all gamblers in the main, much like him. Jimmy recognised that, just like he had been in the past many, many times, these men had been fucked on the river. Deliverance they called it. The odds had been in his favour, it was science after all, but the cards had turned up and defied the odds and he had taken a bad beat. He himself had taken a lot of bad beats over the years, just like the men below. Someone had lost their nerve or a car had failed to start, or a family that should have been on holiday had cancelled at the last minute and were at home when they shouldn't have been. Bad beats all. Or the baddest beat of the lot: being born in the wrong part of London in the wrong kind of family. The kind of family that had no hope outside of crime. No hope because the system had fucked them on the river before they'd even been born, and now the only way out was by the gun or knife, or with a flame and a spike and a packet of temporary oblivion to trade. So he felt a kind of sympathy for them. Not for the rapists, mind, or the child abusers or the soulless killers. For them he'd have a rope waiting, see how the cards fell on the ultimate gamble of all.

The prison guard coughed and Jimmy Skinner turned back to him and carried on walking towards the open cell doors and put the men below out of his mind. One thing you learned playing poker was that you put the past behind you and moved on to your next game. Chasing losses was a sure way to destruction and Jimmy Skinner wasn't that kind of gambler. He didn't play to lose, he played to stay even, so he could play again.

The officer, a wide-set man in his forties with steel-grey hair and eyes as bereft of humour as a warehouse guard dog, stood by the open door of one of the cells and jerked with his thumb to show Jimmy the man inside.

Neil Riley was a scrawny, long-haired man in his early thirties, with skin the colour of church candles and tattoos covering both his arms. Tattoos that hadn't been modelled on any works of the great Renaissance artists as far as Jimmy Skinner could see. He was sat on his bed rolling a cigarette and looked up dispassionately as the policeman entered the cell.

Jimmy fished a new packet of cigarettes out of his pocket and threw it on the bed beside him. The man looked at it, a sneer quirking the corner of his thin-lipped mouth. "You better do better than fucking that."

Jimmy nodded then picked up the packet of cigarettes from the bed, put them in his pocket and slapped the man back-handed, hard across his face.

"The fuck you think you're doing? I got rights, you know."

A snort of laugher came from the guard outside and Jimmy clicked his fingers to get the man's attention. "First rule. You don't swear in my presence."

"Fuck that."

Jimmy hit him hard again, the other side of his face this time, open-palmed.

"Jesus Christ!"

Skinner hit him back-handed again. "Or blaspheme."

Neil Riley scrambled up on the bed, putting his back to the wall and held his hand up at Skinner. "All right, you made your f —" He caught himself. "You made your point."

Skinner nodded. "Good."

"And I don't know what you want to see me for. I don't know anything about anything."

"You know Kevin Norrell, don't you?"

"I knew him."

Skinner leaned in pointedly. "He isn't dead yet, Riley."

The sallow-faced man looked surprised. "I thought —"

"What did you think?"

"I heard he was dead, that's all."

"And where did you hear that from?"

Riley shrugged. "Word gets round. What do you think, this place is a Carmelite nunnery? You think nobody talks?"

Skinner was a little surprised, and ignoring his own rules, said, "What do you know about the fucking Carmelites?"

"I went to a convent primary school."

"I thought that was just for girls?"

"No. Some are mixed up to a certain age."

Skinner caught himself. "Can we get back to the fucking point here?"

"I was just saying."

"Never mind all that bollocks, just tell me who told you Norrell was dead."

"I don't know, what does it matter who told me?"

"Someone took five inches of sharpened steel and tried to make a shish kebab out of his organs with it. Maybe that was the guy who told you, that's what matters."

Riley shook his head. "Get real, Detective. Whoever did it is going to keep his mouth shut, isn't he?"

Skinner glared at him for a moment or two, resisting the urge to slap him hard around the head again just for the fun of it. "Let's get back to the point, shall we?"

"Which is?"

"Which is: you were a friend of Kevin Norrell."

"Says who?"

Skinner looked around the cell. "You see anyone else standing in this fucking room?"

Riley shrugged again. "I knew him a little."

"Come off it, Riley. You think we don't read files? You grew up on the same estate as him. You've been busted together more than once. You knew the man."

Riley hesitated for a moment, as if weighing up his options. Finally he said, "Yeah, I knew him."

"He's on remand. He gets to speak to people. And the information is that you and he were buddy-buddy in here."

"Someone has to watch your back."

"You did a good job of watching his."

Riley held his skinny arms up. "What good would I be? You know Norrell, he didn't need me riding on his wing."

"So what did you do for him?"

"I've been here a while. I know who's who and what's what. I filled him in."

"What was he going to tell Delaney?"

Riley pulled a face, so Skinner slapped him hard again. Sometimes he loved being a policeman. Riley yelped and the guard from outside looked in again. He grinned and nodded to Skinner with approval.

"For Christ's sake, what was that for?"

He flinched and pressed back against the wall as Skinner leaned in, but he didn't hit him this time. "I'll ask the question again. What was he going to tell Delaney?"

Riley shook his head, agitated now. "I honestly don't know. His court case was coming up soon. Preliminary hearings. He told me he had stuff on Chief Superintendent Walker. Maybe he was looking to make a deal."

"He said it was about Delaney's wife."

"He never said anything to me about it. But if he wanted to see Delaney that was a sure-fire way of getting him in."

"What else would he want to see him for?"

Riley shook his head. "Fuck knows, you're the detective."

Some people just couldn't help themselves.

Paul Archer strode angrily down the steps, shrugging into his overcoat. The woman behind the reception desk smiled at him but he ignored her. She wasn't his type and he had taken the afternoon off for more particular distractions than the kind offered in idle badinage with insipid blondes. Paul Archer had the kind of itch that could only be scratched by a certain type of woman. And he knew just where to find her.

Delaney stood in front of the briefing room. On the board behind him were pinned the photographs taken of the dead woman they had found in the woods. Hampstead's very own Black Dahlia, he couldn't help thinking.

"All right, listen up." Delaney raised his voice above the chatter that filled the room and conversations died as they focused their attention on the detective inspector. "Now, as yet we don't have any ID on the woman. We think she was murdered sometime during last night. We're placing her age, give or take a few years, in her mid-twenties."

"Was she killed in the woods, or dumped there?" Audrey Hobson, a uniformed inspector in her fifties, called out.

"Best we can tell, she was killed where we found her."

"An opportunist killing, or was she taken there?"

"We don't know, Audrey. It was lousy weather. It was cold, windy, raining. It's unlikely she'd be in the woods alone at that time of night."

PC Bob Wilkinson spoke out. "It's possible. Like Sally said earlier. Maybe it's some witchcraft thing. She's dressed up as a goth. You know how some of them fruitcakes are. Lesbians and pagans, give them a full moon and they start believing all kind of bollocks."

Diane Campbell glared at him. "Not very helpful, Constable."

Delaney stopped himself from smiling as he held his hand up to quell the beginnings of laughter in the room. "Nothing's discounted. Most likely scenario is that she was taken there, though. Sex attackers don't usually hang around in rainstorms looking for victims."

Sally Cartwright held up her hand. She looked like she should still be in school, Delaney thought, but was glad she wasn't. She may look like a Girl Guide, but he knew beneath that pretty exterior was what his North American colleagues would have called a tough cookie.

He'd had to depend on her more than once and she hadn't let him down. "Yes, Constable?"

"Is there anything in the database matching the MO?"

"Good question. We're running it through at the moment. Until we get the detailed post it's all rather general. No immediate hits."

Diane Campbell stepped forward. "What leads are you pursuing, Jack?"

"A flasher was operating early this morning, near the scene of the crime."

"You think he was involved?"

"Unlikely. But he may have seen something."

"You have a good ID on him?"

"Pretty good. This isn't a run-of-the-mill flasher."

"Go on."

Delaney produced a couple of A3 sheets of paper. He pinned the first on the wall. It showed an artist's rendition of a wild-haired man in his late twenties, early thirties. "This is the man we're looking for, and this . . ." He hesitated before putting up the second picture. "This is his penis."

There was some wincing, some groaning and some laughter at the second picture that Delaney pinned on the board. An artist's rendition, blown up, from the nurse's description, of the man's scarred penis.

"Is that life-size?" Bob Wilkinson couldn't resist it, and now the laughter rippled round the room like a rumbling sea at high tide.

"All right, children, that's enough." Diane Campbell's voice barked and the room fell silent. "Have a look at

115

the picture over there." She pointed at the dead woman's mutilated body. "Any one of you find anything funny in that?" She looked pointedly at Bob Wilkinson.

"No, ma'am."

Delaney's phone chose that moment to ring. He looked at the caller and shrugged apologetically at his boss. "I've got to take this. I'll be right back."

Delaney strode quickly from the briefing room before Diane Campbell could stop him and answered the call in the corridor outside. "What have you got for me, Jimmy?"

On the other end of the phone, DI Jimmy Skinner's voice sounded thin and echoing, the sound of men in the background telling Delaney he was calling from the prison. "Hi, Jack. I'm at Bayfield."

"I gathered. Go on."

"Nobody's talking. I put the hard word on Neil Riley, Norrell's old oppo, and according to him Kevin Norrell was taken down because of the kiddie porn."

"You believe him?"

"I don't know, Jack. Something feels hinky."

"You reckon it has anything to do with my wife?"

"Maybe. But you know as well as I do that you can trust Norrell as far as you could throw him one-handed. Which is ruddy nowhere. The guy's a timeserving prick of the first order."

"Why lie about it?"

There was a pause and Delaney could picture Skinner shrugging at the other end of the line. "The guy was desperate. That much seems clear. Whether it was because he knew there was a hit out on him, or about the trial coming up, who knows? His mate reckons that he had something on Chief Superintendent Walker, perhaps. He was looking to deal. Maybe talking about your wife was the best way to get you in to see him."

"Maybe . . ." But Delaney wasn't convinced. Kevin Norrell had the brainpower of a fermented melon, but even he wouldn't be stupid enough to jerk Delaney's chain over his dead wife. Delaney glanced down at the stairs at the end of the corridor as the sound of high heels clicking rhythmically on the wooden steps grew louder. "Keep on it, Jimmy."

Delaney snapped his phone shut and looked across as Kate came up the stairs and headed towards the briefing room, unwrapping her scarf from her neck and taking off her gloves. If she was a little taken aback to see Delaney waiting outside the door, she didn't betray it in her body language. Delaney watched her confident stride, the determined set to her jaw, but in her eyes he saw something that disturbed him. Something that went against her usual, poised exterior. Something that reached out to him in a primal sense. Something very much like fear.

"Kate."

"Not now, Jack." She sailed past him.

Delaney hurried after her and took her arm. He was shocked to see the way she flinched away. "I'm sorry."

She looked at him, anger flaring behind the fear that was still liquid in her deep, brown eyes. "Sorry for what exactly?"

Delaney hesitated. "I didn't mean to startle you."

Kate nodded, as if his answer had confirmed her thoughts, lessened him once again in her eyes, and he felt the shame of it like a creeping feeling on his skin. "I need to get to the meeting," she said.

She opened the door and walked into the briefing room before Delaney had a chance to say anything more.

Jimmy Skinner was heading down the iron staircase to be taken back through to the reception area when Derek Watters, the guard who had been posted outside Neil Riley's cell, fell into step behind him. He spoke quietly.

"You want to know what was going down with Kevin Norrell?"

Skinner turned back to look at him but the guard gestured him on.

"Just keep walking. I'll talk to you about it, but not here and not for gratis."

"What are you after?"

"A drink. A serious drink. I reckon Delaney's good for it."

"When and where?"

They reached the bottom of the stairs.

"Six o'clock. The Pillars of Hercules. Soho."

Skinner nodded, imperceptibly, as another guard approached.

"All right, Derek. I'll take him from here."

Derek Watters slapped Skinner on the arm as the other guard led him away and back towards the entrance.

At four o'clock in the afternoon, it doesn't matter what time of year, Soho is a busy place. But the White Horse

118

pub, just down the road from Walker's Court, was relatively quiet today; as quiet as it was most days during the week, after lunch and before the workers came off shift. Later on it would be bustling with the regulars who preferred the scruffy traditionalism of a proper London boozer to the trendy bars that had recently sprung up around Soho like mushrooms in an autumn wood. Soho took its name, most believed, from the old hunting cry *Soho,* much like the *Tally ho* that still sounds from blue-blooded lips up and down the shires, hunting ban or no. Less fanciful, perhaps, was that the name just came from a shortening of South Holborn.

The dark-haired man sitting on his own in the pub preferred the first version. As far as he was concerned, Soho was still a hunting ground. The best kind.

The White Horse was a pub he liked to drink in and watch people. A spit-and-sawdust bar with a dirty, wooden planked floor and a look about it as faded as an old man's shirt. The man liked it because he could look at the whores as they worked the street outside, and watch them closer when they came in for a nip of cheap vodka against the elements. Their skinny legs sometimes encased in fishnet stockings and knee-length boots, sometimes bare and cold in red leather shoes, their painted smiles cracking in the sudden warmth like old varnish as they took a brief respite from the cold outdoors.

At the moment, however, there were just a few tourists sheltering from the persistent rain and a couple of old men, seated separately and so far gone on strong

119

beer that time meant nothing them. When they got up in the morning the pub was open and when they went home and collapsed the pub was open, and all that filled the hours in between waking and sleeping was the slow annihilation of thought, feeling and memory. Annihilation by the pint and shot glass.

The man seated at the round table by the entrance door watched the old men with contempt undisguised in his eyes. His right hand caressed his left wrist.

He looked up at the television set above the corner of the bar. He'd been watching the news now for over an hour. No mention of his own artistry that day on the heath. No mention at all. And that made him angry.

The woman reading the news was young, blonde and very pretty. The man took a sip of his drink and watched her lips moving, not listening to the words she was saying. It was all irrelevant. Her lips were full, coloured with a soft, strawberry-pink lipstick. He licked his own lips, as if he could taste hers.

He ran his finger around the circle of moisture on the cracked surface of the wooden table and something sparked in his eyes. Not anger, or self-pity, but desire. He looked up at the television screen again. At the face of Melanie Jones, the news reporter from Sky News, as she smiled at the camera and wittered on about the change in the weather and coastal erosion in some Norfolk village nobody had ever heard of.

It was clear they had no knowledge of what he had done. And it was equally clear that the police had failed to grasp the significance of it. He needed to go to work again. Sometimes it took two pieces of the puzzle for

120

someone to see the connection. Sometimes it took more. Well, if they needed another piece, he'd give it to them. *Can you see what it is yet?* Art is nothing without an audience after all. He smiled to himself taking another sip of his drink and looked at the elderly man at the bar who was watching him with a curious look in his eye, after a moment or two the man looked away and turned his attention back to his pint of Guinness. Some things you didn't want to look at too closely.

Especially in London.

Kate Walker looked at the photographs on the wall. Pictures of a young woman, once vital, now lying on a cold shelf in the morgue. Anatomy of a murder. She looked at the cold savagery of the slashes on the woman's body and felt sick for her race.

Kate could feel the restlessness in the room behind her as she continued to look at the photos. But she needed a moment or two to collect herself. Her heart was racing, as it had been since morning, and her skin was clammy. She'd never felt like this before in one of these meetings. Some people were terrified talking to a large number of people, it was the top fear in the country, bigger even than spiders or snakes, but that had never been one of her phobias. She knew more than most people she ever met and didn't mind demonstrating it. It was a measure of just how rattled she was that she was nervous now. She took a breath or two and turned round and nodded to the assembled policemen and women. "As you already know we're putting her age at mid-twenties. Time of death between one o'clock and two o'clock last night."

The young constable who had been guarding the body from the prurient gaze of the public earlier in the morning raised his hand.

"Can I ask a question?"

"Of course," Kate said. "What is it, Constable?"

"How can you be so sure about the time of death? What are the signs?" Danny Vine asked, his notebook open and his pen ready.

Amusement rippled round the room. Kate glared at them. "All right. Some of you know as much about forensic pathology as I do — in your own opinion. But for the benefit of those who don't, there are a number of ways of determining time of death. It's a science but it's not an exact science. Rigor mortis usually sets in about three or four hours after death with full rigor about twelve hours later. Our victim hadn't reached that stage yet. So that's one thing. Ambient temperature plays a part though. Three to four hours is the norm with mild temperatures."

"It was brass monkeys last night, ma'am."

"Yes, thank you, Constable Wilkinson. You're right, it was bloody cold last night so that skews our calculations. But there are other factors we can use." She looked across to see Danny Vine was taking copious notes. Keen to be a detective, she reckoned. She took a sip of water to allow him to catch up.

"Other conditions factor in. The age of the body, how active the person was prior to death. If they were very active then rigor mortis can set in quicker. We

122

don't know what this woman was doing prior to her murder but at that time of night we can assume she hadn't been jogging on the heath. So we look at other indicators." She pointed to the photos mounted on the display panels.

"The heart, as you all know, is a muscle that pumps blood around the body. Once that pump stops working, at the time of death, blood collects in the most dependent parts of the body. That is livor mortis. Then the body stiffens, which is rigor mortis, and then with no heat being generated post mortem, the body begins to cool and this is the algor mortis stage."

She pointed at the blue staining on the body of the dead woman. "Blood will collect in those parts of the body that are in contact with the ground. Most commonly the back and the buttocks when the person is lying face up. The skin is pale because all the blood that keeps it pink drains into the larger veins. It can take minutes or hours after death, but livor mortis will manifest itself on the skin."

She pointed to a close-up photograph of the discoloration on the woman's face. "These purplish blemishes are what embalmers call post-mortem stain. It takes a few hours but after that the blood becomes what we call fixed. That is, it won't move to other parts of the body if the corpse is moved. So we can use that to also determine where the murder took place. And, in this instance, together with the other factors such as the arterial spray in the immediate area, we can say pretty definitely that the woman was killed in the place where she was discovered."

123

Kate walked back to the desk and took another sip of water. She was aware that Delaney was watching her but determined to keep professional.

"There is a condition, at the time of death, known as primary flaccidity."

"Bob Wilkinson knows all about that," a female officer called out from the back of the room, and laughter erupted. Kate smiled, the grim photos on the wall behind were testament to the seriousness of the situation but the laughter didn't mean anyone in the room wasn't focused on the dead woman, and finding justice for her. Black humour was just a coping mechanism, after all.

She held up a hand. "All right, settle down. Constable Wilkinson is already no doubt well aware that there are medications available on prescription for his particular ailment, so there is no need for embarrassment nowadays."

Bob Wilkinson scowled, taking the ribbing in good heart.

Kate waited for the laughter to subside and then continued. "A dead body will usually stay in full rigor mortis for anything between twenty-four and forty-eight hours. After that the muscles start to relax again and secondary laxity," she smiled apologetically at Bob Wilkinson, "or flaccidity occurs. And it will usually follow the same pattern as it began." She gestured behind her. "Not applicable in this case of course. Another way of gauging how long a person has been dead is by taking the core temperature. And again we have to factor in the ambient temperature. The unseasonably cold weather last night meant that the woman's body will have cooled a lot faster than if she had been murdered at home for example. Wherever her home is."

Kate glanced back at the mottled face of the ravaged woman and wondered if anyone was waiting for her at that home. A distraught parent or worried boyfriend. She assumed she wasn't married as she had no wedding ring, or indications that she had ever worn one.

At the back of the room, meanwhile, Delaney was watching Kate as she pinned different photographs of the murdered young woman to the display board, and talked about the forensic analytical techniques. But those details washed over him, hardly taking in what she was saying. She was discussing putrefaction as another method of establishing time of death. But again it wasn't strictly relevant as putrefaction didn't take place until the second or third day after death and Delaney had seen enough corpses in his time to know about the telltale signs of green discoloration, and the putrid odour that accompanied it. An odour that told him they were already far too late for the victim and had given the murderer a good few days' head start on them. The first twenty-four hours were often critical in a murder case and if the body was putrefying before it was discovered it wasn't a good omen.

Kate turned to the room. "We know the victim is a young female, we know she was murdered sometime in the early hours of last night and we know we are dealing with an extremely sick individual."

A murmur went round the room again, sensing that Kate had finished but she held her hand up for quiet once again.

"One more thing." She walked over to the display panels again and pointed at a blown-up photo of the young woman's neck. "There is an unusual puncture mark on her neck."

"Vampire you think, Doctor?"

A laugh went around the room again. But a nervous one. After all, the woman had been murdered in the dead of night, under a full moon, was dressed like someone out of Bram Stoker and had a couple of pagan symbols on her belt.

Kate let the laughter subside. "I have no idea what to think."

The previously recorded news highlights were playing on monitors throughout the building. Melanie Jones smiling at the camera. It was a practised smile, full of hope, innocence and genuine wonder at the world. A smile that belied the news that she had just been reporting. A third teenager stabbed to death in south London that week. An eighty-three-year-old woman raped and murdered in Nottingham. The foreclosure of a car works in the Midlands that was putting five thousand people out of work. At Sky News the policy was that the viewer should want to kiss the messenger not kill her. And a lot of people wanted to kiss Melanie Jones. The news is a bitter pill, after all, and Melanie Jones provided the sweet, sweet sugar that helped the medicine go down.

At the moment it was her line producer, Ronald Bliss, that was going down. His head nestled between her thighs as she sat legs akimbo on the toilet in the ensuite in his office. She wasn't smiling now. She was looking at her nails. There was a slight chip on her left index finger. She looked across at her handbag which was propped up against Ronald's knees. She'd have loved to get her polish out of it and fix the nail, but thought it might not go down too well. She looked at her watch. He'd been at it for five minutes, breathing heavily through his nostrils and sounding like a St Bernard in labour. Bliss was five foot six and several stones overweight and Melanie hoped the heavy breathing wasn't a prelude to a heart attack. She looked down at the top of his head; he was only thirty-eight but already his hair was thinning badly. She could see the pink of his scalp through the strands of his ginger hair, and frowned slightly. Someone should tell him about dandruff shampoo, but that was his wife's job, not hers. She looked at her watch again, she'd give him a couple more minutes for form's sake then make a few whimpering noises and give him a quick wank, which should keep him happy for a week or so and her own promotion prospects on line.

A buzzing in her jacket pocket and then her phone rang. She took it out and was about to click it off when the man below mumbled, "Answer it, I like to hear your voice."

Melanie curled her lip at him and answered the phone, suppressing a yawn.

"Melanie Jones."

She listened for a while and then went very still. "Call me back in fifteen minutes. I can't talk now." She closed her phone and patted her producer on his head, just once and wiped her palm on the sleeve of her jacket.

"Sorry, Ronald, I think I just came on."

The man looked up, a shifty tremor in his glassine eyes. "I don't mind."

"Next week, eh." She shifted her thighs, squeezing him backward and leaned over to pick her thong. Silk, diamanté-studded, eighty-five pounds from Agent Provocateur. She stood up and the man looked at her hopefully.

"Could you at least leave me the knickers?"

The call she had just received could very well turn out to be the best break of her career and so she was suddenly feeling very generous. She tossed them into his eager hand.

"I want them replaced."

She closed the door behind her. The look of gratitude in her boss's eyes was proof, if she needed it, of just how weak men can be.

Kate walked down the corridor, wrapping the long scarf around her neck and heading for the stairs. She was happy to have put the briefing behind her, her mind wasn't on it. Much as she felt for the murdered woman, she had her own problems today. She headed down the broad staircase and walked to the police surgeon's room. She dreaded what she was about to hear. When she had worked as a police surgeon Kate had had to deal with many cases of rape. She knew that the cases reported were just the tip of the iceberg too. She'd been giving a lecture not many weeks past addressing the issue. She'd been horrified to look at the women against rape website and seen that if anything the situation was getting worse year by year. Ninety-eight per cent of domestic violence goes unreported. Two women a week murdered by their partner or ex-partner. One in six women in the country has been raped and yet only six per cent of reported rapes result in a conviction. And now, most likely, she was one of the statistics. She had no evidence that the man in her bed had assaulted her last night; it was a gut feeling, and the news that he had done it before just made her all the more certain that she had been violated. The thought of it made her feel nauseous again, her stomach lurching as though she were on a particularly choppy Channel crossing. She paused at the water cooler outside the police surgeon's office to take a drink and try and stop herself from hurling her lunch on the smooth tiles of the corridor.

Melanie Jones was standing outside in the car park of the London Apprentice. She was holding a large glass of red wine in her left hand and a Lambert & Butler Superking dangled from her perfectly painted lips.

"Shit," she said looking at her mobile phone, which was staying frustratingly quiet. "Ring, you bastard!" She sucked in a lungful of smoke and paced over to look at the river.

The recent heavy falls of rain had sluiced mud from the banks of either side of the Thames, and the strong

129

winds had stripped dead leaves and detritus from Eel Pie Island, further upriver, to wash down and swirl in the dirty, brown water. Melanie looked at it, her lip curling. Bloody thing was like an open sewer. It was a metaphor for London she thought, she couldn't wait to put the stinking city behind her. The phone call earlier though, if it was genuine, was a career-making opportunity and could have her in America sooner than you could say world exclusive. That had been her ambition ever since she had done a presenting course at Bournemouth University a few years ago. She was born for Fox News. As a teenager she had wanted to be a model, but she was too curvy as an adult, too womanly. Her legs were long for a woman but too short for a supermodel. She'd taken Ulrika Jonsson as her inspiration. So she had started off as a weather girl before being talent-spotted by a Sky News journo at a fundraiser for victims of the Boxing Day Tsunami. She'd rogered him senseless that night on a king-size waterbed and as a consequence he had made the right calls for her and just like that she was in with Rupert Murdoch. Not that she'd ever met the man, but maybe all that would change, and soon. The phone buzzed in her hand and she almost dropped it, her palms suddenly moist with perspiration. She already had the title of her book in mind. *Intimate Conversations With a Serial Killer*.

She took a deep breath and pushed the answer button, her voice like gunpowder soaked in honey.

"Melanie Jones. Talk to me."

* ★ ★

Caroline Akunin was standing at her window drinking a cup of white tea when Kate walked into her office. She found herself standing a lot more often these days, the baby was definitely making its presence felt. Sitting behind the sturdy police desk for any long periods of time was just not possible any more. She ran a thoughtful hand across her stomach and smiled sympathetically at Kate as she came in through the open door.

"I hope I haven't kept you waiting?" Kate asked.

"Of course not." The police surgeon's perfect teeth flashed in a dazzling smile.

"I had a briefing to attend first. It went on longer than I thought."

Caroline Akunin gestured to the chair in front of her desk as Kate shut the door behind her. "Why don't you sit down, Kate?"

Kate sat in the chair and gestured at the woman's prominent belly. "How's it going? The pregnancy." It seemed to her an inane thing to say but suddenly she wanted to talk about anything other than the reason she had come. Now she was sitting in the police surgeon's office she didn't want to hear anything that would confirm her worst fears. If you don't name the bogeyman he can't get you, after all. That's what her mother had always told her. But, as in a lot of things, she had lied.

Caroline smiled again; Kate could easily see why her Russian husband had fallen in love with her. "You know how it is. The first nine months are the worst."

Kate forced herself to return the smile. The truth was she had no idea how it was. Motherhood was not high on Kate's agenda. Just thinking about the modern world, the pollution, the global warming, the disaffected hopelessness and the violence of youth, the gun deaths and knifings, the rape, assault and mutilation of women throughout the country, the fear, as essential and as constant a part of London life now as the Victorian smog used to be, and she didn't think it ever would be. Who would want to bring a child into this world? But as she looked at her friend Caroline's beatific face, a living sculpture in maternal happiness, she knew she could never convey the darkness of her thoughts to her, so she changed the subject back to what she feared the most.

"What can you tell me about what happened last night?"

Caroline Akunin sighed and pulled another chair across closer to her friend. "I can tell you what our tests have shown so far."

"Go on."

"There are no physical signs of rape. No bruising, no abrasion."

"I know that."

"Of course, sorry."

"Don't apologise, Caroline. Just tell me straight. I need to know."

"Okay. Well, there are no pubic hairs."

"None at all?"

"Just yours, Kate."

"And there are no traces of semen?"

132

"None."

Kate blew out a sigh. "Thank God for that, at least."

"I guess."

Kate leaned her head back and looked at the ceiling. "Doesn't mean, of course, that nothing happened."

"No, it doesn't."

"Any traces of lubricant?"

"Nope."

"Lubricant- and spermicide-free condoms are readily available."

Caroline nodded. "Let's face it, Kate, he could have put a condom through a dishwasher before he used it."

"Reused. Nice image."

Caroline shrugged sympathetically.

"Don't tell me there's traces of Fairy Liquid power-ball?" She tried to smile but couldn't manage it this time.

"There's nothing, Kate."

"What about date-rape drugs? Rohypnol, one of those?"

"I'm still waiting on the blood work."

Kate clenched her hand angrily. "There must be something he used, Caroline. Something has to show up. If this was taken to the CPS they'd laugh in our faces."

"Let's see what the blood tests show."

"You said he's already been charged?"

"Cautioned, charged, released on police bail and due in court this week."

"Can you give me the details?"

Caroline stood up and shook her head sadly. "Sorry, Kate. You know I can't do that. Completely against the rules. Client confidentiality and all that. Not to mention that it could jeopardise the case."

Kate looked up at her, sensing there was something she wasn't saying.

Caroline smiled apologetically. "You'll have to excuse me for a moment. One of the downsides of being pregnant is that you have to go to the loo every five minutes."

"Okay."

"I might be some time." She grinned at Kate again, more broadly this time. "Why don't you make yourself at home? Read something." She gestured at her desk on which were stacked a pile of magazines and a single, blue folder. Kate looked at the name on the folder, *Helen Archer*, and smiled gratefully back up at the police surgeon.

"Thanks, Caroline."

"Take your time."

Caroline left and Kate pulled the folder towards her, took out the documents and started to read.

Helen Archer's hand shook slightly as she went into her house, closed her front door behind her and double locked it. On the way back home, with the wind howling and throwing the fallen leaves against her bare legs, she had jumped at every barking dog or creaking tree branch, flexing its long, skeletal fingers as though deliberately taunting her.

She walked across the polished oak floor of her hallway, kicking off her low-heeled shoes and letting her feet sink comfortably in the luxurious pile of the cream-coloured carpet in her lounge. She went straight to the walnut sideboard next to the fireplace, poured herself a large brandy and took a healthy swig. It was expensive brandy, as smooth as the silk on her bed upstairs, but she still gasped a little as it went down. Coughing and catching her breath she took another sip, slower this time, and felt the warmth of it spread through her body. She crossed over to her curtains and pulled them shut, then switched on a couple of side lamps and dimmed the main light. A red light was blinking on the answerphone on top of the coffee table in front of an enormous, red, buffalo-hide sofa, something her ex-husband insisted they buy and she hadn't got round to replacing. Its overwhelming size was a constant reminder of him. She punched the play button on the answerphone. It was his voice again and her fingers tightened on her brandy glass, her knuckles white.

"Don't be like this, Helen. We need to talk. We need to sort things out." His voice was calming, soothing. As though he were talking to one of his patients. "Call me back. You don't want to make me angry." And there was steel in his voice now. Unsheathed. Brutal.

She clicked the phone off, ignoring the blinking light that signalled there were many more messages.

She drained her brandy and then poured another, sipping at it as she looked at herself in the large, gilt mirror that was above the fireplace. She flicked her hair from side to side and ran her fingers softly through her thick tresses. It was honey-blonde again, the same colour as it had been at twenty-six when she had first met Paul. Not entirely her natural colour, but not far off it. He had asked her to change it in the early days and she had refused. But he had asked time and again, and by that time she had found herself falling in love with him. And it wasn't such a big deal, was it? Only a hair colour. She had dyed it a deep brunette, the colour he wanted. The colour of one of those women from the original *Charlie's Angels*. And she quite liked it at first. Made her look like a different person. Like putting on a mask. But the collar and cuffs hadn't matched he'd said. The curtains and the carpet. He thought he was so damned amusing. So he had made her shave her body hair. Shaved quite nude, just like he did himself. He had told her that it was for health reasons. She laughed drily as she remembered his words, but she knew better than that. It was because he thought it made his cock look bigger, that was the simple truth. The brandy was chasing away her nerves and replacing them with anger. How could she have been so wrong about a person? How could she have thought she loved him? He'd seemed so gentle with children, and she always thought that he wanted some of his own. That was one of the reasons why she married him. She'd always wanted a family and she had made that clear to any man who ever wanted to get serious with her. At the age of twelve she had known how many children she wanted and that hadn't changed since. She took another sip of her brandy and unconsciously rubbed her stomach as she looked down at the flickering flames roaring hungrily around the logs now.

It wasn't long after the honeymoon that the excuses started. It was always his career, a new posting, a promotion. Just as everything was settled and he promised they could start a family, he got offered something new. More money to pay for school fees, he had said, and it meant they had had to move to London. Then there was a new house to find, and to decorate and renovate. And the new job meant he had to focus on that so the family would have to wait for another short while. And that short while became a year and then another year. Then one day Helen realised she was well into her thirties and he was never going to change.

Except he did.

He became violent. She swallowed more of the brandy, its taste bitter in the back of her throat now. She felt a little disorientated, her eyes momentarily out of focus, and she suddenly felt hot, a little giddy. She put the back of hand on her forehead and it was damp with perspiration.

"Overdoing it on the brandy again?"

She spun around, her mouth open in shock, her arm dropping, spilling the brandy from her glass into the rich pile of the carpet.

"How did you get in?" Her voice trembled as she looked at the man in front of her.

"I always kept a spare key in the garden shed. If you didn't want me here you should have changed the locks."

"Get out!" Helen screamed at him and threw the brandy glass. The man laughed as it missed him by five feet and smashed against her new Liberty-print wallpaper that she had always wanted but had never been allowed.

Paul Archer shook his head, the laughter in his eyes dying in an instant. "Seems like you never learn, Helen. No matter how many lessons you're given, you never learn. But as someone once remarked . . . repetition is an excellent learning tool."

Helen shook with terror as Paul Archer moved towards her. She tried to get away but she could only make a few steps towards the door and then her legs wouldn't move, her muscles useless, she felt her knees buckle and she slid, almost in slow motion, to the floor. She tried to get up but couldn't. She watched helpless as her ex-husband looked down on her as he took off his shirt, which he folded neatly and put on the sofa, then unbuckled his belt and lowered his trousers. She tied to move backwards but couldn't. She could barely scream as he stood above her naked, stroking himself with his right hand, hardening. Her eyes flicked to the right, to the broken brandy glass, lying against the wall. If she could just reach that she could take that smile off his face for good.

Delaney leaned against the wall in the small entrance to South Hampstead station watching the commuters as they spilled out of the lift and bustled for the exit. A couple of uniforms were waiting outside and Sally Cartwright stood next to Delaney looking at her watch.

Across from them was the ticket office and station master's room. The door opened and an angry-looking man, with dark, wavy hair and an accent spooned with silver, glared across at them.

"Haven't you people got anything better to do?"

Simon Elliot, a police surgeon in his thirties, came out behind him and shook his head at Jack. He wasn't the one they were looking for. Delaney shrugged at the angry man with the posh voice and held his hands out apologetically.

"We're just doing a job here."

"Your family must be very proud of you."

The man walked off in a huff and Sally looked at her watch again.

"Keen to be somewhere, Constable?"

"Like I said earlier, we're having a drink a bit later. You're welcome to join us."

Delaney looked at her deadpan. "You know me, Sally. I don't drink during the week."

"Just a bit of a headache was it this morning, sir? A migraine?"

"Along those lines."

Delaney listened as another train pulled out of the tunnel many feet below, feeling the ground vibrate beneath his feet, and watched the indicator that showed another lift was on its way up. So far they had interviewed two of the three potential suspects identified by Valerie Manners and had no luck with either of them. Any resemblance to the flasher on the heath's southern common disappeared below buckle level.

★ ★ ★

Kate felt nauseous as she finished reading the statement. Helen Archer explaining in clinical detail the assault her ex-husband had made on her. No, not assault, she corrected herself mentally, the rape. As she read the clinical words she could picture all too clearly in her mind what had happened. Helen suspected that Paul Archer had laced her brandy with some sort of sedative, some kind of date-rape drug. But the levels hadn't been strong enough, clearly, as she could still remember what had happened. She had remembered being powerless as he had knelt beside her on the carpet, lifting her legs apart, raising her skirt, taking off her underwear and violating her as she tried desperately for her limbs to work again. And finally they had. As she recognised the telltale signs, the little mewing noises, the tightening of his buttocks, the widening of his eyes as he sucked his breath quickly in over his teeth, his wife had summoned enough strength to jerk his body sideways, off her and out of her and shuffled away like an injured crab as he jerked in spasm and came, spilling his seed into the carpet.

Evidence.

The lift doors opened and about thirty or so people came out into the small concourse that formed both the entrance and exit to Hampstead station. Delaney was relieved to see that their third suspect looked to be among them, although he could only see his curly, brown hair. He had his head down reading the *Evening Standard*, but he looked up as the group spilled though the lift doors. He was an IC1 male, in his early thirties, wearing a charcoal-grey suit and his eyes flashed with shock and then anger as he saw Delaney. They recognised each other almost immediately. Delaney knew he was not one of the men in the security footage that Valerie Manners had identified as a possible suspect. But he looked a little like him, even though his hair was far longer and curlier than it had been when Delaney had last seen him.

The man looked ahead, saw the uniforms chatting outside on the street and, panicking, he grabbed a young woman and shoved her straight at Delaney and Sally Cartwright then took off at a run, out of the exit and down the street, flashing past the uniforms.

Delaney left the detective constable to pick the young woman up and went after the man, shouting at the officers to follow as he raced up the street.

The man ahead shouldered past a couple of people waiting at the bus stop, the briefcase in his hand waving wildly as he ran pell-mell towards the road that led to the common and the southern reaches of the heath.

Delaney breathed heavily, his lungs on fire, feeling the muscles in his thighs burn as he hammered his legs down on the hard pavement. He swerved around the people waiting at the bus stop and shouted for the man to stop.

He didn't.

Delaney cursed through panted breath and picked his pace up. He was beginning to regret his two visits to Roy's burger van. A bacon sandwich or two is one thing going down, it's an altogether different thing coming up, and if he didn't catch the guy sprinting ahead of him soon he was either going to throw up or have a heart attack, probably both.

He spurted forward, blowing fast now. Christ on a bicycle he needed to do more exercise. He flicked his eyes heavenward in the slightest gesture of apology for the blasphemy of his thoughts then dived forward to rugby-tackle the man round his legs and bring him down hard on the pavement.

At school Delaney was considered a great prospect for the game. Natural speed combined with courage bordering on stupidity, a keen intelligence and the ability to read the play on the hoof made him a superstar of school rugby in his early teens. As he grew older and taller and filled out in the shoulders, he was not only playing with boys much older than himself, he was playing better than them. There was talk of national trials. But then, at the age of fifteen, Delaney discovered girls and his ambitions for glory on the muddy field were swapped for ambitions of a more comfortable kind, and certainly not of a team nature. He played his last game of rugby when he was eighteen years old and so it was more than twenty years since he'd practised the move.

He missed the man entirely.

Smashing down on to the cold, slick pavement he cried out and skidded forward like a clubbed seal on ice, his right shoulder wrenched out of its socket again, a recurring legacy of a motorcycle accident in his mid-twenties.

The man ahead turned back to look, the smile on his face and the smart remark on his lips quickly dying as

Sally Cartwright charged up to him and, not bothering with the technical rules of the game Delaney had once played, tackled him high, wrapping her arm round his neck and pulling him violently to the ground. At Twickenham she might have got a yellow card, in South Hampstead she got a shout of encouragement from the two uniformed officers who followed closely behind and grabbed the man, pulled him roughly to his feet and cuffed him.

Delaney took a moment or two to catch his breath, his face like a satisfied shepherd's sunset.

"You all right, boss?"

Delaney got to his knees, his right arm dangling uselessly by his side, and looked up at Sally, who was grinning a little too broadly for his liking, and gasped hoarsely. "I wore him out for you."

"Course you did, sir."

Delaney stood fully up, dusted the wet leaves from his trousers with his good hand and walked over to where the tackled man was watching him, amused.

"I take it you don't play for the London Irish, Delaney?"

"I play on the only team that counts, you little shite."

The man winked at Sally and indicated Delaney. "You get to an age and suddenly you can't perform, if you know what I mean."

Sally smiled back. "Oh yeah, and how's your performance been of late?"

"I've had no complaints, darling."

Sally pretended to be surprised. "Really? Only an elderly nurse we were talking to earlier said you could only manage to fly the flag at half mast this morning."

The guy looked over at Delaney. "What's she on about?"

Sally turned to her boss. "Do you know him then, sir?"

Delaney nodded. "This here is Andy Ware. Aka Chemical Andy. Small-time drugs dealer, full-time pain in the arse. The last time I saw him he had a skinhead haircut. Peroxide blond."

"Yeah, well, you got to move with the times, haven't you? I do a lot of business with the brothers nowadays . . ." Correcting himself. "*Did* a lot of business. All behind me now of course. I've gone legit."

Sally looked him up and down, unimpressed. "What's up then, Chemical? Couldn't you get hold of any Viagra? Or was it just too cold for you this morning?"

"The fuck are you talking about, woman?"

Sally gestured towards his groin. "The little man, flashing it on the heath this morning, were you?"

"I haven't been flashing anything." He swirled his hips. "And let me tell you, there ain't nothing little about this baby."

"What are you doing here, Andy?" Delaney cut him short.

"I live here. Last I knew that ain't a crime."

"You caught the train just after eight this morning. What have you been doing all day?"

"Working. Like I say, I'm out of the life."

"Working at what? Somehow I can't see you as an estate agent."

"Like I give a fuck what you see me as."

Delaney leaned in. "We can do this down the nick if you prefer it?"

The man shrugged. "Community service."

"What?"

"With the CAB, helping people with their finances."

Delaney turned to Sally. "He's a semi-qualified accountant. Left university with a degree, a bad haircut and a habit."

"Fuck the habit, I left university with fifteen thousand pounds' worth of student loans to pay off."

Sally flashed him a less than sympathetic look. "So, you're telling us you weren't flashing the wiener this morning."

Chemical Andy flashed his teeth again and pumped his groin forward. "I told you, sweet cheeks, this here ain't no chipolata. I'm talking jumbo sausage, darling, you bring your own sauce."

Delaney glared at him. "Just answer the question."

"What, you serious? You think I'm some kind of pervert?"

Sally nodded. "Yeah. We do. Why did you take off when you saw us otherwise?"

Andy Ware shook his head. "Because I know the way you people work. You be putting something on me."

His eyes slid sideways a little, not holding Delaney's gaze.

Delaney sighed and turned to Sally. "Look in his briefcase."

Andy Ware struggled futilely against the grip of the uniformed officers as Sally opened the case.

"No way, man. That's my private property. That's cold, man. You got no cause. You got no right."

Sally opened the briefcase and pulled out several packs of white powder. "And you got the right to remain silent."

"Fuck that."

"And the right to brag about the size of you hot dog to the boys of E Wing. I'm sure they'll have plenty of sauce for you."

Delaney nodded to the uniforms. "Take him to the car."

The uniforms led him off cursing. Sally smiled and looked at Delaney. "You think he's good for it?"

"Doubt it somehow."

"So where does that leave us?"

Delaney let out a long painful sigh and let the pain show on his face. "In need of a drink."

"What's up, boss?"

"I've dislocated my shoulder."

"Shall I take you down to the hospital?"

Delaney held his right hand out, wincing. "Just take my arm, both hands, and hold it tight."

"Sir?"

"Just do it, Sally."

Sally, puzzled, did as she was asked.

Delaney took a quick, sharp breath then wrenched his shoulder, snapping it back into place. "Jesus, Mary, and all the sweet saints!" He staggered backwards, Sally still clinging to his arm. "All right, you can let go now."

Sally released her grip and Delaney put his left hand against a lamp post.

"You all right, sir?"

146

Delaney nodded at her, breathing deeply. "You get off to the pub, I'll process laughing boy back at the factory."

"You going to join us later?"

"Yeah, I reckon I've earned a pint today."

"Or twenty."

"You're getting the idea."

He watched Sally walk away, waited until she had turned the corner then staggered to a bus shelter, leaning against it with his good arm, fighting hard not to throw up as he took great gulping breaths and waited for the agony in his shoulder to subside.

Kate closed Helen Archer's file and pushed it to the back of the desk as Caroline Akunin came into the room. "When's the trial coming up?"

"A few days."

"Not easy for her. Having to relive that all over again in court."

Caroline sat opposite her and took her hands. "How are you doing?"

Kate shook her head, blinking back tears.

"He's not going to get away with it."

Kate gestured at the blue folder. "How confident are the CPS on this?"

Caroline shrugged. "As confident as they can be in these cases. There is physical evidence."

"That he drugged her?"

"Not of that. But bruising. DNA. Semen secretions on the carpet."

"So he'll go down for it? For her at least?"

"He claims it was consensual. That she said she regretted the split. She asked him round, they drank a lot of brandy and then made love on the carpet in front of the fire."

"You're joking?"

"No. He admits it was rough sex, but entirely consensual. It's what you would expect him to say, Kate. You know that. If he is going to deny rape, then he has to play the consensual card, given the physical evidence."

"So it's his word against hers?"

Caroline nodded sadly. "Always is. That's why only six per cent of them get prosecuted successfully."

The phone on Caroline's desk rang and Kate gestured towards it. "You better get it."

Caroline answered the phone. "Hello. Speaking." She listened for a while. "Okay, thank you."

He face was impassive but Kate could see something was worrying her as she hung up the phone. "Bad news?"

"It's your blood work, Kate."

"Go on."

"There's no evidence of Rohypnol."

"Which doesn't mean to say there wasn't any."

"No, of course not. Depending on the strength of whatever it was he used, it could have been flushed through your blood and out of your system before the tests."

"I know."

"There's something else . . ." Caroline hesitated.

"What?"

"You're pregnant, Kate."

★   ★   ★

Delaney pulled his car into the White City car park, and, as he stepped out of it, he had to shield his eyes from a bright light suddenly shining at him.

Melanie Jones from Sky News stepped forward, smiling like an evangelist, and looked over at the long-haired cameraman who had his video camera on his shoulder and pointed straight at the policeman as though to launch an RPG. "We running?" she asked him.

The cameraman nodded and Melanie turned back to face Delaney. "Melanie Jones, Sky News. What can you tell us, Detective Inspector Delaney, about the dead woman who was found on South Hampstead Heath this morning?"

Delaney was too long in the tooth to be caught on the back foot like that. "It's an ongoing investigation, I'm afraid. I'm not in a position to comment at present."

"Sky News has learned that there was mutilation of the body. Was this the work of a serial killer?"

"When we have information, we'll call a press conference." He made the words a dismissal.

Melanie Jones called after him as he walked away. "What is the significance of the belt buckle, Inspector?"

Delaney's turned back to look at her, his eyes hardened. "I beg your pardon?"

"The Green Man belt buckle? What's so special about it?"

Delaney walked towards the police station entrance. "Come with me."

Melanie enjoyed matching her long stride to his. His reaction had pretty much told her that her source was genuine. The cameraman dropped his camera from his shoulder and followed at a more sedate pace. Delaney walked through reception and up to the security door. He quickly typed in the code on the small pad and opened the door. Melanie Jones walked through, but as the cameraman went to follow Delaney blocked his path. "Not you." He called across to the desk sergeant. "Keep an eye on him for me, will you, Dave?"

Slimline Matthews nodded tersely and came around from behind the desk, showing his massive frame. "Sure thing, Jack."

Delaney closed the door behind him.

"What the hell do you think you're doing?" The reporter's normally smooth voice had nothing honey-like about it any more.

"Come with me." Delaney took her none too gently by the arm and marched her along the corridor. He opened the door to an interview room and pushed her into it, closing the door behind him and leaning against it. He crossed his arms. "Start talking."

"No, I won't start talking. Who the hell do you think you are?"

"My name is Jack Delaney. I'm a policeman."

Melanie snorted. "I know who you are, for fuck's sake, what I want to know is what the hell you think you're doing?"

"You kiss your mother with that mouth?"

Melanie took a deep breath and smiled, full wattage. "I tell you what, let's go back outside, let my cameraman through and we'll do this properly."

She walked up to the door but Delaney made no motion to move out of her way.

"You mentioned the buckle."

"So?"

"So how did you know about it?"

"If you don't let me out of this room right now you'll have bigger problems to worry about than that."

Delaney gripped her upper arm. She kept herself in very good condition, that much was clear, but she gasped as he tightened his grip. "No details have been released about the belt buckle. Why don't you tell me how you know about it?"

Melanie met his gaze, unfazed. It was a long time since any man had scared her. "How about you take your hand off the merchandise?"

Delaney released his grip. "Believe me, whatever you've got to peddle, I'm not in the market for, honey."

"I got a call. The belt buckle. He told me to ask you what belt buckles were for. He said it was a clue. Seems he was right."

"Who was it?"

Melanie smiled. "Back in the market, are we?"

"Just answer the fucking question."

"I don't know. Male voice, could be twenties, could be thirties."

"You didn't get his number?"

Melanie shook her head. "It was withheld. He said he was the artist responsible for this morning's installation piece on Hampstead Heath."

"What else did he say?"

"He said you were obviously no student of art history so he was going to have to give you some more clues."

"He actually mentioned me by name?"

"Yes."

"And that was it?"

"Just that and the belt buckle. He said he'd be in touch with me again." Melanie rubbed her upper arm. "This how you treat everyone who has information for you?"

"You came in here pointing a camera and looking for a story. Not exactly trying to be a model citizen." Delaney moved away from the door but Melanie Jones did not try to leave.

"You have your job to do, Jack. I've got mine. You're smart?" She made it a question. "You'll see how we can help each other here."

Delaney shook his head. "Like you helped Alexander Walker last month?"

Melanie tilted her head slightly, looking up at him. "Is that what the attitude is all about?"

"He was a poster boy for the worst kind of corruption in the police and you wanted to make him a media celebrity."

"We're both on the same side here, Detective Inspector. You got any children?"

"What's that got to do with anything?"

"Financial security, Jack . . ."

"Don't call me that."

"For life. For you, for your family, for your children. The inside story on how you brought down Alexander Walker. And how you worked with me to bring down a serial killer."

"He's not a serial killer. And I work with you the day Johnny Cash starts his comeback tour."

Melanie Jones shook her head, deadly serious now. "We have to work together, whether you like it or not, Detective Inspector. He's contacting me and this guy is a serial killer. You know it, I know it and, more importantly, he knows it."

Delaney would have responded but the door burst open and Superintendent George Napier barrelled past him into the room. He smiled apologetically at the reporter.

"I am really sorry about this, Miss Jones."

Delaney glared at him. "With respect, sir. I am conducting an interview here."

"No you're not, Delaney. Your interview is over."

Melanie Jones brought the full force of her professional smile to bear. "It's quite all right, Superintendent. The detective inspector and I were discussing the case."

"It's not all right, Miss Jones. I will not have members of the press treated in such a cavalier fashion in my station. Your cameraman has told me how you were manhandled, Miss Jones."

"A small misunderstanding."

Delaney held his boss's gaze. "No misunderstanding on my part, sir. I don't care if she's press, public or a member of the royal frigging family, she has information on an ongoing murder case then she gets treated just the same by me."

Napier goggled at him. "Have you listened to a word I have said, Inspector?"

Delaney smiled sardonically at Melanie Jones. "I'm just doing my job, sir."

"Wait outside, Delaney. I'll speak to you later."

Delaney nodded pointedly at the reporter then walked out, closing the door loudly behind him, and took a moment to compose himself. He'd have liked to have gone back inside and slapped his boss but he knew what the consequences would be, and although in times recently past he wouldn't have much cared, right now he needed his badge and the authority it brought. He still had personal matters to take care of and his warrant card was going to help do just that.

He walked through to public reception area where the long-haired cameraman was watching him with a smug and amused expression on his face as he lounged against the counter. "Your boss had a word with you, did he?"

Delaney walked up to him, the smile on his lips far from friendly. He grasped the camera out of his hands, slid the broadcast-quality Betacam tape out of it and put it in his jacket pocket.

The cameraman was outraged. "You can't do that!"

Delaney ignored him and nodded at Dave. "Napier will probably be looking for me in a minute."

"Want me to tell him where you'll be?"

"Tell him I got called away. Urgent business."

Dave smiled knowingly. "Have one on me."

Delaney cocked his finger at him, pulled an imaginary trigger and headed towards the entrance.

The cameraman called after him. "Oi!"

Delaney ignored him, walking outside and closing the door behind him, silencing the cameraman's outraged protests.

He looked up at the sky and thought about what Melanie Jones had told him. The moon was low in the sky, leaking a sulphurous light over the dark car park; a few clouds scudded over it as he watched, throwing a shadow over his face, but his eyes still glittered.

Derek Watters had been a prison officer for twenty-two years and married for twenty-three. He had left school at the age of sixteen and worked in a number of different jobs over the next year or so, never really settling into any of them. But after walking into a recruiting office, he had decided that when he turned eighteen he was going to join the army. His mates threw him a big party at the local pub, the Roebuck, to celebrate his eighteenth and give him a bit of a send-off before he took the Queen's shilling. Derek's mates had all had a whip-round and organised for a strippergram as well. A girl whose real name was Audrey but was calling herself for the purposes of erotic entertainment Sergeant Sally Strict. She was nineteen, dressed in a policewoman's outfit and had breasts like coconuts, the young Derek Watters had thought. Heavy, full, magnificent. Exotic fruit indeed.

Derek had always been more of a headlamps than a bumper man, still was. And Audrey's headlamps on that night dazzled him. Literally. She'd made him walk around the pub on all fours barking like a dog and then given him eighteen lashes with a soft suede whip. One for each of his years. Then given him his birthday treat. She hadn't done a full strip, she was just a fun telegram girl she'd said. But she had gone topless and let him

155

cradle his face in her ample bosom. It was the best night of Derek's life thus far.

It turned out that Audrey was a student, training as a nursery nurse. The strippergram work was just to help pay for her fees. Derek had taken her card and a couple of days later he'd finally sobered up and found the courage to call her up and ask her out on a date. To his delight she had said yes. And on the third date she'd taken him home to her digs at college. Donned the policewoman's uniform once again and then took it off for an audience of just one. Took it off very slowly. All of it this time. And if Derek had been happy before he was fit to burst now.

But that "now" was twenty-three years ago, he thought bitterly as he trudged up past the hordes of office workers who were spilling down the short steps into Piccadilly Circus station. Twenty-three years ago; and three weeks after her strictly non-Metropolitan Police regulation knickers had hit the floor of her eight foot by eight foot bedroom, he had got the phone call. He was having Sunday dinner at his parents' at the time, roast pork and parsnips, thinking life didn't get much better. No, it got worse.

Audrey was up the stick, he was the father, and his plans for joining the army were right in the shitter.

She wouldn't hear of him joining up. She wanted him home with her, not swanning off overseas whenever Maggie wanted to win another election. She wanted them to get married as soon as possible, and it wasn't just one baby she wanted, it was three. And there was no way she was walking up the aisle looking like Alison Moyet with a pillow stuffed under her jumper. Derek wasn't even thinking about marriage let alone a family but abortion was out of the question, seemingly. Audrey had her way; they got married and had three kids. Derek's application to join the police force was turned down and he ended up in the prison services. And the worst of it was, she refused to wear the uniform ever again. After her third baby her stomach had thickened and her back broadened and her once coconut-like breasts were now like flabby pumpkins that were long past their Halloween best.

So, he was going to put the touch on the copper and his CID mate. The information he had should be worth a couple of C notes and he was going to put the money to good use. A feisty little Irish tart he liked to visit when he had enough folding squirrelled away.

He smiled to himself as he pulled out his mobile phone and stood outside Boots on the north side of Piccadilly Circus, turning the collar of his raincoat up as the wind had freshened. There was moisture in the chill air. An hour ought to do it, he figured. Give him time to get some cash from DI Jimmy Skinner, a couple of drinks to set the ball rolling and then round to the auburn-haired strumpet for another round of Sergeant Strict and the love truncheon. He punched in the number and grinned expectantly.

Delaney took a sip of his Guinness and wended his way through the crowd at the Pig and Whistle over to a back table where Sally Cartwright and a bunch of other people were sitting, He nodded to some of them, all uniform, all fresh-faced and eager. Cops really were getting younger these days, he thought.

"Glad you could make it, sir." Sally pulled out a chair for him. "I think you know most people."

"Sure."

Delaney nodded generally and shifted uncomfortably in his seat, the pain in his shoulder throbbing and reminding him that his own youth was far behind him. He took another pull of his Guinness. Creamy analgesic by the pint glass.

Sally gestured at the young, black constable. "This is Danny Vine."

"Nice to meet you again, sir."

Delaney flashed him a quick smile as he shook his hand, pain lancing into his shoulder and making him regret it. "Please don't call me sir. Not in here, anyway."

"Sure."

"And this is Michael Hill."

She smiled at the blond-haired man in his mid-twenties. Delaney picked up the slight catch in her voice and the sparkle in her eye. Danny Vine had competition. He nodded at the man, not risking another handshake. He recognised him from somewhere, but couldn't quite place him. "I know you?"

"You'd have seen me earlier, sir."

"Like I said, no sirs. When you're out of uniform I'm just plain old Jack Delaney."

"I'm not uniform."

"Oh?"

"I'm the police photographer."

158

Delaney nodded a little guiltily. "Sure, I thought I recognised you." The truth was he hardly noticed any of the myriad support staff when he was working. Especially if they were all kitted out in white spacesuits. Some detective.

"Any developments on the case, Inspector?" Danny Vine asked. He was clearly eager to show he was keen. Sally had better look out, Delaney reckoned. Youth and energy were dangerous enough, particularly when you added testosterone to the mix.

"Nothing new. We'll track down who she is tomorrow with any luck. Give us somewhere to start."

"How are you going to do that?"

Michael Hill this time. Delaney sensed that they weren't really interested in talking to him per se, but thought that if they got on his good side they'd get on the good side of Sally Cartwright.

He was relieved to see Bob Wilkinson coming in and heading up to the bar. He smiled apologetically at Sally. "Sorry, got to have a word with Bob."

Sally nodded back distractedly but Delaney could tell she had other matters on her mind. Young love, he thought as he worked his way back through the noisy hubbub, God and all his angels save us from it.

"Inspector."

"Get us a pint, Bob, for Christ's sake."

Bob smiled at the barmaid and jerked his thumb at Delaney. The barmaid, a button-nosed temptress called Angela something, Delaney never could remember, grinned at him as she poured a fresh pint of Guinness. "Shot with that, Jack?"

"No. Being a good boy tonight."

Angela laughed, a throaty, husky laugh that started somewhere low. "Can't see that somehow."

Delaney winked at her. "Turning over a new leaf. Jack Delaney. Modern man."

"Yeah, you and Hugh Hefner." She put the pint on the counter. "Let it settle and if you want a top-up give me a whistle." She moved off to serve some others at the end of the bar. Her hips swinging like a Tennessee two-step.

Bob looked at Delaney watching her. "They reckon if a woman swings her hips like that, she isn't ovulating."

Delaney looked back at him. "That a fact?"

"Mine of them, me. Fuck police work, I should have been a black-cab driver."

Delaney couldn't be bothered to wait for the Guinness to settle properly and took a long gulp. "Got a stupid question for you, Bob?"

"Shoot?"

"What's a belt buckle used for?"

Bob Wilkinson shrugged. "Well, in the good old days it would be used to keep your women and children in line." He grinned. "Nowadays just to keep your dignity, and your trousers up."

"Yeah." Delaney nodded.

Bob frowned. "Why do you ask that?"

Delaney shrugged and immediately regretted asking Bob the question. "I have no idea." He took another pull on his drink and as he put the pint down on the bar and gestured to Angela for a top-up, his mobile phone rang. Irritated, he pulled it out from his pocket but his expression changed as he saw who was calling.

"Delaney."

"Jack, it's Kate."

"I saw. What's up?"

"I need to talk to you."

"What about?"

The large group at the bar started singing loudly. Kate said something on the other end of the line but Delaney couldn't catch it. "Hang on, Kate, I'll take it outside."

Angela watched him, puzzled, as he walked towards the exit. She picked up Delaney's unfinished pint. "Does he want this or not?"

Bob grinned at her. "I may be the fount of all wisdom, darling, but what I am not, is a psychic."

"No, what you is, is an arsehole."

Bob nodded with a self-satisfied grin and took a sip of his pint. Some things you couldn't argue with.

Jimmy Skinner liked coming to Soho for very different reasons to the prison officer from Bayfield Prison. Jimmy had two vices. One was Internet poker and the other was Scotch. Unlike Delaney, however, he didn't drink it like lemonade. He treated himself every now and again with a small glass when he had won a high stakes game. He never drank when he was playing. That way disaster lay. You played the odds, you trusted the maths. What you didn't do was get drunk and risk all on chance, on the vagaries of the turn of a card. Lady luck was for losers.

Soho had a couple of great places to shop for the whisky connoisseur. One was on Old Compton Street and the other was on Greek Street. Just down from a bookshop specialising in spanking magazines and one of the entrances to the Pillars of Hercules, which was why he was more than happy with where Derek Watters had suggested they meet.

He stepped out of the whisky shop, pleased with himself. In his carrier bag a bottle of Johnny Walker Blue Label. A blended whisky but at one hundred and sixty pounds it wasn't the kind of stuff you found on special offer in the alcohol aisle of Tesco's. It wasn't about the money for Jimmy Skinner, it was about the victory. And victory always deserved to be marked, in his opinion.

He looked up at the narrow, black clouds scudding across an already dark and crimson sky then suddenly down again as he heard the sound of an engine screaming in high revs and the concurrent sound of tyres screeching on tarmac. He looked up the street and the carrier bag in his right hand slid from his open fingers. The bottle inside it hit the pavement hard and smashed. But Jimmy Skinner didn't register it all. He was too busy shouting, straining his lungs in the face of the gusting wind.

"Look out!"

But for Derek Watters as he spun round to the sound of the tortured engine, it was too late. Far too late.

The jet-black Land Rover Discovery hit into him still accelerating. The bull bar on the front of it crushed his ribs, splintering them and piercing his heart before the

162

front of his head smashed down onto the bonnet. He was thrown back into the street as the driver stamped on the brakes and then into reverse, the tyres biting and screaming once more. As Jimmy Skinner ran across the road the back of Derek Watters head slapped hard down on the road with the crunching sound of a coconut being cracked by a hammer.

The Land Rover roared backwards into Soho Square, then drove round the green and, accelerating once more, shot up Soho Street and out into the busy traffic of Oxford Street, oblivious to the blaring of horns and sudden screeching of brakes, and disappeared as it turned left heading towards Marble Arch. Skinner watched it go, trying to see the number plate, but it had been taped over. He knelt down and put his fingers to Derek Watters's carotid artery on the side of his neck, though it was a movement made more by instinct than expectation. But, surprisingly, the prison officer had one last breath in him. As his eyes clouded over he looked at the tall, thin, bone-faced policeman kneeling beside him and sighed more than spoke: "Murder."

Then his eyes froze, motionless, and Derek Watters, forty-one years old, who never got to serve his country by bearing arms, died on a chill, wet street in a city that had a heart as cold as a solar system where the sun had died out many millennia ago.

Delaney sat behind the wheel of his car taking a moment to collect his thoughts. Adjusting the rearview mirror he looked at himself. He didn't know what had got Kate Walker so agitated, she wouldn't tell him on the telephone, just told him to meet her at the Holly Bush pub in Hampstead. He knew it well enough, it was just up the road from his new house. What he didn't know was what had got her so rattled; he could hear it in her voice, the thinnest form of politeness covering someone close to breaking point. It had something to do with what happened in the hospital car park that morning, he'd bet his life on it. Whatever it was that had gone down, the clear fact was that Kate needed his help. She didn't say it in so many words, but it was expressed in her barely restrained emotion. She needed his help. And that was the one thing Jack Delaney couldn't walk away from.

He'd put the mirror back in position, switched the engine on and slipped the gearstick into first, when his phone rang. He angrily slipped the gear back into neutral, glanced at the cover of his phone and snapped it open.

"Make it quick."

"Jack. It's Jimmy Skinner."

Kate Walker sat at the long wooden bar in the Holly Bush. Comforted on the one hand to be surrounded in the warmth and hubbub of familiar faces and voices of the early-evening crowd, and yet starting every time the front door opened. She wanted it to be Delaney coming through that door but was terrified of the notion that it would be Paul Archer walking in instead. She didn't know what made her suggest this pub to Delaney. She wasn't thinking straight. Hadn't been since she had

164

woken up this morning to find that man in her bed. She took a sip at her Bloody Mary. Cautiously. She had no intentions of getting hammered again tonight; besides, she was pregnant. God knows what she was going to do about that. And maybe she hadn't been raped. Maybe she was blowing things all out of proportion. She certainly had drunk a lot last night, maybe they had gone back to her flat, got paralytic and just passed out in bed. But if that was the case, why couldn't she remember any of it?

She looked at her watch again. Where the bloody hell was Jack Delaney? It had taken all her nerve to call him in the first place and if he stood her up now, leaving her alone at the bar like a jilted teenager, she would kill him. She downed her Bloody Mary and gestured at the barman for another. After all, two wouldn't hurt. Would they?

The ambulance pulled away from the kerb and drove slowly down Greek Street towards Shaftesbury Avenue. It had no need for sirens and lights. The police cars that had cordoned off the area, blocking traffic from Soho Square, Bateman Street and Manette Street, pulled away too. Nothing to see here either. Not any more, at least. Delaney leaned back against the painted glass of the porno bookshop and put a cigarette in his mouth. He held the packet out to Skinner who shook his head then lit the cigarette with a lazy scrape of a match.

He inhaled deeply and looked up at the night sky. It was like a carmine canvas that an artist had dragged thick, soot-stained fingers across. Like the black fingers of blood that had crept along the cobbles where Derek Watters had been murdered. He exhaled a thin stream of smoke and looked back at his colleague.

"Definitely not an accident?"

Jimmy Skinner shook his head.

"Professional hit?"

"I'd say so. The guy didn't have a chance. Walking along the street when suddenly out of nowhere . . . Bang!" Skinner slapped one hand hard against the other.

Delaney took another thoughtful drag on his cigarette. "And that was all he said. The one word."

"Yeah. 'Murder.' Hardly the most insightful final utterance, seeing as I had just watched him being splattered halfway up Greek Street."

"What's going on, Jimmy?"

Skinner shrugged drily. "Looks like somebody doesn't want anyone talking to you."

Delaney nodded in agreement. "Looks like."

"I'd watch your back, if I were you, Jack. Somebody going to all this trouble, easier maybe to just take you out."

A cloud cleared the moon, throwing for a moment a spill of yellow light that reflected in the black orbs of Delaney's eye.

He threw his cigarette on to the road, the sparks flaring briefly then dying out as he crushed it under heel. "Maybe."

Kate sipped on her third or fourth drink. She wasn't drunk, just couldn't remember how many she had had.

Time passes in a different way when you're lost in thought. No matter what Einstein said, some things aren't relative. She tasted the fluid in her mouth, thin and liquid and she realised that all she was drinking was melted ice, any vodka in the glass long since gone. She rattled the glass and held it out to the barman, who refilled it and added the drink to her tab. She swirled it in her hand, watching the splash of red wine, which the Holly Bush always added to a Bloody Mary, spin like a star system in a universe of its own. Like a black hole. Like the eye of Sauron.

Some time later she looked at the oak-framed mirror above the bar and could see the front door to the pub opening and a man with curly dark hair entering and her heart pounded suddenly in her chest and she struggled to breathe. She knew the symptoms. It was a panic attack. And being the doctor that she was, Kate knew that sometimes panic was absolutely the appropriate response.

A single, skeletal leaf was cartwheeling along the road. It was a dry, brittle, frail thing and it came to rest, finally, in the damp gutter that was already clogged with the decomposing corpses of leaves from the semi-denuded trees that lined the street. A street of wealthy people, whose lives behind the closed oak doors and wrought-iron gates were consumed with problems other than mortgages and council tax or the National Health Service. This was a street of financiers, of publishers, of authors and literary agents, of property developers and quantity surveyors, of Harley Street

167

doctors and surgeons . . . and of a forensic pathologist who had, just that very day, sickened of death, and handed in her notice. The man in a car across the road from her house didn't know that, however, and it wouldn't have made any difference if he had. Her job, after all, had brought her to his attention in the first place.

He looked down at the pointed toe of his cowboy boot as it rested on the accelerator pedal and was glad he had gone for the snakeskin rather than the leather option. He could relate to snakes. The ability to move silently and unseen. The ability to shed one's skin. The ability to bare one's teeth and terrify. He smiled to himself humourlessly, and the light from the watching moon lent his teeth a cast the colour of old ivory. He looked across once more at the empty house and waited.

Hunters knew how to wait after all.

Jennifer Cole looked at the images on her Macbook laptop with professional detachment. A woman in a corset wearing old-fashioned seamed stockings and posing like a Vargas pin-up come to life. She was a full breasted woman in her late twenties, her bee-stung lips painted red with a hint of purple, the tip of her tongue visible and wet with promise, the pupils in her dark painted eyes wide with desire. She wasn't making love to the camera, she was fucking it. Jennifer flicked through the next pictures, some in uniform, some topless, some in elegant lingerie from Agent Provocateur. The burlesque look was very popular at the moment. A hint of goth, a hint of forbidden pleasure. Pain and pleasure, sugar and spice. She spent a lot of money on her lingerie and the photos that she used to update her webpage at least once a month. She probably didn't have to do it so often, but the truth was she enjoyed the ritual of it. The costumery and the perfumes, the candlelight and the moonlight. The black and red satin sheets. The artistry.

It had been a long time since Jennifer Cole had needed the money she made from her services. She had got into it, as most did, from need. But that need had passed. She was selective now too. She didn't work every night and was extremely choosy about her clients. After all, that was the main thrill for her, the power she felt. She didn't feel degraded or used, just the opposite. It was her decision, her choice to make. And it was never something she regretted. She knew about the human body, how it functioned, how it was put together, what parts needed maintenance. Sex was just part of that. And it was fun.

She flicked forward to the last of the images. She was wearing a long fur coat that she had bought on a cruise trip to the Norwegian fjords one year. The real thing, never mind the paint-throwing hypocrites with their leather belts and shoes. It was mink, thick and luxurious. Her hair was piled high on her head with silver threads adorning and confining it. She wore silver boots with high platform soles and heels. The coat was open, her breasts jutting with the pride of the goddess Diana, her sex cupped in the sculptured, rounded vee

169

of a silk thong, and in her right hand a long, silver-handled riding crop.

Her small silver mobile phone rang and she answered it slowly, patting her hair as she looked at herself in the mirror. Her pupils widened as she licked her lips and purred.

"Hello. How may I help you?"

If she'd been a cream cake, she would have eaten herself.

"Angelina. It's me."

Angelina, her stage name as she liked to think of it, had been taken from an early American feminist hero of hers, Angelina Grimké, and not, as some had assumed, after the famous actress. She looked at the photo of herself holding a crop and thought it must have been an omen of sorts that he should have called just then. "Hello, bad boy. How have you been?"

There was a pause, then his voice, husky with desire. "I don't think Santa is going to have me on his nice list this Christmas."

"You've been naughty?"

The voice on the other end was breathy. "Ooh, yeah."

She could hear the need. "I hope you're not being naughty right now?"

"Not just yet."

"You want to come and confess to a superior mother?"

"Not today."

"Oh?"

"I want you to come to me."

"It's going to cost more."

"I don't mind paying. Bad men pay for their sins, don't they? Sooner or later we all pay."

"If they know what's good for them."

"I know what's good for me."

Jennifer Cole had only met the man recently. He had visited her a couple of times at her flat in Chalk Farm but she recognised the soft burr in his voice and knew one thing for sure: he was good-looking with kinky tastes. Just her kind of man. She didn't do this to pay the rent, after all.

"Where do you want to meet?"

"I thought we could go for a drink first."

"It's your dollar, babe. You spend it how you want."

"That's what I want."

"Where?"

"Camden?"

"Sure. Tell me when and where." She listened then hung up the phone and looked at her picture on her laptop again. Only the hair colour was wrong. Her midnight cowboy liked brunettes. She picked a wig off a stand and slipped it over her head. She stood up and picked up the long riding crop from one of her bedside cabinets and gave it a swishing flex in the air. She slammed the crop down hard on the bed with a satisfying thud and smiled. Christmas was coming early to Camden.

Hampstead was huddled against the weather. The scudding clouds had taken on weight and mass now, and although the wind still blew at a constant rate the swollen sky above was black and unbroken. The air was cold and threaded with moisture. Delaney looked up at the night sky, the moon now hidden behind the low wall of cloud that hung over the spread city like a biblical judgement. It shouldn't be so dark this early at this time of year, he thought as he looked at the entrance to the pub, deliberated for a second or two and then tapped a cigarette from a crumpled packet into his hand and searched through his pockets for his matches. The scent of the perfume Opium suddenly filled his nostrils and he realised a woman had come up to stand beside him. She was in her late twenties in a fake-fur coat and was holding a lighter out to him. Delaney was taken aback for a moment then leaned forward so she could light his cigarette.

"Thanks."

"Not a problem."

Her voice had the lyrical smoothness of the confident rich, one whose education had eschewed affectation.

Just like Kate's.

The woman closed her lighter and Delaney wondered why someone such as her would approach him, but then realised as the woman walked away and joined her friends that the gesture was just one of solidarity, of friendship. The fraternity of smokers in exile, gathered in groups outside every pub and bar throughout the country, united by the stigma of nicotine.

The woman's friends laughed a little and whispered something to her. She turned to look back at him curiously and Delaney realised he had been staring. He looked away and sipped some smoke from his cigarette into his mouth, then drew it deep so that it burned his lungs. Delaney was sure he saw something akin to pity in the young woman's eyes and the thought of it stung more than the hot smoke. What the hell was he thinking of, buying a house in an area like this? He looked at the window of the pub behind him, bright with colour and noise, he looked through it at the shining faces with smiles full of porcelain, and voices ringing with the confidence of a golden future. He looked at the fashionable ties and slicked-back hair, at the Barbour jackets and coloured, corduroy trousers, and he thought of the dark-haired woman who waited for him at the bar and who fitted in among that crowd like a Hunter Wellington at the Chelsea Flower Show. He told himself he hadn't moved to be near her. It was to be near his daughter and his sister-in-law and her family. But as he ground out his cigarette on the cold slate beneath his feet, he realised the biggest sin was lying to yourself. The trouble was that, contrary to received opinion, the truth did not set you free. Sometimes the truth was an iron cage of your own fashioning.

He walked through the door, the sounds and chatter around him muted somehow, the light a softness like warmth as he threaded through the crowd and saw her waiting for him at the bar.

"Hello, Jack."

He could see in her eyes that the drink she held in her hand was not her first. But her gaze was steady and the warmth of her breath was sweet. Her lips had been stained by the tomato juice and Delaney wanted

173

nothing more than to put his arm around her alabaster shoulder and kiss her.

Instead he pulled over a stool, sat beside her and gestured to the barman. "Another one here please, and I'll have a large . . ." He hesitated for a moment. "I'll have a large Bushmills. Straight up. No ice, no spittle."

Kate handed her drink over to the barman. "Vodka tonic please." She smiled at Delaney. "You can only drink so much tomato juice."

"Of course."

Delaney waited for her to say more but Kate turned her attentions back to the barman and handed Delaney his drink when it arrived. He took a sip of his whiskey and before he could ask her why she had wanted to see him, Kate spoke.

"I'm pregnant, Jack."

And for the second or third time in his life the world rocked on its axis. Kate was saying something else but Delaney couldn't hear it. All he could hear was the blood pounding in his temples. He took another sip of his drink and tried to catch her words but failed. "I'm sorry?" he managed at last.

"It's not a question of anybody being to blame, Jack."

"No, that's not what I meant. I meant I didn't hear the rest of it."

"I don't know what the rest of it is, Jack. That's what I'm saying. I don't know what to think, I just wanted you to know, that's all. And I didn't want to tell you on the telephone."

Delaney nodded, still taking it in. "I'm the father?"

174

Kate looked at him, trying to read his eyes, cursing herself for drinking too much again and clouding her judgement. "Yes, Jack. You're the father."

"I see."

Kate took another swallow of her drink. "Is that it?"

"I don't know, Kate." He shrugged. "What was that business this morning, in the hospital car park?"

Kate shook her head, the colour drained out of her face and Delaney couldn't work out if it was through fear or through anger. "This has got nothing to do with him."

"If he's hurt you in some way, I want to help."

Kate had to fight back the tears but she was damned if she was going to let him see her cry. "You're a knight in shining armour, are you, Jack?"

"Hardly, but I could see something was wrong. I can be a friend, can't I?"

Kate pushed her glass away and stood up a little unsteadily. "You know what, this was a bad idea. We have to talk, but not now."

She picked her coat up off the back of her chair and would have walked away but Jack held her arm, gently, as he stood up himself. He looked into her eyes and could see the need in them as naked as a flame. He wanted to wrap her in his arms and hold her and tell her that he was there for her in every way that she wanted. But the visions of the dead man in Greek Street and the comatose body of Kevin Norrell held him back. The violence visited upon his wife four years ago was still a force loose in his world, a force that he could neither identify nor control. So in that moment,

175

between breathing and speaking, as he looked into Kate Walker's eyes, he knew that the past still had a grip on him as tight as the clasp of a drowning man. He could not offer Kate the emotional lifeline she so clearly needed. "Let me know what you decide."

Kate looked at him, the hurt sparking in her eyes. He wished he could kiss it away, but he knew, also, that the kind of pain she was feeling took a lifetime of disappointment to build, and its healing was way beyond the small amelioration provided by such short-lived gestures.

"Fuck you, Jack." She brushed his arm aside and walked quickly to the door. Delaney let her go. Turning back to the bar again and looking at his reflection in the mirror hanging on the wall behind the counter, he felt his face burning with shame.

Outside, Kate made no effort to hold back the tears that were now streaming down her face. What had she expected of the man after all? She'd had no illusions, no dreams that the fact of her pregnancy would drive him begging for forgiveness into her arms. What had she expected of him then? The truth was that she didn't know, but the cold reality of the encounter was too much for her to bear. He wanted to be friends, he wanted her to let him know what she decides! Christ, if she had had a shotgun in her hands right then she would have cut him in half with it. She dashed the back of her right hand across her eyes. What the hell had she been thinking? She should have known Delaney would be as emotionally available as a piece of the frozen

Donegal turf or wherever it was he came from. But the trouble was she knew exactly what she was thinking, even if she hadn't been honest with herself. She wanted to tell him all about Paul Archer, about what she thought he had done to her. She wanted to tell him everything and she wanted him to take care of it for her. She wanted him to fold her in his arms and tell her that he loved her. How stupid was that? She wiped her hand across her eyes and crossed the road, barely registering the horn blaring from a passing car that had to swerve to miss her. She hated herself for being so weak and formed a fist of her right hand. If she had to do it all on her own then that was how it was going to be. Damn Delaney. Damn all men, if it came to that. Kate Walker had been her own woman for thirty-odd years and she wasn't about to let that change now. She took a deep breath and wiped her eyes dry. She knew what she was going to do.

Delaney finished a second whiskey in five minutes. He looked at his watch. He should never have let Kate go off on her own like that, she deserved to know what was going on. He had no intention of letting the matter of Kevin Norrell drop. Norrell had something to tell him that would lead him to his wife's killers. Derek Watters's murder proved that much. He had never bought the idea that the attack on Kevin Norrell was just some sort of rough justice in prison. Kevin Norrell was an ignorant, ill-bred, psychopathic Neanderthal with as much conscience as a rabid stoat, but he wasn't a nonce. Delaney was pretty sure about that. So that

177

meant the attack on Norrell and Watters's murder was to stop them both from getting information to him. He should have told Kate that. She would have understood. But her revelation that she was pregnant had taken him completely by surprise. He needed to talk to her. He finished his glass and considered for a moment as the barman gestured to see if he wanted another. He shook his head and headed for the door.

It took Delaney a matter of minutes to reach Kate's house. He crossed the road and looked up at the windows. There were no lights on. It had been ten minutes since she had stormed out of the pub. She should definitely be home by now. He hated to think of her in there alone with the lights out, curled up on her sofa sobbing. He walked up to the door and rang the bell. After a short while he rang it again, but there was no answer. He banged his fist on the door a few times and called her name out but still there was no answer.

"Come on, Kate. If you're in there open the door. We need to talk. Jeez, I know I've been a prick, just let me talk to you."

Apart from a curtain twitching in her neighbour's property there was no response. He glanced at his watch and then looked up the road. There was no sign of her. He took out his mobile and quickly tapped in her name. After a few rings her voice on an answerphone cut in asking him to leave a message. He hesitated and then closed the phone. He hated leaving messages and what could he say anyway? He looked up once more at the dark windows. If Kate was at home she clearly wasn't ready to talk to him just yet. He pulled his overcoat closed and set off back down the road. He was tempted to keep going as he neared his new house, keep going further down the hill and then turn right into the Richard Steele pub. Take the prescription in iron-rich Guinness and amber measure, repeat as necessary, but for the first time in a very long while he realised he didn't want to be alcohol-numbed; he knew he was going to need a clear head about him.

He took his key out of his pocket, opened his front door, and went inside.

The scream was cut off very quickly. His hand was around her throat like the strike of a snake. Silencing her to a barely audible gurgle of horrified panic. The sound a kitten might make if you held it under muddy bathwater. Her legs kicked weakly and she felt a sharp pain in her neck. She gasped, fighting for breath, and reached out her right hand, snaggling her fingers in his thick curly hair, but before she could clench her hand and pull, the power seemed to drain from her muscles. Her body flopped like a marionette with its strings cut. He moved forward catching the droop of her body on his chest. She could feel the hardness of his prick as he pressed excitedly against her. Then the lights seemed to dim, she fought to blink her eyes open but, like her leg muscles, they refused to respond. She looked down, drool from her mouth falling to drop on the toe of his snakeskin cowboy boots. She felt a warmth rise from her lower body as though she were being lowered slowly into a very warm bath and then she was aware of nothing at all.

179

* * *

Paul Archer paused for breath, the sweat running down his forehead into his eyes and forcing him to blink. His breathing was ragged, gasping as much for oxygen as with desire. The woman on all fours beneath him was breathing hard too, whimpering, although he could make out no words, the gag he had tied made pretty sure of that. He placed his strong hands on either side of her perfectly shaped buttocks, raising them up to cup her waist and, positioning himself again, began to thrust deep into her, with the relentless and perfunctory rhythm of a gardener using a trowel to dig into hard earth. Stabbing at her. Her breathing was harder now, a yelping sound coming with every thrust, her luxuriant, dark hair flicking with the movement. Archer smiled coldly. Turn and turn about. He wasn't a misogynist, though he had been called one many times. He didn't despise women, he loved them, in fact, especially those that knew their place. And if they didn't, well, he enjoyed teaching them it.

A trickle of sweat ran down his nose and he released one hand to wipe it, wincing as a fresh stab of pain came with the movement. He gripped the woman's body again, not caring if he hurt her as he dug his fingers in and pulled her towards him. He had paid for his pleasures after all, hadn't he? Paid in so many ways.

Day Two

DC Sally Cartwright shivered and flapped her arms, trying to spread some warmth into them. Seven thirty in the morning now and she had been freezing her tits off on the heath since six o'clock. An old-fashioned bicycle, complete with front basket, was propped up against a tree with a puncture repair kit open on the ground beside it. A couple of concerned citizens, male naturally, had already offered to help her fix her tyre. She had moved them along. Their motives were not entirely based on the Good Samaritan principle, she guessed, but she also knew that neither of them matched the photofit of the flasher that they had been given by Valerie Manners, and neither looked the type, to be fair. Even so, she was learning that in matters of sexual deviancy you shouldn't judge a book by its cover. The most mild-seeming and normal of men were often capable of appalling crimes. You only had to look at Ted Bundy to see that. She slapped her arms again, unhappy to be made to wear a nurse's uniform, but Delaney, in a particularly filthy mood this morning, had insisted, arguing that the uniform itself might be the trigger. Maybe only nurses provided him with the desire to wag his wienie? Who knew, but she wasn't going to argue with her boss. Not with him in that mood, and what he was saying might well be the case. But if Delaney was right why hadn't the flasher been reported before? Why hadn't other nurses come forward? Either way she still felt a little foolish in the outfit, and was all too aware of her colleagues hidden away in the bushes and trees, looking at her. The honey trap. The wriggly worm on the hook. The bait in black suspenders. Although she had drawn the line when her colleagues had suggested that suspenders were an essential part of the nurse's uniform. Male colleagues, again, of course. But she knew better, and there was absolutely no way she was going to be wearing anything other than a very thick pair of tights and industrial-strength knickers under her skirt at that time of the morning on a cold, wet and windy South Hampstead Heath.

She flapped her arms again, feeling particularly conscious that Danny Vine was over there in the trees somewhere. Hidden, with the others, out of her range of sight, but with a good view of her. She smiled a little to herself as she thought of him. She'd had a good time the night before, being the centre of attention between him and Michael Hill, and she wasn't above playing the two off against each other. She was young after all, she was entitled to a bit of fun, she worked hard enough, God knows, to be allowed to let her hair down now and again, and misbehave a little. Not that playing men against each other was misbehaving, it was redressing the balance, if you asked her. And anyway, she wasn't

182

sure which of them she preferred. Danny Vine was confident, fit, attractive, but he knew it. She could tell he was used to women eating out of the palm of his hand, but she knew how to deal with his type. Michael Hill, on the other hand, was quieter, but that meant he listened, he took interest and really paid attention. And while she didn't normally go for the blond-haired, blue-eyed Nordic type, she couldn't deny she was attracted to him. She was attracted to them both, in fact, so didn't feel any great rush to choose between them. She had gone off for a pizza with Danny after the pub last night but had agreed to go out with Michael tomorrow night for a drink and a curry. She smiled a little to herself again, lost in her thoughts, and then started as someone rustled through the leaves right behind her. She spun round to see a middle-aged, bald man staring at her. He was wearing a bright yellow duffel coat with a Burberry scarf wrapped round his neck.

"Can I help you at all?" he asked.

Sally shook her head. If this was the curly-haired man in his twenties or thirties who had flashed Valerie Manners yesterday morning, then he'd had a really, really bad night. She shook her head. "No, that's okay, thanks, I've got it covered." Unconsciously she pulled the cloak she had been given a little tighter around her shoulders.

The man made no move to go. "I'm very good with punctures. I've got a bike myself. Well, several actually." He shrugged and smiled. "You know how it is."

Sally had absolutely no idea. "I'll be fine, thanks."

"You work at the South Hampstead?"

183

"I'm sorry?"

The man gestured. "Your uniform."

Sally sighed, this man obviously wasn't going to go away. She reached into her pocket and pulled out her warrant card and held it out for him to see. "No, I work at White City police station. I'm a detective constable. And I'm working here." She didn't hide the impatience in her voice

The man didn't seem fazed, however, he just smiled good-naturedly. "Oh, I see. Well, I'll let you get on. My name's James Collins. Mr Collins. I'm the obstetric surgical registrar at the hospital. Didn't like to think one of our own was stranded."

Sally smiled back, embarrassed now. "Oh, well, thanks again." She nodded self-consciously as he walked away, she had been sure that the man was a pervert, that he was hitting on her at least. It was the uniform she guessed, what was it with men and uniforms? She looked down at the unflattering cut of it, the plain colour, the thick tights, the simple, black elasticated belt and didn't understand it at all. And then a thought struck her.

"Boss!" Sally's voice came out louder than she intended, almost a scream.

Delaney came crashing through the undergrowth closely followed by Danny Vine. Bob Wilkinson brought up the rear at a leisurely pace.

Delaney looked around, confused. "What the hell happened, Sally?"

"I had a thought." She could see he wasn't looking too impressed and rushed ahead before he could say more. "About the belt buckle, sir."

184

"What belt buckle?"

"That the dead girl was wearing. The silver buckle. The Green Man in the woods."

She had his attention now. "Go on."

" 'What are belt buckles for?' he said."

"Get on with it, Sally."

"Well, traditionally, when a nurse qualifies, they are often given a belt buckle by a loved one to mark it. Often silver. Often an old one. Victorian. That kind of thing."

Delaney nodded, pleased.

"I think she's a nurse, sir."

Delaney waved at Danny and Bob Wilkinson. "Okay, guys, I think we can call this off for now. You two get back to the station."

Wilkinson looked at his watch and nodded. "Five past bacon-butty o'clock." He crooked his finger at Danny Vine. "Come on, Kemo Sabe."

Danny glared at him. "That had better not be a racist remark."

Wilkinson looked at him as though highly offended. "I am a white male English policeman in his fifties, what are the chances of me being racist?"

Danny laughed. "Absolutely none at all."

"I'll even drink my tea with you."

Delaney watched the uniforms walk away, the future and the past of the Metropolitan Police, and figured a blend of the two wasn't perhaps such a bad thing.

He turned back to Sally and nodded at her, pleased. "Brains as well as beauty. Not sure there's a place for that on the job."

Despite herself Sally felt herself blushing. Compliments from Jack Delaney were like goals from England trying to qualify for Euro 2008. Which, as her grandfather said at the time, were fucking few and fucking far between.

"Come on then, you can drive."

Sally blinked. "Where to?"

"South Hampstead Hospital. You should fit right in."

Sally pulled her dark, woollen cloak about her, feeling like a character from a *Carry On* film, and set off following her boss to where his car was parked just off the common.

A few moments later, about thirty yards from where Sally had been, a dark-haired man zipped himself back up and scuffed up some wet leaves with the sharp toe of his boot to kick over the evidence of his shameful pleasures. Though, in truth, he felt no shame at all. Just the thrill of the hunt . . . the thrill of it beginning all over again.

Last night was just another chapter. Long way to go yet.

Delaney's expression was grim as he pushed open the main entrance door to the South Hampstead Hospital, the muscles in his jaw flexed and bunched as though he were chewing on gum rather than memories. Sally stole a sympathetic glance at him as they walked up to the reception desk. She knew why he didn't like hospitals, knew exactly why he didn't like this one in particular. His baby had died here after his wife, wounded badly by shotgun fire, had had to undergo an emergency Caesarean section. Very premature and traumatised by the injuries to his mother, the baby had survived only a matter of moments after the procedure. Delaney's wife survived her son's death by no more than a few minutes. Sally Cartwright knew that her boss still carried the guilt for both their deaths like a member of Opus Dei carries a scourge to beat themselves with daily. Delaney had never let the scar tissue heal, each day he'd make it bleed afresh.

She remembered reading the details of his wife's murder the day before; something about it had struck her as odd, but she didn't feel now was the right time to discuss it.

Delaney held his warrant card up to the bored-looking receptionist who betrayed no emotion at the display. Police and their warrant cards were, after all, not a rarity at any city hospital.

"I want to see whoever is in charge of the nurses here."

The receptionist glanced back at her horoscope. Sally could see it was written by Jonathan Cainer. "Depends what wards they work on. They all have their own senior sisters."

"I don't know what ward she worked on. Isn't there someone from personnel who deals with them all?"

Sally could hear the irritation in his voice. The receptionist picked up the phone. "I'll see if I can find someone to talk to you. Can I ask what it is about?"

"It's about police business. Tell them that," Delaney said curtly.

The receptionist sighed heavily and punched some numbers into the telephone keypad. Delaney walked across to read the notices pinned on the adjacent wall on the other side of the reception desk and Sally smiled apologetically at the woman behind the counter. "He doesn't like hospitals very much."

"Not really interested."

Sally shrugged. "What's he say for Capricorn?"

The receptionist looked back at her, frowning. "What?"

"Jonathan Cainer. He's very good, isn't he?"

The receptionist pointedly turned the page. "I don't know. I only buy it for the Sudoku."

Sally shrugged again, and wandered over to join Delaney as he was studying a poster advertising an STD drop-in clinic.

"Something you're worried about, sir?"

Delaney gave her a flat look. "You may have done well with the belt buckle, Detective Constable, but don't push it."

"Sir." Sally grinned, she knew Delaney wasn't annoyed. Not with her at least.

A little while later, a short woman dressed in a navy-blue suit, with iron-grey hair cut fashionably short, strode briskly up to Delaney and thrust out her hand.

"Margaret Johnson. I understand you have some questions regarding one of our staff?"

Delaney shrugged. "Possibly about one of your staff, Mrs Johnson."

"Why don't you come through to my office?"

Margaret Johnson's office was surprisingly colourful and cluttered. She moved a stack of files from one of the chairs facing her desk and gestured at them to take a seat.

"What can I do to be of assistance?"

"We are trying to identify someone. We think she may have worked here."

"And she's dead?"

"How would you know that?" Sally asked.

Margaret Johnson looked at her sadly. "Call it an educated guess. If she wasn't dead she herself could tell you who she was, especially if you knew where she worked."

Delaney placed a file on the desk in front of him. "I'm afraid these photos are going to be rather unpleasant to look at."

"That's okay, Inspector."

"You know all the nurses who work here?"

"I would have interviewed them all at least once, yes."

Delaney opened the file. "We're trying to find out who she is. She wore a belt with a distinctive buckle. It's why we think she might have been a nurse."

He took out a ten by eight black-and-white photo of the belt and buckle and handed it across to her.

Sally leaned in. "We thought it might have been a qualifying gift. She was found near the hospital and we figured she may have worked here."

The woman nodded. "It's a possibility. It's the sort of buckle that a nurse might well have. When you say she was found . . . may I ask what the circumstances were?"

"She was murdered," Delaney said shortly. "Her throat was cut and her body was slashed. Repeatedly, and with some force."

Margaret Johnson swallowed and nodded at the folder, steeling herself. "I had best take a look then."

Delaney handed the file across to her and Sally could see moisture forming in the older woman's eyes as she looked through the photos one by one.

"The poor woman." Her voice cracked, and she brushed the back of her hand across her eyes. "I'm sorry."

She handed the file back.

"I'm sorry you had to see those, but we need to know," Delaney said.

"I meant I'm sorry because I can't help you."

"Mrs Johnson?"

"She may well have been a nurse. But she didn't work here."

The man looked at the answerphone by his bed. It was an old-fashioned one that he had never got around to replacing. You could have it through your line on BT so you didn't need a separate piece of equipment, but he had never cared for that. He liked the mechanics of things. He liked taking them apart to see how they worked. Always had. As a kid he had opened the backs of clocks to see the hidden, inner workings.

He looked again at the blinking light on the machine and felt no urge to play the message. He knew what it would be, but he had no time for petty distractions.

Not today. Today he was on a high. He was floating. He was invincible.

He looked at the scuffed toes of his cowboy boots and reached down to peel a wet leaf from one of them. He held the leaf to his nose, smelling the mossy tones of it, the woodland smell, the faint but sweet smell of organic matter beginning to decompose. He rubbed his other hand on the crotch of his trousers, feeling himself harden again as he drew in another deep sniff of the leaf and looked at the photos he had taken of a young detective constable dressed in a nurse's uniform. She certainly was very pretty.

Delaney thanked Margaret Johnson once more and closed the door to her office behind him. He had made her look at the photos again and then asked her to pull the records of all the nurses currently working at the hospital. One by one they had gone through the records, looking at each passport photo attached to each nurse's personnel file and by the end of it were none the wiser. Margaret Johnson had been right. The dead woman had not been working at the South Hampstead Hospital. At least they knew that now, if precious little else.

Delaney could see Sally Cartwright's upbeat mood had been dented a little. Not because she would have wanted the glory of making the nursing connection, of that he was sure. She was disappointed, just like he was, that they hadn't been able to identify the woman. If they could do that then it was a start to identifying her killer. Put a name to her and then maybe they could

191

track the sick bastard down before it was too late. Before he struck again. But in Delaney's heart, he knew that it was a distinct possibility that it was already too late. He turned to his assistant. "Come on."

"Where are we going, sir?"

"To the clap clinic."

"I beg your pardon?"

Delaney laughed drily, amused at the shocked look on the young detective constable's face. "You start going out with uniform, it's best you know where it is." He smiled again as Sally's face reddened and walked towards the stairs. "Come on, it's on the third floor."

Sally called after him and hurried to catch him up. "I hope you know that from reading the poster, sir."

Delaney walked up the first flight of stairs and looked at the signs pointing off to the maternity clinic and back to A&E and felt a fluttering in his heart. He stopped by the window and pulled out his mobile phone. "You go on, Sally. I'll meet you at the top."

"Sir?"

"I need to make a call."

Sally continued up the stairs and he waited before she was out of sight before he hit the redial button on the phone. After Kate's answerphone message kicked in again he closed the phone, the blood draining from his face as he gazed down the familiar corridor.

The nurse was a small dark-haired woman in her early twenties with delicate, almost oriental, features. Her hands were small too, but precise. She moved a pillow under the woman's head. The woman's eyes were closed, her breathing operated by an artificial respirator. The mechanical pumps making an obscene sound. Her body was invaded with tubes and wires, and the beat of the heart monitor sent out a contrapuntal and discordant rhythm to the respirator. She was living in form only.

Delaney stood at the foot of the bed as the nurse finished adjusting the pillow so that the woman's dark hair fanned neatly on it. There was no twitch beneath her eyelids, no smile tugging at the corner of her lips, and there never would be again. She was dead. All it needed was for Delaney to let them turn the machine off.

The consultant was sympathetic. "If there was any hope at all I would advise against it. Of course I would, but the brain stem has suffered too much damage. For all intents and purposes she is already dead."

Delaney looked at him for a long moment, scared to ask the question but needing to know the answer. "And the baby?"

The consultant shook his head sadly. "I'm sorry."

Delaney's head nodded downward as he gave permission. He couldn't hold back the tears any longer. His world went dark as the obscenity of the pump ceased and the heart-monitor line became still.

Delaney looked out of the window, his hand still clutching the phone like a rosary. He'd lost his wife and his baby in a matter of heartbeats four years ago and it had all but destroyed him. Now, though, he was being given a second chance. The woman he had come to love was carrying his child. His stupidity had almost lost her, but he'd be damned if he'd let anything or anyone come between them now. He opened the phone and hit speed dial. The phone rang at the other end and on the fifth ring cut into Kate's voice.

"This is Kate Walker. I am unavailable right now but leave me a message and I promise I will get back to you as soon as possible."

"Kate. This is Jack. I'm sorry." He sighed. "I'm sorry about everything. Call me."

He closed the phone and nodded to himself. He wasn't going to let history repeat itself. It was time to do the right thing. Finally.

Agnes Crabtree was sixty-eight years old and her knee joints were feeling every year of them that morning. The damp weather didn't help and Agnes's mood was even more depressed than usual. Six bloody months of winter nowadays. It would be April at least till there was a bit of warmth again and her aching bones might get some respite. Some doctor had been banging on about seasonal disorder on morning television earlier. SAD or something. And it was bloody sad. She made it up the flight of stairs and rested. Putting her bucket of cleaning materials on the floor and caught her breath. Not that she wanted to be breathing too deeply. The whole place smelled of piss. And not cat piss at that. Just as well she only cleaned on the inside of this flat, she reckoned. She groaned as she leaned over to pick up her equipment and fumbled a key into the lock of the flat. She took one or two steps into the flat, saw the long coloured scarf on the floor first and then registered what it was attached to. She tried to scream but her throat seized up with shock. She quickly stepped back, the pain in her knees ignored. The front door closed in her face and she finally found herself able to scream. She screamed again and stumbled backwards, her legs trembling. Her shaking hand went to her mouth and she took another step backwards, tripping over the can of Mr Sheen that had fallen from her dropped bucket. Her arms windmilled in the air as she lost her balance and crashed down the stairs. Her screams died as she landed at the bottom, her old head slapping on the wet concrete to lie at an odd angle, her eyes closed and a thin trickle of blood leaking from the corner of her mouth.

Delaney put his case on the table and pulled out a file. He removed the e-fit picture and handed it to Dr Andrew Burke, a silver-haired man in his early thirties. Delaney reckoned that maybe the rigours of his job, the sights he'd seen on a daily basis, had sent his hair prematurely grey.

The man shook his head as he studied the picture. "Sorry, he doesn't look familiar. He might have been in yesterday, you say?"

"Might have been."

"I'll get Suzanne. She was on the morning shift yesterday. She might recognise him."

The doctor left the room. Sally picked up the picture that the doctor had left on the desk. "Why do you think he came here?"

"It's pretty common."

"What is?"

"Flashers. Think about it, he gets to expose himself and have the goods handled at the same time." He shrugged with a rueful smile. "And if he's got a thing about nurses . . ."

Sally grimaced. "Please tell me you're joking."

Delaney grinned again. "It's a sick world we live in, Sally."

"You can say that again."

"A pound to a penny our boy likes to get his pickle tickled."

Sally frowned. "Don't they stick little spoons up?"

Delaney nodded and Sally grimaced again. The office door opened and the doctor came back in followed by an Afro-Caribbean woman, five foot two and weighing close to a couple of hundred pounds by Delaney's reckoning, but she fitted into her neat, dark blue uniform like a Horse Guard on parade.

Andrew Burke gestured towards her. "This is Suzanne."

"How can I help you, Inspector?" Her voice was thick and rolling, like a wave of wind through a field of molasses cane.

Delaney held the photo out to her and she nodded. "Yes, bless him, he was here yesterday. If it's who I think it is."

"Why bless him?"

"The poor lad. He's had some disfigurement."

"Scarring to his penis?"

The nurse nodded. "Indeed. And then he got a bit embarrassed when we did some tests."

"Embarrassed?" Sally asked.

The nurse smiled at her. "He got himself a little aroused. It does happen."

Sally's scowl deepened.

Delaney took the photo from her. "If you could let me have his name and contact details it would be very useful."

"Sure. It will take a few minutes."

"Quick as you can."

Suzanne looked up sharply at the seriousness in his voice, and hurried away to get the information.

Outside the clinic Sally could barely contain her exuberance.

"You think he's our man, sir?"

"He's our flasher, that's about all we know for sure."

"Should we call it in, send uniform round?"

"We'll take care of it, but first, as we're here, let's see if the Kraken has woken up."

Sally looked at him puzzled. "Sir?"

A stray dog slowly approached the motionless body of Agnes Crabtree, tentatively sniffing the air, and moved closer. It was a ragged thing. A composite of hair and bone and appetite, scabby, starving and neglected. It nuzzled Agnes's face with its jaw and scented the fresh blood that had spilled along the pitted line of her chin into a small, brown stain on the wet stone. The smell made the dog's stomach rumble and flex with pain. He opened his jaw wider and, taking the old woman's ear between his teeth, gave a little tug. Agnes Crabtree groaned and shifted but did not awaken and slumped again, her breath exhaling in a wet, barely audible sigh. But the dog had long gone by then, his tail between his legs and his meal forgotten. In his experience human beings never meant anything but pain.

Delaney looked down at the still motionless body of Kevin Norrell as Sally picked up his medical chart at the foot of the bed.

"He's lucky to be alive."

"If he makes it."

"What do you think he knows?"

"People talk in prison. They brag. Someone may have told him something. Maybe he was involved himself." Delaney shrugged.

Sally hesitated then put Norrell's chart back and looked at her boss. "Yesterday I looked at the reports, boss. The incident . . ."

Delaney, hearing the hesitation in her voice, glanced over at her. "Just spit it out, Sally."

"The hold-up at the petrol station."

It flashed back unbidden into Delaney's mind. The darkness of the night split by the sound and the flare of lighting cracking. Of glass exploding, of tyres squealing and a woman's voice screaming, then silence. Those shards of glass flying through the night air like barbs of conscience to bury deep into Delaney's brain. The guilt hooking him, ever since, like a bloodstained puppet to jerk and twitch under the hand of a punishing god.

"What about it, Detective Constable?" he asked simply.

"They robbed the place. And then they left, shooting out the window. Why would they do that?"

"Because they're mindless thugs."

"Maybe. But three heavily tooled-up villains and a driver? Sounds like a professional job to me."

"Go on."

"For a petrol station?" Sally shrugged. "Makes no sense. Everyone knows they don't have the sort of cash on the premises to merit that kind of operation."

Delaney took it in, the realisation giving him a feeling in his stomach akin to a lift dropping several floors quickly. Sally was right, he had been the worst kind of idiot. Four years of alcohol-induced rage, but it had been directed at himself not at the people really responsible. He'd been flailing around in his own misery and self-disgust to see what Sally had seen almost immediately. No self-respecting, professional outfit would target a petrol station, it made no sense.

"So, it wasn't a robbery?"

"No, sir, I don't think it was." She looked at her boss sympathetically. "I think it was a warning, and your wife just got in the way."

"Warning to who?"

"I don't know, sir."

Delaney looked down at the sleeping figure of Kevin Norrell. The comatose man knew something, he was certain of that. But Sally had provided him with somewhere to start at least. Four years of nothing. Dead ends and false trails. And now his bright-eyed detective constable, fresh out of college, was seeing things he should have seen straight away. He cursed himself for a fool and then realised he didn't have the time for any more self-pity. It was time to put matters right.

"Come on then, Sally."

"Where to?"

"Work."

Delaney held the piece of paper the Afro-Caribbean nurse had given him tightly in his hand. The flasher was called Ashley Bradley, he was twenty-eight years old, on unemployment benefit and lived at 28b Morris Street in Chalk Farm, just a couple of stops down on the Northern Line from South Hampstead Tube.

He was heading for the exit when he saw a familiar face waiting at the lift. He stopped and waved Sally ahead. "Wait for me in the car, Sally." He tossed her the keys. "You can drive."

Sally looked over to where Delaney's gaze was focused and her mouth twisted in disapproval. "Do you think that's a wise idea, sir?"

"Just do it, Constable."

Sally walked on to the exit and Delaney crossed over to the lifts just as they opened. The man turned round as Delaney approached. "Do you want to step away from me or do you want me to call security?" he said, a little nervous catch in his voice.

Delaney pushed him into the lift.

"What the hell do you think you're doing?"

He tried to force himself past Delaney and back out of the lift, but Delaney blocked his way, pushing the button for the fifth floor. The doors closed and Delaney turned to face him.

"You and I need to have a little talk."

Paul Archer crossed his arms across his chest. "The only person you need to talk to is a lawyer. Because you better believe I am calling the police."

Delaney pulled out his warrant card. "Can you hear my knees knocking?"

Archer leaned forward to read it and laughed humourlessly. "Even better. You'll be out of a job as well."

"Kate Walker was upset yesterday, I want to know why."

"What business is it of yours?"

Delaney leaned in. "Just answer the fucking question."

Paul Archer smiled, which Delaney figured was a big mistake. He was moments away from smashing the smug look off his face and spoiling his looks for good.

"Whatever is between Kate and me is our concern and certainly none of yours."

"You want to tell me now or do you want to be eating your meals through a straw for a couple of weeks?"

"Is that a threat, Inspector?"

Delaney stepped in closer. "Does it sound like a threat?"

Archer moved back into the corner of the lift. "Don't touch me." His hand involuntarily went up to touch his nose. "She tell you she was fucking me the night before?"

Delaney was taken aback. "Last night?"

Archer's eyes flickered as he corrected himself. "Not last night. The night before. She picked me up in the Holly Bush and took me back to hers. I told her it was just a one-night stand, but she wanted more."

Delaney didn't say anything, taking it in.

Archer could see his words had hit home. "Your problems with her are nothing to do with me," he said as the lift door opened and he hurried past Delaney out of the lift.

Delaney watched him go then stabbed his finger on the ground-floor button. He couldn't blame Kate, it was exactly the sort of thing he would have done. He remembered that night, he remembered the hot breath of Stella Trant whispering in his ear. He had no moral high horse to ride on. He had no justification for being angry with Kate. But rationalisation was one thing, emotion another. The truth was he was fucking furious. He slammed his open hand hard against the side of the lift as the doors opened. A couple of nurses stepped back as he stormed past, but if he felt at all apologetic for startling them it certainly didn't show on his face.

Out in the car park Delaney opened the passenger door to his car, and got in, banging it behind him. Sally tried to fire up the engine as Delaney pulled out his mobile phone and punched in some numbers. The Saab coughed ineffectually a few times but turned over eventually after Sally gave the accelerator a couple of prods with her foot.

"When did you last have this serviced, sir?"

Delaney didn't answer. Instead he looked out of the passenger window as his call was answered.

"Jimmy, it's Jack. Have you got anything for us?"

"Nothing new," Skinner answered.

"I'm just leaving South Hampstead Hospital, we've got a lead on the flasher."

"Right."

"Norrell hasn't regained consciousness and the other guy is holding to his story."

"You believe him?"

"I believe they went after Norrell because they thought he was a nonce. But I don't believe that was why they were sicced on to him in the first place."

"You being careful, Jack?"

"I'm doing what has to be done."

"Keep me posted."

Jack closed his phone and gestured at Sally. "Come on, move it."

"Chalk Farm, sir?"

"Not just yet."

"Sir?"

Delaney looked at his watch. "Pinner Green."

Sally nodded and pulled the car away as Delaney's phone rang. He looked at who was calling and answered it. "Hi, Diane."

"Where are you, Jack?"

"Just following up a lead."

"The boss wants you in for a press conference."

"I'll get there when I can."

"This lead, is it in connection with the South Hampstead Common case, or something else?"

"You wanted me back on the job, didn't you, guv?"

"Just don't let it get in the way. This turns out to be a serial killer and you fuck up on us, Jack, there's no way I can keep your nuts out of the vice."

"Nice image."

"Just don't let me down . . ."

"You got it."

"And don't call me guv!"

Delaney closed his phone. Trouble was, he was good at that. Letting people down.

Jack Delaney and his wife had been eating dinner that Saturday night four years ago in a restaurant at the top of Pinner High Street. Just down from the church they had been married in, a Norman-style edifice that stood on top of the hill like a small, suburban castle. The restaurant served a pan-Asian menu, or Pacific-rim fusion as the owner liked to call it. Whatever it was called, though, it wasn't to Jack's taste, he'd never really liked Chinese food. But it was his wife's favourite restaurant. It was their anniversary that evening and the truth was that Jack had a lot of making up to do to her. They had been arguing too much of late. Mainly about his job and the hours he worked. The risks he took. The danger on the streets, the growing proliferation of guns and knives in the hands of teenagers who, with no future ahead of them, valued others' lives as cheaply as their own were valued in turn. It was the same arguments that policemen and policewomen had with their spouses up and down the country and all around the world. But that wasn't all there was to it. Behind it all Jack knew the real reason for the growing tensions between them.

Sinead wanted to go back home. To leave England behind and return to her native Dublin, or move even further out into the country. Even as far as to the heathen, blighted, wind-blown and rain-soaked fields of Cork, whence Delaney had dragged his own sorry Irish arse. Jack had pointed out to her many times that he was ten years old when his parents had moved to England. Although he would hate to admit it to his colleagues, Jack felt that England was more of a home to him now than Ireland. His memories of it were fond enough, but mainly he remembered the lack of work, the lack of money, the struggles his parents had to put food on the table and leather on their feet. The opportunities London offered in the seventies for a man such as his father and a woman like his mother, God rest her soul, who were prepared to put in a long day's work were too good to refuse. And so the family had moved, like many before, across the waters to the mainland. His mother had died when he was eleven years old, run over in the early hours on her way to work by a hit-and-run driver whom the police never found and whose soul, Jack still hoped, was rotting in hell. And so it was his father who had pushed Jack into joining the police. A man needed a profession or a trade, Jack's dad reckoned, and as the boy had maybe the brains but not the inclination for a university degree he should look at the army, the navy or the police force. The idea of serving in Northern Ireland put any notions of joining the armed forces out of Jack's head. He couldn't see himself pointing a rifle at his Northern brothers, Catholic or Protestant, and he certainly couldn't envisage pulling the trigger. But the thought of joining the police had some appeal to him. Maybe it was the spectre of his mother's death, maybe it was just the knowledge that if he didn't join the police he'd go the way of his cousins who lived in Kilburn and made their money on the other side of the legal fence. And so he worked hard enough at school to get the right kind of grades to apply to the Met. Which he did when he was eighteen and hadn't regretted it since.

But lately Sinead had been, subtly at first, and then not so subtly, pushing him to take early retirement. Plenty of people left early, took up another profession. Something safer, something with regular hours. A job that meant she wouldn't be looking at the clock with dread, but with pleasure at the certainty of his arrival home at the given hour. The sound of a phone ringing wouldn't set her heart racing and her mouth dry every time she answered it, terrified that this call would be the one bringing the news she lived her life in fear of. And, moreover, their young girl, Siobhan, was three years old now. A walking, talking miniature human being with her future all before her. And she reminded him, time after time, although the bulge in her belly made it plain, that she was pregnant again and she wanted a secure future for all of them.

206

The trouble was that Jack Delaney didn't know what he would do back in Ireland. He was too young to retire. Too old to start a new career. And in truth he didn't want to. Jack loved his job. He loved the freedom of it, and although he might work long hours, they weren't hours spent behind a desk or in a neon-lit office, not for most of the time anyway. He got results and at the end of the day that was what really mattered. It's what mattered if you had a decent boss, that is. Someone who was more interested in banging up criminals than brown-nosing their way into senior management. And Jack's boss, Diane Campbell, was diamond.

So Jack didn't know what he was supposed to do. He loved his wife, really loved her. But the tensions over the last few months had put a strain on them both. And Jack had made a mistake. He'd had an affair. Not even an affair really, just a one-night stand, but the guilt of it ate away at him on a daily basis like a virus. Like a flesh-eating disease. And, because he felt guilty, he got angry, and covered it up by arguing with his wife. It was a vicious circle and Jack wasn't at all sure how to get out of it. But he had made an effort tonight and was grateful that he had had. They had had a lovely meal and a lovely evening. For the first time in ages they hadn't argued. They'd enjoyed each other's company, they'd made each other laugh and Jack couldn't for the life of him understand why he had strayed. And especially with whom.

As they had left the restaurant and started up the car engine, Sinead had insisted they get more petrol. Jack would have argued, he was well aware that they had enough in the tank to get home three times over, but it was one of his wife's pet foibles, she never let the petrol gauge drop below a quarter of a tank. And so they had turned right at the bottom of the hill and drove out of Pinner up to Pinner Green, where there was a petrol station that would be open at that time of day. It was a hot summer night, the heat still cooking the air and only the faintest breaths of wind. Venus was bright in the night sky and Delaney took it to be an omen. He pointed at the star. "If men are from Mars and women are from Venus. And if men like bars, what do women like?"

Sinead laughed and slapped him on the arm. It was a musical laugh, like the sound of trickling mountain water over cool slate.

Delaney spun the wheel, turning into the forecourt of the petrol station. The adverts finished and the Cowboy Junkies started to play. "Blue Moon". One of Delaney's favourites. "Now you can't tell me that isn't proper music."

His wife laughed again. "I can't tell you anything, Jack. I've learned that much by now."

Delaney had got out of the car and popped open the petrol tank; he was reaching for the fuel nozzle when the plate-glass window of the shop exploded. Delaney instinctively raised his arm to protect his eyes from the storm of flying glass. His wife's scream carried over the sound of the shotgun blast and two men came out of the shop. Thickset men dressed in black with balaclavas covering their heads, shotguns held waist level, sweeping the forecourt in front of them.

They shouted at Delaney, but he couldn't hear them; their shotguns trained on him and he watched them frozen for a moment, until his wife screamed at him and her words finally registered.

"For Christ's sake, Jack, get in the car."

And he did, watching as a Transit van drove through the forecourt with its back doors open. One of the men jumped in and the other ran to catch up. Delaney turned the key in the ignition and gunned the engine, not listening as his wife shouted at him, putting the car in gear and screeching after them, swerving to avoid an incoming car.

The second man jumped into the van, half falling back with the motion and landed with a bone-jarring crash on his knees, but a hand to the inside wall of the van steadied him and he brought his shotgun round to bear on the pursuing car. Delaney's wife screamed and the sound ripped into Delaney's consciousness like ice-cold water as he realised what he was doing. Too late. The shotgun fired again and Delaney's windscreen exploded, the car spinning out of control as the screaming blended with the screeching of brakes and the crumpling of metal . . .

Delaney shook his head to clear the thought and frowned as he pulled the car to a stop outside a block of upscale apartment buildings on the left-hand side of Pinner Green heading towards Northwood Hills.

"What's up, boss?"

209

"The petrol station."

"What about it?"

"It's not here any more."

Jenny Hickling turned back to the fifteen-year-old boy who was following her. Nervously flicking his long and greasy hair like a girl.

"Get a move on for fuck's sake. I ain't got all fucking day."

"All right, keep your knickers on."

"That supposed to be funny?"

The boy shuffled after her. His jeans were hanging off his scrawny arse gangsta-style, and although he swaggered as best he could, Jenny reckoned he wasn't as cocksure as he thought he was. She knew the type, posh kids bunking off from the grammar school up the road, dressing like hoodies and trying to talk the talk. About as convincing as her uncle Gerard who used to dress up as Marilyn Monroe at every opportunity, complete with a blonde wig and five o'clock shadow. She reckoned the boy was cherry. She'd probably get away with only a couple of strokes and the scratch of her fingernail across the business end before he'd shoot his load. She'd agreed to give him a blow job but she reckoned she wouldn't have to. She wasn't bothered about giving him a suck, it was just she weren't going to let him stick it in her mouth unprotected and she hated the taste of latex. It reminded her of the washing-up gloves her bitch of an Irish mother used to wear when she washed her mouth out for swearing. Before Jenny grew too big of course. She had believed the threat that

210

if she tried to do it one more fucking time she'd wake up with a fucking carving knife in her throat, if that wasn't what her pervert English teacher, Mr Gingernut Collier, called a contradiction in fucking terms. She looked back at the kid who was still limping along behind. He wanted it, that much was clear, but he was still nervous as shite. His older brother was at the University of Middlesex, wherever the fuck that was, and he had nicked some gear off him. Primo gear, he had called it, like something he had heard on late-night TV. But if Jenny guessed right the prissy boy wouldn't know primo gear from a knobbly stick up his arse.

She turned the corner into the backyard of a block of flats. The bottom corridors weren't overlooked, and if she had a penny for every dick she'd dealt with back there she'd have a good pound or two and no fucking mistake.

"Will you get a fecking move on?"

She walked up the step into the covered walkway where the wheelie bins were kept and stopped dead in her tracks. The body of Agnes Crabtree lay right in front of her. One leg trailing up the steps and her head at an angle God hadn't intended. She was pretty sure of that.

She turned back to the pimply teenager who had turned white as a sheet and was running away as fast as he could move. Which wasn't very fast; she almost laughed when he tripped over and landed head first in a puddle, but the smile died as soon as it was born as she realised the little gobshite had taken the gear, primo, or otherwise with him.

211

She pulled out her mobile phone and dialled 999. "Ambulance. There's an old lady here not looking so tickety-fucking-boo."

She gave the woman on the other end of the line the address, then grimaced when she asked her how old she was. "I'm fourteen, so I won't be here when they get here, all right." She closed the phone down, then cursed, they'd be able to trace her from her phone number. But she reckoned the woodentops, as her mother called them, would have better things to do than chase up a bleeding truancy.

She looked down at the body of Agnes Crabtree. "I hope they sort you out, missus." Then she set off in pursuit of the pimply boy, though she reckoned his knob must have shrivelled to the size of an acorn at the sight of the dead woman, if it hadn't retracted up inside him altogether.

Delaney looked out of the passenger window as they drove along the Western Avenue, at least the rain had stopped, but the flyover was clogged fairly solidly as they moved slowly towards White City. He looked over to where the old dog-racing track used to be and realised how much London had changed over the last twenty years or so. And not for the better. Delaney had a theory that a city could only take so many people. Too many rats in a cage meant that some, already feral, turned psychotic and in his experience humans were no different. It might not be against the laws of God for so many millions of people to be crammed together in one space, but it was certainly against the laws of nature. We are the architects of our own destruction sure enough, he thought drily. He should have got out of London when he had a chance. If he had listened to his wife four years ago things would have turned out very different.

He'd never have met Kate, and once again Delaney's stomach gripped with the guilt of it all. London might be a mess but he himself was a walking fucking disaster area. And he knew it. Maybe this was it though. Maybe he had a chance to rewrite history, almost. A second chance. Maybe Kate was his salvation.

The traffic cleared and Sally was able to floor the accelerator and they drove past the White City police station and soon they were at Chalk Farm.

He had to live on the third floor Delaney thought as they trudged up the steps, out of breath and figuring, yet again, it was time for a new fitness regime. A man clattered by in army fatigues and a woollen hat. Delaney stood aside to let him pass. The man was probably carrying, which was why he was so keen to get past, but Delaney had other fish to fry. He carried on to the third floor where Sally Cartwright was already waiting for him, not a hair out of place nor the slightest evidence of any exertion on her part.

"What are you waiting for, Sally? Bang on the door!" he snapped.

Sally smiled thinly and rapped hard on the door. After a short while with no response Delaney stepped forward and banged harder, and they heard the sound of a chain being lifted and the face of a small, white-haired, elderly woman peered out.

"I'm not interested in Jehovah or shoe brushes."

Delaney knew how she felt. He held out his warrant card. "Detective Inspector Jack Delaney, and this is Constable Sally Cartwright."

"He hasn't done anything wrong." She tried to shut the door but Delaney held it open with his hand.

"Who hasn't done anything wrong?"

The elderly woman shook her head. "I should speak to a lawyer first. That's right, isn't it?"

Sally smiled at her reassuringly. "What are you talking about?"

The woman shook her head again. "I don't know anything about it, and he was with me the whole time."

"Is Ashley Bradley your son?" Sally asked.

The woman shook her disarrayed white hair. "He's my grandson. I told them never to get that dog, I knew it would end in tears."

"Where is he, Mrs Bradley?"

The woman shook her head. "You just missed him."

Delaney cursed himself. "Army-type clothes and a woolly hat?"

"That's right. He's gone. But he's been with me all the other times."

"Can we come in, Mrs Bradley?"

"The woman shook her head nervously. "I'm having my Weetabix."

Delaney would have responded but his phone rang, startling him out of his introspection, and he snapped it open. "Delaney."

"Jack, it's Diane."

"I'm on it."

"Never mind that. Where are you?"

"Chalk Farm, why?"

"Good. I need you to get to Camden Town."

"What's going on?"

"We think there might be another one. And it's bad, Jack. Really bad."

"Give me the address." He listened as Diane gave him the details and closed the phone. "Come on, Sally, we're out of here." He turned back to the old lady. "We'll be back."

They hurried back down the stairs and Delaney pulled out his phone again, hitting the speed dial. It rang for a few times, again, and then cut into Kate's voice message again. He snapped the phone angrily shut. "Where the bloody hell is she?"

"Sir?"

Delaney hadn't realised he had spoken aloud. "Don't worry about it, Sally, just get us to Camden."

Just as a human face is a map, in most cases, of the kind of life a person has had — sad, happy, hopeful, despairing — so a building has a personality every bit as decipherable. Grosvenor Court in Camden Town was built in an era that had more hope than it deserved. Hope that experience soon wiped off its facade, just as the bright green paint was now faded, scabby and sore.

The apartments were built on three sides of a square, with a car park in the middle. A single police car blocked the back entrance. Sally pulled Delaney's Saab to a groaning stop alongside the police car and they both got out.

It wasn't even lunchtime yet but Delaney was yawning expansively. He had hardly slept the night before. After Kate had left him in the Holly Bush and wouldn't answer her door to him he had gone home, where, for the first time in four years, he didn't even contemplate drinking himself into his usual oblivion. But the night had brought no relief in sleep, as he knew it wouldn't. It was part of the price he had to pay.

Danny Vine was waiting at the bottom of the stairs with Bob Wilkinson and the police photographer, Delaney couldn't remember his name, and a couple of SOCOs. They were waiting for Delaney to see the scene before recording every detail. Bob nodded at Sally and Delaney as they approached. "I hope you haven't had breakfast." He wasn't joking.

Delaney didn't reply. He hadn't eaten since the bacon sandwich he had had for lunch yesterday, but sensed this wasn't the time for small talk. He could see it in the pale faces of the three men watching him.

"Who called it in?"

"The cleaner. She walked in on it. Staggered back and fell down the stairs. Nearly broke her neck. She came round in the ambulance and the paramedics alerted us."

Delaney walked up the stairs and two uniformed policemen at the top stood aside. Their faces were drained, one was shaking visibly. Delaney pushed open the door and stepped into the darkness of the room, Sally following closely behind.

216

Delaney's eyes didn't need time to adjust to see what lay on the floor. What had once been a human being was now rendered into a thing of slaughter and his world tilted on its axis once more. Delaney's heart felt like it had been gripped by a hand made of frozen steel and he gasped out loud. He fought to catch his breath. He wanted to tear his eyes away from what he was looking at but couldn't. Among all the blood and ripped flesh, among the blood sprayed on the walls and the tissue splayed over the floor and the guts strewn like the wet, grey tubing of a squid's tentacles, was what was left of a once beautiful woman; she had hair the colour of blue midnight, lips as sweet as an Elgar cello concerto and a scarf trailed around her naked body soaked in her blood. A long, thick and multicoloured scarf, just like Doctor Who used to wear.

"Kate . . ." Delaney's voice was a tortured whisper.

And the roaring in his ears was like an ocean now.

Delaney gagged, again, and turned and stumbled from the room. Outside he turned and half ran, half fell to the end of the walkway, where he bent over and retched, sank to his knees, coughed and retched again, gagged until there was nothing left in him to throw up.

Superintendent George Napier looked at his wristwatch and took a sip of coffee. One of the first things he had done when taking over the office was to bring in his own espresso coffee maker. A hand-pumped La Pavoni machine, a design classic in shiny chrome. He ground his own beans, a particular coffee he ordered over the Internet called Jumbo Maragogype — the elephant

217

bean. He swallowed and sighed. One cup of real coffee and ten minutes to himself, if he could organise it, was a small luxury he could rarely afford.

The telephone on his desk rang and he deliberated for a moment or two before answering but finally snatched it up.

"Napier."

He listened for a moment, the frown on his forehead deepening. He nodded finally. "I'll take care of it." He replaced the phone in its cradle and sighed as he looked at his cup of coffee. The moment was ruined. "Bloody Irishman!" he said and slammed his hand on his desk, causing his phone to rattle and his precious coffee to spill out on the perfect order of his highly polished desk. But Napier didn't even register it. "Damn them all," he said and slammed his hand down again.

"It's not her, sir."

Delaney could barely hear the words. He wiped the sleeve of his jacket across his mouth and looked up to see Sally standing above him. "What?"

"It's not her, sir. It's not Dr Walker. It's her scarf, by the looks of it, but it's not her. That woman. She's wearing a wig." She could barely get the words out. "She was wearing a wig." She corrected herself.

Sally took a step towards him and then had to put her hand on the wall. She looked down to the car park below. Taking a few deep breaths herself. Her face was the colour of a white lily pressed in an old hymnal.

* * *

Delaney took a long swig of water from the bottle that Sally had just given him and wiped his mouth as Diane Campbell came up the steps and walked over to join them.

"You got anything for me?"

Delaney shook his head. "Just got here, Diane."

"Is it the same guy?"

Delaney shrugged. "It's the same kind of butchery. Worse than the first."

"Is he escalating?"

Delaney gestured helplessly. "Seems to be, but honestly, I don't know, boss. We're pretty much in the dark here."

"What about the suspect? The flasher?"

"We've tracked him down but he wasn't at home."

"Why don't you get out of here and go and find him then?"

"Shouldn't I stay here, process the scene?"

"I've got it covered. The super is on his way over, cowboy. He wants your balls in a chocolate fountain and served up at the ambassador's party."

Delaney grimaced. "The guy from the hospital made a complaint?"

Campbell shook her head dismissively. "You can tell me about it later." She jerked her thumb back towards the murder scene. "For now we have more important things to worry about than some paediatrician you've been having a pissing competition with. Now fuck off before he gets here."

Delaney gestured to Sally Cartwright and led her back down the stairs. Campbell watched them leave for a moment and then put a cigarette in her mouth and then barked at the uniform standing by the open door. "Get me a sodding light!"

Delaney held his warrant card up again for the old lady at the door to read, but she knew very well who he was. She backed away resignedly as Delaney and Sally walked in. Delaney told the two uniforms that were with them to wait outside and keep an eye out for Ashley Bradley, and if the little bastard ran they had better damn well catch him.

Mrs Bradley led Delaney to the back of the flat to her grandson's bedroom. Delaney didn't consider him likely for the two killings. It was a very big step from flashing nurses on the common to murder and mutilation. It did happen of course. Serial killers were often profiled as having been cruel to animals in their youth, going on to sex offences like peeping through windows and flashing before maturing into full-time psychopaths. It was pretty bloody rare for it to happen overnight, mind.

The door to Ashley Bradley's bedroom was locked and his grandmother didn't have a key. Delaney didn't even apologise as he used his shoulder to smash the door open. But what he saw inside made him rethink the matter entirely and curse himself for every kind of fool in God's cruel Christendom.

Superintendent George Napier stood at the top of the stairs at the flats in Camden Town, glaring at Diane

Campbell as she took another satisfying drag on her cigarette.

"Is that absolutely necessary?"

Diane jerked her cigarette back at the crime scene where the suited-up SOCOs were now processing every square inch. "Have you seen what he did to her in there?"

"You know damn well I haven't."

Diane took another drag on her cigarette and pointedly blew out a long stream of smoke. "Talk to me about it when you have then."

Napier looked far from happy but let it rest. "Where's Delaney?"

"Following up a lead."

"I've had a complaint that he assaulted a paediatrician at South Hampstead Hospital yesterday morning and then physically threatened him again today."

"I'm sure he had his reasons."

"I don't give a damn if he had his reasons or not. I will not have members of my police force roaming around assaulting members of the public."

"I'll have a word, sir."

"You'll do more than that. I want him suspended pending a full inquiry."

"Why don't we get his version of events before we do anything?"

"The man's a loose cannon, you know that, Diane. But he's gone too far this time. I want him closed down."

"Can't do that, sir."

"You'll do as you're damn well told. This ain't Dodge City, Chief Inspector."

"Why don't you tell that to the press?"

"What are you talking about?"

Diane pointed her cigarette behind the superintendent. "Melanie Jones seems to think the killer has some kind of connection with Jack Delaney. She wants to liaise with him about it."

George Napier swore under his breath as he turned round to see Melanie Jones and her cameraman coming up the stairs towards them.

"How the hell did she know about this?" he hissed.

"Seems the killer has a thing about her too. Likes to call her up for cosy chit-chats."

Napier turned his back on the approaching reporter. "Jesus Christ, Diane. This kind of thing can ruin careers."

"If Jack is suspended, sir, I guess she can deal with you."

Napier glared at her. "You've made your bloody point, Diane. Let's not push it, eh?"

Delaney stood in the centre of the small room. A bed in the corner, a wardrobe, a desk with a laptop computer on it and a digital camera beside it. A stack of pornographic magazines at the base of the bed with a waste-paper basket beside it full of old tissues. He picked up a couple of the magazines and flicked through the titles, voyeuristic stuff mainly, peeping Tom-type shots. Posed for the camera as though the subject was unaware the camera was there. And every spare inch of every wall of the room covered with photographs. Photographs of women genuinely unaware they were being photographed. A lot of them from South Hampstead Heath. A lot of them in nurse's uniform.

Sally waved a hand under her nose. The odour in the room was overpowering and distinctly unpleasant. The smell of stale sex. Solitary, self-administered sex. She crossed to the curtains, opened them and after struggling with the catch managed to release the window, letting a little fresh air into the room. She glanced at the waste-paper basket and grimaced at Delaney. "The greatest love of all."

But Delaney wasn't listening, he was staring at the photos on the wall.

"Have a look here, Sally." He was pointing at a photo on the wall near to the desk. It was of a dark-haired woman dressed goth-style and walking on the South Hampstead common.

Sally looked at the picture. "It's hard to tell, sir. The make-up makes them all look alike. Goths, I mean."

Delaney tapped at the picture. "Blow this up and I'll bet you we'll see a belt buckle with two green men on it."

"It does look like her."

"Check all the others."

Sally and Delaney methodically worked their way along the photos. After five minutes Sally stopped and looked at a picture.

"I think this is the second one, sir. She's got blonde hair, but I think it's her."

Delaney walked across and looked. The hair colouring was different but the face was the same, she was dressed in a nurse's uniform from South Hampstead Hospital. It felt like someone had punched him in the stomach. He deserved it. "Shit!" he said.

"Sir?"

"We let the sick fuck get away."

There is a connection between life and death. Delaney believed in that, if he didn't believe in much else. When he was four years old and living in Ballydehob, he had been bundled out of the house one day during the summer holidays. His two older, twin cousins, Mary and Clare, had taken him down to the old railway viaduct over the river. It was a scorching hot day and he had been given ice cream and lemonade in the village, then taken down to the river and up on the viaduct where they allowed him to pick up pebbles and throw them into the water cascading far below.

A crow had landed on the spur of green land under the entrance to the viaduct where they were standing, high overhead and just by the lamp post. The girls, older than him by some eight years, looked on Jack as their own little walking, talking doll. They told him that the crow was actually a raven. When Jack threw a pebble and it took off squawking in the air, the girls had said that it was a bad omen. The raven was an omen of death. And Jack, as susceptible to superstition as an Irishman from Cork is wont to be, believed them. But when they returned home late that afternoon, with the sound of laughter and bustle coming from the house like it was almost Christmas, Jack, swinging between them, dangling from their longer arms like a curly-haired monkey, picked up on the atmosphere and smiled even more broadly for no reason at all. But as soon as they entered the chaos of the house it became clear why Jack was being treated to a trip out with his beautiful cousins. His mother had given birth to a daughter. A young sister for Jack. And although he didn't really understand what was going on he knew it was a special day.

Before the day was spent, however, eleven o'clock at night with the moon hanging low and enormous in the summer sky like a swollen exotic fruit, his silver-haired grandfather, eighty-three years old, had died. And Delaney would never see a crow or a rook again without shivering slightly, although in his heart, deep down, he knew the raven had not been meant for his grandfather. But there was a cycle to life, and death was part of that. Jack grasped that from a very early age.

How that connection worked, though, in the case of the murdered and mutilated woman that had been obscenely decorated with a scarf just like Kate Walker's, Delaney wasn't quite so sure. But he knew evil wasn't an abstract concept.

He was far from hungry. After what he had witnessed a short while ago he felt as if he might never eat again. But his energy levels were low and his brain told him he needed nourishment, so he was standing outside the burger van chain-smoking and trying to wash the memory of what he had witnessed from his mind. He held his cigarette to his lips and realised his hands were

225

still shaking. He couldn't keep the images away and he knew what would be written in the pathologist's clinical report.

Her left arm was placed across the left breast. The body was terribly mutilated . . . the throat was severed deeply, the incision through the skin jagged, and reaching right round the neck. The body had lost a great quantity of blood. There was no evidence of a struggle having taken place. The scarf was draped around her savaged neck. There were two distinct, clean cuts on the left side of the spine. They were parallel with each other and separated by about half an inch. The muscular structures appeared as though an attempt had made to separate the bones of the neck.

The abdomen had been entirely laid open: the intestines, severed from their attachments, had been lifted out of the body and placed on the shoulder of the corpse; while from the pelvis, the uterus and its appendages with the upper portion of the vagina and the posterior two-thirds of the bladder, had been entirely removed.

"Inspector?"

Delaney, startled out of his reverie, looked up at the florid face of the short-order chef.

"You want onions with this?"

Roy held up the burger and Delaney shook his head, not sure he had the stomach for it right then.

"You all right, sir?" Sally asked.

Delaney didn't reply, pulling out his mobile phone and tapping in some numbers. After a while the call was answered. The familiar voice purring with self-content.

"Melanie Jones."

"Melanie. It's Jack Delaney."

"I was just about to call you,"

"Why?"

"Because he just called me again."

"And . . ."

"He said to give you another message."

"What was it?"

"He said for you to start with the man in the mirror."

"What's that mean?"

"I don't know, Jack. That's all he said. Then he hung up."

Delaney clenched his fist. "Do you have any idea what he did to that woman?"

"They haven't given me any details, no."

"I find out you're jerking me around and I am going to visit vengeance on you like a biblical fucking angel."

"Great line. Can I use that?"

Delaney spoke quietly but furiously. "Do you believe me, when I say it?"

"All right, yes. I believe you. You're the arch-fucking-angel of death and justice. I'm telling you what he's told me. What more do you want me to do?"

"I'll let you know." Delaney cut the call off. He quickly scrolled to Kate's number once more and snapped the phone angrily shut when it cut into her answerphone yet again. Where the bloody hell was she?

Sally walked over to him, holding out his burger. Delaney snatched it off her, took one look at it and threw it in the bin.

"Oi!" Roy shouted out.

Delaney glared up at him. "Not now, all right?" He turned to Sally. "Come on."

"Where are we going?"

If Sally was hoping for further enlightenment, it wasn't forthcoming as Delaney was already striding quickly away.

Roy leaned over the counter and called after him. "Jack Delaney. International man of misery!" He grinned, pleased with himself, then went back to reading his Peter F. Hamilton.

In Hampstead village itself, a light drizzle had started. And the wind made the air far colder than it should have been for the time of year. Kate locked her car door then pulled her coat tighter to herself, hugging her arms around her body as she walked, head down, across the road.

She walked up to the front door but hesitated before knocking on it. She had taken the morning off to meet with this woman, but now that it came to it, she wasn't sure she could go through with it.

After she had left Delaney the previous night, she had stood outside the Holly Bush for a moment or two, furious and hurt. Really hurt and hating herself for it. She couldn't face being alone that night so she had flagged down a passing cab and told the driver to take her out of Hampstead. When he had asked her where to go she honestly had no idea, but then told him to take her to Highgate. She needed a friend. But at her friend's front door she had hesitated, wanting to ring the bell but fearing conversation. Knowing that if she articulated her thoughts she would break down in tears. The rain had started falling in earnest when Kate finally pushed the doorbell. The chimes sounded as though from a different world. A world of comfort and security. A world that Kate felt as though she had been ripped away from and was not sure she would ever find her way back to.

The door had opened and it had been like standing in front of an open fire after a winter storm.

"For God's sake, Kate! How long have you been out there? You look like a drowned rat."

Kate had stumbled in and Jane had put her strong arms around her, stroking her wet hair as the tears poured down Kate's cheeks and she sobbed like a hurt child.

The next morning, back in Hampstead village at another front door, Kate took a deep breath and willed her finger forward, knowing if she pushed the bell the world might change for ever.

The chimes played a tune Kate felt sure she should recognise but couldn't quite place. The door opened and Helen Archer looked out at her. She was a beautiful woman somewhere in her thirties, Kate guessed, with long blonde hair the colour of antique pine with threads of amber gold. Her eyes were startling, wide and doll-like. But Kate could see behind those painted eyes an innocence that had been betrayed long ago. A hurt that was beyond restoration. She had seen it before, in her own eyes.

"You must be Dr Walker."

"It's Kate, please."

The woman stepped back and gestured with her arm. "Come in, Kate."

Across the road Paul Archer rolled down his window and stared at the door as it closed behind the pair of them. He put a hand subconsciously to his nose.

There was nothing kind in his eyes.

Roger Yates was sitting behind his desk in a plush office. It was a partner's desk, green leather on the top with a rich patina on the wood which only comes after a few hundred years. There was nothing repro about the office. The paintings on the wall were originals and insured for many thousands of pounds. Roger believed that the outward expression of wealth was one of the main pleasures in life. What would be the point of being as rich as Croesus if poorer people weren't made aware of it? It would be like having a supermodel figure and wearing a burka, if you asked him. Sackcloth and ashes were all very well for the Jesuits and the Presbyterians but his shirts were made in Jermyn Street of silk, not hair, and he always turned left when boarding an aeroplane. Not that he wasn't a generous man. He gave more than most people's salaries to charity each year, and he always made a point of buying the *Big Issue*. And he was popular. For some reason his opulent lifestyle and big gestures didn't engender envy in people. He bought himself a new jag every year and had never had it keyed once. The *Big Issue* seller always smiled when he saw him, not at all resentful that his watch alone could have housed him in fine style for a year.

Maybe it was down to his good looks. He had always been a handsome man, six foot tall, a generous head of hair. Naturally perfect teeth housed in an effortless smile, and blue, honest eyes that held your gaze and commanded trust.

Roger was an accountant. He'd been to Harrow and Oxford and somehow felt he should have done something more glamorous as a career. But he came from old money, and the Yateses had been in finance in one way or another since the Great Fire of London; Roger's career had been mapped out for him long before his name had even gone down for prep school. In truth, he was secretly glad of the arrangement, not that he'd ever really admit it to himself, because Roger liked order in his life. He liked to know what the next day would bring, what the next week would bring, what the next year would bring. He liked to be in control. He liked discipline. Which is why the morning, which had started badly — he had had to cancel a golf tournament, something he had been looking forward to all year — had gone from bad to worse, and the reason for it, the one main thing in his life that Roger wasn't content with and seemed powerless to do anything about, was now standing, larger than life and twice as ugly, in front of his desk.

"Roger," Delaney said.

"Jack, what the hell are you doing here?"

"I've been great thanks. How about yourself?"

Roger leaned back in his chair, his scowl deepening. "Let me think about that for a moment. How have I been? Well, I'll tell you." He held his hand out to count off on his fingers. "Firstly I had to cancel a golf tournament this weekend. And that's because ... Secondly my wife is coming out of hospital. My wife who was stabbed by a homicidal nut job that you brought round to my house."

"I didn't bring him round."

"And thirdly," Roger Yates continued, pointing his fingers at Delaney, "I have to take care of your daughter, because her father is a drink-sodden car crash of a man with the social responsibility of a mentally damaged animal."

Delaney fought the urge to punch him. "I do feel responsible."

"You bloody well should do."

"And I am grateful."

"As I told you before, Jack. Many times. You can show that gratitude by keeping out of my sight."

"I need a favour."

Roger sat back in his chair, genuinely astonished. "You are bloody joking?"

Delaney pulled out a piece of paper with an address written on it and put it on the desk in front of him.

"I want to know who owns this building, who built it and who sold it. I want the financial trail."

"And you can't do this through your own department, why?"

"Because it's linked to Sinead's death. The people responsible for your sister-in-law's murder."

Roger looked at the paper but made no move to pick it up. "I don't think so."

Delaney looked at him for a moment. "You want me to tell Wendy you refused to help?"

Roger glared at him for a moment before snatching the paper up. "Get the hell out of my office."

Delaney glared back at him for a moment then nodded, turned his back and walked out the room, closing the door loudly behind him. Roger Yates simmered with fury for a moment then picked a golf ball off his desk and hurled it against the opposite wall, narrowly missing a Chagall which was worth more than Delaney's annual salary. He looked at the address written on the piece of paper then snatched up his telephone and punched a button.

"Sarah, I've got a job for you." He sighed angrily. "Well, cancel it. This is urgent. My office, now."

He slammed the phone down. "Fucking Irishman!"

Helen Archer sat down in a chair which she had carefully placed opposite the sofa where Kate was sitting, took a sip of her tea and looked at her visitor with puzzled eyes. "I don't see why we need to talk about him. The court case is in a couple of days."

"I know."

"And you're with the police, you say?"

Kate shook her head. "I work with the police. I'm a doctor."

"You're a police surgeon?"

"I used to be. Not any more. I'm a forensic pathologist."

The frown on Helen's forehead deepened. "I don't understand. Has somebody died?"

Kate took a deep breath. "I think your husband might have raped me."

Helen looked at her, shocked. "What do you mean *you think* he might have raped you?"

Kate shrugged, blinking back tears. "I think there were drugs involved." She wiped the back of her hand across her eyes. "A date-rape drug. Rohypnol, something like that . . ." She paused for a moment. "Like he used with you."

Helen flinched. "How do you know that?"

"Like I said, I work with the police," Kate said. "I looked at documents. I shouldn't have done, but I needed to know about him. I needed to know if it was true."

Helen stiffened, lifting her chin, challenging. "Is that why you came here? To see if I was telling the truth."

"Not that. To see if it really happened with me. I want to know about him."

"You want to know about Paul?"

"I'm sorry."

Helen Archer sighed, her fingers clutching her ring, the knuckles white. She took a deep breath. "Don't be sorry," she said finally. "None of this is your fault."

"I'm still sorry. You have enough to deal with."

"I know what it's like to not be believed. To have a man rape you and others believe him when he denies it. I know what it's like to be attacked. To be attacked by a man you trusted, who you once loved." Helen blinked back tears now. "I know what it's like to be hurt."

Kate bit her lower lip, not noticing the pain, and said again, "I'm sorry."

Helen came across and sat beside her on the sofa. "It's not your fault," she said, taking Kate's small, cold hand in her own. And Kate cried now, the tears running down her cheeks.

The curly-haired man leaned back against the wall and looked with disdain across the road where a group of office workers had gathered for a cigarette. The smokers' room was now al fresco by law after all. He had never been a smoker. He had tried it once, buying a pack of ten Camels off a boy at school when he was twelve years old. He had only smoked one of them and hadn't cared for it at all, never felt the urge to smoke again. In his book it was a sign of weakness. He looked at his watch. One o'clock. He slipped headphone buds into his ears, turned on his portable radio and listened to the headlines he had been waiting for.

A few minutes later he turned it off again. The fools still hadn't made the connection. A small mention of a woman found dead. Being treated as murder but that was it. No mention of the one on Hampstead Heath. No mention of what they signified. He laughed out loud, quite careless of the curious looks he was getting from across the street. Idiots the lot of them. Delaney smoked, didn't he? Another idiot. He couldn't see a clue if it was served up on a silver plate for him.

He looked at his watch once more, started whistling a Michael Jackson song and wandered back towards his office. In a couple of hours he'd be off rota. Then the fun could begin again.

Helen's eyes were like cold flint as she remembered. "There was no evidence of any date-rape drug that they could find. I got away whilst he was dressing. Locked myself in my bedroom and called the police from there. But he had plenty of time before they arrived to rinse out the decanter. Replace the brandy. Clean the carpet where it had spilled."

"Yes."

"They took me down the police station. It was horrible, Kate. You could see it in the eyes of the men. They didn't believe me. My voice was slurred, I'd drunk a lot of brandy, laced or otherwise."

Kate looked at her sympathetically. She knew what it was like, she'd drunk far too many vodkas to have any control, to have any defences that night. Helen was blaming herself for that much at least, and Kate could well understand how she felt. The *if only* that changed lives for ever.

"The police surgeon on call was different. She believed me. She treated me like the victim I was in all this." Her voice hardened. "But I'm not going to be a victim any more, Kate. I'll see that bastard in court and make him pay."

"I know."

"And do you know what the worse thing was, Kate?"

"Go on."

"On our fifth wedding anniversary I bought him a watch." The bitterness sharp in her voice. "A Rolex. An

236

eighteen-carat white-gold Rolex Oyster Perpetual Cosmograph Daytona. Seventeen thousand pounds' worth."

Kate nodded, not sure what to say.

"A big manly watch for a big manly man. He had his arm over my throat and around my head, pinning me down, so that the watch scratched my cheek and was pushed against my ear. And he was grunting with each thrust like an animal, like I was some kind of mechanical toy." Her nostrils flared wide as she breathed deeply. "And I could hear the tick-tock of the clock before each thrust. Tick, thrust. Tock, thrust. Tick . . ."

She took in another gulp of air and looked at Kate with eyes filled with sadness.

"I bought that watch as a symbol of my love for him."

Delaney drummed his fingers impatiently on the dashboard of his car as Sally drove them away from Roger Yates's office.

"Back to White City, sir?" Sally asked.

"Not just yet. Take us back to Bradley's flat. I want to look at those photos again."

"Sir."

"If they let us that is. This will have been bumped over our heads."

"What do you mean?"

"If he's a serial killer now the glory boys from Paddington Green will be all over this like a rash."

He pulled out his phone and pushed a speed-dial button, putting it on loudspeaker as he rummaged in his pockets. "Slimline, it's Jack Delaney."

237

"Shoot."

"I need a favour."

"This the kind of favour that might cost someone his job?"

"Probably not."

Delaney could hear him sighing on the other end of the line.

"Go on then."

"I want you to get one of the guys to triangulate a number, locate a mobile phone for me. But keep it off the books."

"Whose phone is it?"

"Just get me the location, Dave."

"Give me the number then."

Delaney pulled out a piece of paper and read the number to him, then closed the phone. Sally looked across at him but didn't say anything.

The SOCO team was leaving as Sally and Delaney walked up the steps to Bradley's flat. His grandmother was watching them go, less than pleased.

She recognised Delaney and grabbed his arm.

"Here. Can't you do anything about them? You should see the mess they're making."

"Sorry. Nothing I can do."

"They won't let me back in my own house. And I've got *Murder She Wrote* to watch in a minute."

"Sorry."

Delaney gently took her hand off his arm as a uniformed female officer came across.

238

"They say I've got to go down the police station, Detective Inspector. What's he done now then?"

"They'll tell you all about it there."

"I told them they should never have got that dog. Twelve years old he was when he bit him. Right in the privates." She shivered and shook her head. "Made a terrible mess it did."

"Come on, Mrs Bradley. I'll make sure they get you a nice cup of tea," the uniformed officer said as she led the old woman away.

Delaney looked at the photos in Ashley Bradley's room. They'd all be taken down, sent to the command centre that would now be running the case. Everything Delaney wanted to do would have to go through them, which made him practically redundant. Only Delaney didn't want to be off the case. The killer had made it personal, dressing the last victim in a scarf like Kate's. Or maybe it *was* Kate's. The idea that the bastard might have her somewhere and be taunting him with the knowledge turned his stomach. He had called her office and had been told that Kate had called in, saying she wouldn't be in until later that day, but that could have been done under duress. The damn woman wasn't answering her phone and Delaney had no way of knowing if it was deliberate or not.

He brought his mind back to the subject in hand and tapped a few of the photos. "A lot of these interior pictures are taken in the same place. He obviously has his favoured hunting grounds like South Hampstead Heath and the common." He tapped another photo, an

239

interior shot this time. "And I reckon I know where this is."

Sally looked at where he was pointing. "Where, sir?"

"That shopping arcade at the bottom of Bayswater."

"Whiteleys?"

"That's the one." Delaney tapped on another photo. "Look at him, he's hanging around the entrance to the ladies' toilet there."

"Why?"

Delaney looked back at her. "Why? Because he's a sick fucking pervert. Come on."

They were heading for the front door when Delaney's phone rang. He snatched it out of his pocket and looked at the caller ID. "What have you got for me?"

He grabbed a pen out of his pocket and wrote an address on the back of his hand. "One other thing, Dave. Get Bob Wilkinson and some backup to get down Whiteleys in Bayswater. It looks like a favourite hangout for our boy. Second floor near the ladies' toilets." He closed his phone and reached into his pocket.

"Give me the car keys, Sally."

"Sir?"

"Just give me the keys." He took the keys from her and thrust a ten-pound note in her hand. "I'll see you back at the factory."

Sally would have responded but Delaney was already flying down the steps taking them two at a time.

Kate held Helen Archer's hand for a moment as she stood on her doorstep. "I'll be there at the trial."

Helen squeezed her hand back. "Thanks, Kate. Don't worry. He's going to pay for what he's done to us. He's going to pay big time."

Kate stood for a moment or two on the step after the door had been closed. Troubled. Little flashes of memory were coming unbidden into her consciousness. It was something Helen had said. "He's going to pay big time." She was in her lounge, drunk. There was music playing. Some country folk record. Alison Krauss maybe. She'd bought it because she thought Jack Delaney might like it. But she had never gotten the chance to play it to him.

"Here you are, you. Alison bloody Krauss and the . . ." Her words slurred slightly and she took a moment to steady herself. "Alison Krauss and the Union Station. You ever heard of them?" She turned round to the man in her living room. A tall man with dark curly hair who she had only just met. She must have invited him back, but she couldn't remember doing it.

"Can't say I have," Paul Archer said.

"Well, here she is." She pushed play on her CD player and music filled the room. Fiddles and guitars. She walked over to the sideboard and poured herself a large glass of Scotch. "Join me."

The man shook his head. "Mixing vodka and whisky?"

Kate beamed and took a big swallow of it. "Ish a cocktail."

Archer smiled back at her. "You're going to pay for that in the morning. Pay for it big time."

Kate put her hand on Helen Archer's door to steady herself. She must have invited him back. What else was there that she couldn't remember? She turned around and almost fell back against the door with shock.

"What the hell are you doing?"

"I need to speak to you."

"No." She shook her head and tried to push past. "I've got nothing to say to you."

But he held her arm, and she had to look up at him again. At the dark curly hair and the dark brown eyes. But in those eyes she didn't see scorn or hate or self-importance. She saw hurt, pain and concern. Enough to break her heart. She stopped struggling, all resistance gone, the bones in her body like soft fabric.

"What do you want, Jack?"

"We need to talk."

Heavy drops of rain splashed onto the windscreen of his car and Delaney turned the ignition a notch and flicked his wipers on, but made no move to start his engine.

Next to him, Kate sighed and pulled her coat tighter to herself, as if cashmere and wool could protect her from her emotions. "What do you want to say, Jack? I haven't got the energy for an argument."

"I know. And I'm sorry. I've been trying to get hold of you all morning."

"How did you know where I was?"

"I got the boys to triangulate your mobile."

242

"Is that legal?"

"I needed to speak to you."

"And it couldn't have waited?"

"I thought you were dead, Kate."

Kate looked over at him, shocked. "What are you talking about?"

"There was another murder. Another bad one. Mutilation . . ." He shook his head at the memory. "We think it's the same man."

"What's that got to do with me? I've given my notice in, you know."

Delaney took her gloved hands and held them tight. "No, I didn't know. But she was wearing your scarf, Kate. The victim. It was either yours or one exactly the same. It was deliberate."

"And you thought it was me, you thought the victim was me?"

Delaney nodded. "For a moment. And what he did to her . . ."

Kate sat there for a moment, letting him hold her hands as she took it all in.

"I don't want to lose you again, Kate."

She felt the tiny pinpricks in her eyes again. God, but the man's timing was bloody excellent. She finally collected her thoughts and squeezed his hands back.

"You're right. We do need to talk. But not here. Not now. There are things we need to take care of first. Things I need to do."

"I've been all kinds of fool, Kate. I won't deny that. But it stops here for me, it stops right now."

Kate nodded, unable to meet his eyes. She knew if she did kiss him, then all control on the train wreck of her life would be lost for ever. She took her hands out of his clasp. "Take me home first, Jack."

"It might not be safe."

"I need to see if my scarf is there."

Delaney hesitated for a moment and then fired the engine up and pulled the car away from the kerb. Kate stole a sideways glance at him and saw something she wasn't sure she had seen before in his eyes. She couldn't be certain, but it looked something like hope.

The busker, in tie-dyed jeans and a floral shirt, sitting near the bottom of the stairs had a small, portable amplifier to boost his voice and the sound of his guitar to echo around the mall. He flicked his long, braided hair and started singing. A John Lennon song. Ashley Bradley scowled as the music started up, he was never a fan of the Beatles. Any of them. Smug bastards in stupid suits, you asked him.

He flexed his knees a little bit more and held the bag he was carrying a little lower. At the bottom of the bag was a hole, and through the hole, pointing upwards, protruded the lens of a video camcorder. Just a little hole, which was great, because camcorders could be really small now and it made his job a lot easier. The one thing in the world that Ashley Bradley was truly grateful for, apart from stretch fabric, was technology. Technology was a marvellous thing. It gave him the Internet and it gave him the camcorder, with the built-in hard drive, which he was now positioning

244

under the skirt of the young lady in front of him on the escalator. He liked to imagine what colour panties she was wearing, not that he really minded. Others did, of course, some of the guys he swapped files with on the web were very specific. Had to be white and cotton or no deal. Or leather. Or a thong. But for Ashley, the colour of them didn't matter at all, because it meant he had lucked out. Ashley Bradley was a commando hunter. But they were rare. And part of the thrill for him was the anticipation. He wouldn't know if he had bagged one until he got home and downloaded what he had shot so he could see it on the computer screen. And it had been some weeks since he had a result. He had a real good feeling about the woman in front of him. She looked like butter wouldn't melt, and in his experience they were the worst. He'd have loved to have had a rummage through her drawers, he reckoned he'd find all kind of toys.

He could feel the escalator begin to flatten out which snapped him out of his reverie; he moved the bag back towards him, looked up and saw two uniformed policemen at the top of the stairs staring straight at him. He turned around and began running down the stairs, pushing people out of the way but not getting very far. He leapt over the side of the escalator on to the steps travelling downwards and began running down them as the two policemen above him gave chase. At the bottom he clattered into a group of foreign-looking nuns, and after he had pushed them aside, the young black copper was nearly on him. He darted left and was putting his foot down but hadn't

245

seen the busker who was sitting on the floor, tripped right over him, smashing his guitar into the ground and splintering the wood. The busker's shocked, amplified voice filled the shopping centre.

"You broke my fucking guitar!"

Danny Vine and Bob Wilkinson, who arrived a little later, had to drag Bradley bodily away to save him from being strangled by the outraged New Age hippy. "Fucking muppet! I'll fucking kill you!"

Kate sensed as soon as she entered her house that something was wrong. She walked down the hallway to the kitchen. She looked at the hooks hanging on the back of the kitchen door and shook her head. "It's not here, Jack. What the hell's going on?"

Delaney shrugged. "I don't know. But I'm going to find out."

Kate shook her head. "No, *we're* going to find out. Who was attending at the scene from my office?"

"Patrick Neally."

Delaney's phone rang, echoing loudly in the stone-flagged kitchen as he pulled it from his pocket.

"Delaney."

"It's Bob Wilkinson."

"Go on, Bob."

"You might want to get down the nick."

"You got him?"

"Yeah, you were on the money. But I'd get down here quick if I were you. The shiny boys from serious crime are all over him."

"We're on our way."

Delaney put his hand on Kate's arm and steered her out. If she felt displeasure at his touch she didn't display it. "Who have they got?" she asked.

"Ashley Bradley."

"He's the killer?"

"He had pictures of both victims on his walls and he's a class-A pervert, we know that."

"Why the bloody hell would he take my scarf though?"

Delaney fished his car keys out as Kate locked her front door behind her. "I don't know, Kate."

But he had an idea.

Ashley Bradley sat uncomfortably on the hard, plastic chair. The central ridge cut into him painfully. He wasn't wearing underpants, he never did when he went out on a mission, but he now wished that he had been. He shifted again and adjusted himself.

Delaney watched, through the one-way mirror, as the suit- and tie-wearing finest from the serious crime squad interviewed him. He flicked the switch so he could hear the words.

"You want to tell us about the photos on the walls of your bedroom?"

"It's not a crime."

"Yes it is, Ashley."

"No it's not. It's perfectly legal to take pictures of people in public places."

Delaney was amazed, as ever, at the calm arrogance of degenerates caught right in the act. People who looked at child pornography were only doing it for research. Convicted child abusers claimed it was a form of love as

247

ancient as humanity. Delaney would have liked to have gone into the room and given Ashley Bradley some tough love right then. The kind that draws blood.

His mobile phone rang and Delaney, seeing the ID, flicked the switch off on the intercom.

"What have you got for me, Roger?"

"The properties in Pinner Green. A development company was set up to buy out the existing businesses there and convert them to luxury apartments. Took about a year to set up. The petrol station, independently owned, was the last to be sold. Given the time of the development and the time the last of the luxury apartments were sold at the height of the market two years ago . . ."

"Go on."

"We're looking at millions of pounds' worth of profit."

"And who owned the development company?"

"An outfit called Blue Heaven Property."

"And who owns that?"

"It was just set up for this venture. But it links to a shell company called Hunter Developments."

Delaney sighed. "Get to the point, Roger."

"That's just it, Hunter Developments, like I say, is a shell company. The trail leads offshore. Financed out of the Cayman Islands."

"And what does that mean?"

"It means we don't know who owns the development company."

"And there's no way of finding out?"

"None that I'm capable of."

"How then?"

"I don't know, Jack. These guys are probably operating outside the law. This is your area of expertise. You deal with it."

The line went dead. Delaney closed his phone and cursed. He may not know who was behind what happened, yet. But at least now he had motive and that was a start. He flicked the intercom switch on and listened to Ashley Bradley flatly denying any involvement in the murders. As he watched him, and listened to him speak, Delaney thought he was an unlikely candidate for a serial killer. But then he was also aware that they didn't always hunt alone. Yes, sometimes they had an accomplice, someone who had graduated up from flashing at cantankerous nurses and filming the undergarments of unwary shoppers at shopping malls. But, if the smart-suited and career-enhanced coppers interviewing the suspect had asked for his opinion, he would have said that Ashley Bradley wasn't involved at all. He could read people, that was his talent above all else. And, although he had thought, when he first saw the photos Bradley had on his wall, that he had made a big mistake in letting him pass them on the stairs, listening to him now he didn't think he had. They had the wrong man. He'd put money on it.

Upstairs, Kate Walker was sitting in Jack Delaney's office, at his desk, and drinking a cup of coffee from his mug. If someone had told her this morning she would be doing that she would have thought them mad. At the moment though she didn't have time for introspection. She was looking at the preliminary report from Dr

249

Patrick Neally, her colleague who had attended the murder scene earlier that day. She had asked her assistant to email it through. Strictly speaking she should have gone to him first, but she didn't have the time for professional niceties. And, in any case, she was working out her notice, so she thought, stuff it! She also had the photographs and notes from the scene of crime, which she was leaving till last. The report didn't make for good reading. Whoever had done this to another person was beyond reason. The mutilation was sickening even to her, who had seen enough horror over her years as a forensic pathologist to despair of the human race entirely. This was a degree of magnitude more gruesome than anything she had ever seen.

But it was to get worse.

Delaney was walking down the front staircase, heading for the exit to the car park. He needed a cigarette. Actually he needed a drink. Not needed it, he rationalised, but wanted it. When did want become need? he wondered. When you had no control over your desires? Well, that was something he always had. Not like the sad bastard being interviewed right now.

What Delaney needed to do was think, and the quick spikes of nicotine in his blood helped him do that. He was fumbling in the right-hand pocket of his leather jacket for his cigarettes when George Napier walked up to him, a smile on his face, Diane Campbell right behind him, not smiling at all.

"Delaney."

250

Delaney's heart sank. Napier smiling. Not a good sign. "Guv." He nodded at Diane, who raised her eyebrows back. "Ma'am."

"Good work today, Delaney. Nipped him in the bud."

"Sir?"

"Bradley."

"I don't think we should get ahead of ourselves, sir."

"Now is not the time to piss on your own parade, Delaney."

"I'm sorry?"

"We have a press conference set up. We want you to make the statement."

"Aren't we jumping the gun a little?"

"Not at all. The press are going to be all over the serial killer aspect. Sky News have held off until now, but as we have the perpetrator in custody they have asked for first bite of the cherry."

"How did they know we have someone in custody?"

"Are you deliberately being obtuse, man?"

Delaney smiled at Diane. "Must be my Irish upbringing, sir."

"I've been in contact with her to control what goes on the news. We made a deal. I, for one, honour my deals."

"And if he's not the killer?"

"Of course he's the killer. He's got pictures of the two women hanging on his wall, and we have him exposing himself on the heath right by one of dead victims."

"All we have him for, sir, with respect, is just that. Flashing his johnson at medical workers and sticking his zoom lens up the skirts of happy shoppers."

251

Delaney turned to his line boss. "Can you talk some sense into the man?"

"Maybe we should let Delaney interview him first, sir," she said quickly.

Napier goggled at her. "And while he's doing that, Paddington Green take the credit for our collar? I don't think so."

He looked at his watch. "We're set up outside."

Delaney shrugged and put a cigarette in his mouth. Napier snatched it out and handed it to Diane Campbell. "Can't you keep a bloody leash on him, Diane?"

"He needs castrating, sir, if you ask me. But I trust his instincts."

Napier thrust a sheet of paper into Delaney's hands. "Just smile at the pretty reporter and read the statement, Delaney. Think you can manage that?"

"Not sure, sir. Not one for multitasking. Maybe the chief inspector should do it."

"And maybe I should remind you that there is a complaint against you, Delaney?"

"And I'm sure Detective Constable Cartwright will tell you that I merely defended myself."

"Just play ball with me, Delaney. And I'll play ball with you. This is a team here, and what counts is we get results. You clear on that?"

"Sir."

He thrust the sheet of paper into Delaney's hands. "Then put one on the scoreboard for White City and read the bloody statement."

★ ★ ★

In the CID room, Jimmy Skinner called for hush, even though nobody was talking and turned the volume up on the television mounted on the wall. Sky News was playing, with the breaking news banner ticker-taping along the bottom — *man arrested in connection with two recent murders*. Delaney was facing the camera, looking as happy to be there as a pig in a pork-pie shop. The camera cut back to Melanie Jones who had her serious face on.

"Detective Inspector Delaney. I understand you have been responsible for the arrest of a suspect in two particularly gruesome killings. The first on South Hampstead Heath yesterday, and the second discovered this morning in a rented flat in Camden Town?"

"A man is helping us with our inquiries."

"One man responsible for both murders? So we are looking at a serial killer here?"

"If I could just read out the prepared statement?"

"Of course."

Delaney looked at the camera. " 'We can confirm that a man has been arrested this afternoon and is being questioned here at White City police station in relation to the unlawful killings of two women. These women have not as yet been identified and we would urge anyone who knows them to contact the police as soon as possible.' "

The pictures taken from Ashley Bradley's bedroom wall of the two dead women flashed up on the television screen.

In the CID room Kate looked at the photographs as they appeared on the screen. She couldn't see why Jack

Delaney had thought that one of them was her. But with a wig on, and wearing her scarf, perhaps it was an easy mistake to make. The women in the photos looked young, confident and full of life. She hadn't as yet looked at the scene-of-crime photos from the Camden flat. She looked at the screen as the camera shot cut back to Melanie Jones.

"What can you tell us about the man in custody, Detective Inspector?"

Delaney looked down at the piece of paper that his boss had given him. There was no more to the statement and he had been told not to answer any questions.

"There is nothing I can add to my statement about the man in custody. However, we do believe that the man responsible for these crimes has very low self-esteem. He also has an uncontrollable anger towards women and we think this is down to a very serious form of penis envy."

Melanie Jones reacted, smiled a little as she recovered herself. "I beg your pardon?"

Delaney looked at her, deadpan. "We believe that he feels himself to be extremely inadequate in the eyes of women, and that this is down to some kind of genital deformity."

Behind the camera Delaney could see that George Napier was absolutely fuming. He'd better watch his stress levels, he thought, he was a heart attack looking to happen. He could see Melanie Jones was about to ask another question but he held his hand up.

"I am sorry but that is all the information I am able to give at this juncture. Once again, I would urge anyone who has any information about these women to come forward."

The images of the two women appeared on the television screen once more.

Delaney headed back to the building. Napier would have followed after him but Melanie Jones approached him and he stopped to try and fight some of the forest fire Delaney had started.

In the CID office Jimmy Skinner grinned at the television screen. "Way to go, Jack." He winked at Sally Cartwright. "Looks like you might need a new partner."

Kate looked across at him. "I'm assuming he made all that up?"

"The bit about the deformed wing-wang? I doubt that was in the script."

"Why did he say it then?"

"The killer is fucking around with Delaney. Sending him messages. I guess he thought he would send one back."

"Is that wise?"

Skinner laughed out loud. "Wise? This is Jack Delaney we're talking about. He's not famous for having the wisdom of Solomon."

Delaney gave the custody sergeant a quick, grateful nod as he opened the door to the holding cell. He stepped inside and the sergeant closed it behind him. He looked down at Ashley Bradley who was sitting on the bed holding his head in his hands.

"You got anything to tell me, Ashley?"

"Who are you?"

"I'm the sugarplum fucking fairy. Now answer my question."

Ashley Bradley shook his head nervously. "I have no idea what you're talking about."

"You don't know who I am?"

Bradley shrugged.

"I'm Jack Delaney. Detective Inspector Delaney. That make matters clearer for you?"

"You've come to let me out?"

Delaney barked a short, humourless laugh. "Now why in the name of all that's fucking holy would you think that?"

"Because I haven't done anything wrong."

"We caught you filming up the skirt of some woman with no knickers on, you twink."

Bradley sat up, more animated now. "Are you saying she wasn't wearing anything?"

Delaney sighed. "You want to stick with the programme here, son."

"I want that tape back. That's my property. It's legal to film people in public places, I looked it up on the Internet."

Delaney glared at him, his voice ratcheting up a few decibels. "Up her fucking skirt isn't considered a public place, you sick dipstick."

He crossed over to Ashley who flinched back against the wall. "What the hell is the mirror and the buckle about?"

Bradley shook his head. "I don't know what you're talking about."

Delaney looked in his eyes. Could see the fear and the confusion, but couldn't see any guile. In truth, he hadn't expected to. He turned back to the door and rapped on it for the custody sergeant to let him out.

"Wait a minute."

Delaney could hear the desperation in his voice and turned back half hopeful. "Yes?"

"About that tape . . ."

"What about it?"

"If you could get it back for me, I'd make it worth your while."

Delaney slammed the door on him.

The curly-haired man was sitting at his usual table in the White Horse again. Nursing a pint of Guinness. He took a sip and spilled some as he put the glass back down on the table, his hand was shaking so much with anger. The barman picked up the remote control and changed the channel from Sky News to Sky Sports.

He took another sip of his pint. The Irish beer was far too bitter for his taste but he drank it anyway. That clown Delaney had just made a big mistake. He was helping the guy after all. And, all right, he might have teased him a little with a practical joke. But he'd been helping him. Leaving him clues. Getting that retroussé-nosed reporter to put her candy-coloured lips to good use. Delaney should have been orgasming by now. He should have been coming in his fucking detective trousers for the help he was giving to him and his career. Instead he was dicking about on national television. Deformed genitalia! He'd give him deformed genitalia. He looked at the woman who was standing at the bar sipping on a bottle of Gold Label. Her thin shoulder showed bone, but her arms had muscle on them, like a female javelin thrower, with just as strong a grip. In her thirties with ancient eyes and buttocks that had been kissed by more bricks than a stonemason's trowel, he reckoned. He watched as she took another gulp of her Gold Label. Strong barley wine, proof against the elements. Probably proof against any leakage in her mouth from a poorly fitting condom too, he thought. Gold Label, it was like Domestos, killed ninety-nine point nine per cent of all germs dead.

He could relate to that.

Detective Inspector Jack Delaney was a germ.

Kate hesitated for a moment before opening the envelope containing the scene-of-crime photographs. Something Jack had said niggled at her. There was something she was sure they ought to be seeing, something right before their eyes. She opened the envelope and spilled the black-and-white photographs on to her desk. One slid to the back of the desk. She picked it up. It was a close-up of part of the woman's neck and it showed the same deep puncture wound as the first victim had.

She picked up the phone and dialled her own work number. When her assistant answered, she asked if the blood-work report was in. She listened, making some notes as she did so. There were high levels of tranquilliser in the first victim's blood, and she'd bet her mortgage that the second victim's blood work would show the same.

She thanked her assistant, told her not to make any appointments and hung up the phone. She sorted through the other photos and looked at them, shuddering to see her own scarf hung about the throat of the mutilated woman like some kind of macabre decoration. She looked at the next photo, a close-up of the victim's right hand which was holding a small, broken mirror.

She looked at the report again. It was the sort of compact mirror you might find in a handbag. And it was broken. Suddenly her synapses started firing like fireworks on Guy Fawkes Night and she put the pieces together. She remembered what Jack had said and she looked at the second photo once more, the woman laid out, posed for the camera, with her scarf as a final flourish. And she remembered.

"Sweet Jesus!"

Delaney was heading towards his office. The newscast had generated hundreds of calls, people phoning in claiming to know the identity of one of the dead women, and each one had to be checked out. It wasn't what Napier had in mind but maybe some good had come out of the news piece after all. He had his hand on the office door when his mobile phone rang. He looked at the caller ID but didn't recognise the number. "Jack Delaney."

"Jack, it's me."

Delaney didn't need to ask. He could hear the lazy, hypnotic lilt to her accent. He remembered it as a voice filled with mischief, with amusement. But today, her voice was as serious as a heart attack.

"What do you want, Stella?"

"I saw you on the television."

Delaney sighed. "I'm a little bit busy here."

"One of those women. I know her. She's in the life, cowboy. At least, she was."

Jack didn't even stop to consider the irony of the expression. "Who is she, Stella?"

The lightning cracked through the air like a jagged spear. Moments after the thunder rumbled overhead and the rain started in earnest, splattering against the window like a hailstorm. Kate looked at her watch, it was only five o'clock.

She pushed the print icon on Jack's computer and watched as the sheets began to spill from his printer. A couple of desks down Sally looked up from her computer monitor and saw her expression.

"Something wrong?"

"Yeah, Sally. Something's very wrong."

Delaney pushed the door of the CID room open with the flat of his hand.

"The second victim's name is Jennifer Cole. She was an escort. High-class call girl. She had her own website." He pulled a chair out and sat next to Sally. "Type in London Angel, one word, dot co dot uk."

Kate collected the papers she had printed out and walked over to Delaney, as an image appeared on the screen. A healthy, sexy, vibrant image of the woman who had been butchered like a sacrificial cow.

"You better have a look at this, Jack." Kate handed Delaney the documents she had printed out.

Delaney skimmed his eyes over as he read the first page. "She wasn't missing any teeth. What is this?"

Kate took the pages off him and read sections aloud. " 'The left arm across the left breast. The instrument used at the throat and abdomen was the same. It must have been a very sharp knife with a thin narrow blade, and must have been at least six to eight inches in length, probably longer. He should say that the injuries could not have been inflicted by a bayonet or a sword bayonet. They could have been done by such an instrument as a medical man used for post-mortem purposes, but the ordinary surgical cases might not contain such an instrument. Those used by the slaughtermen, well ground down, might have caused them. He thought the knives used by those in the leather trade would not be long enough in the blade. There were indications of anatomical knowledge —' "

"What is this?" Delaney interrupted her.

"It's a report, Jack, but not from our murders."

"Whose then?"

"They didn't come from my office, I just printed them off the Internet. He's been sending you messages all along. Start with the man in the mirror, Jack! It's your namesake."

"What is?"

"The scarf instead of a handkerchief. The mirror found with the second body. The guy is dressing the victims up like Jack the Ripper victims."

Delaney looked up at her, taking it in. "He's copycatting."

"Not exactly, no. But . . ." she shrugged.

"How many were there?"

"At least five," said Sally. "All prostitutes. Some reckon as many as eleven."

"Jesus!"

The lightning flashed again. The thunder was almost simultaneous now; they were right under the storm. Delaney looked across at the pane of glass and back at Kate. "You can't be fucking serious."

"There's another thing," said Sally.

"Go on."

"As you know they never found the identity of Jack the Ripper."

"Yeah, of course I know that."

"One of the suspects, not one of the main ones but one of them nonetheless . . ."

"Go on."

"Walter Sickert."

"The artist."

"Some people claimed he was the Ripper himself. A lot of people thought he might just have been an accessory. An accomplice to the real killer."

"And?"

"And, Jack . . . He had several operations on his penis," Kate interjected.

"That's right," said Sally. "He had what Jimmy Skinner would call a deformed wing-wang."

He leaned his forehead against the pane of glass. He hated the rain, but the cool glass seemed to ease the heat in his forehead. He looked at his watch, five o'clock, but it was already as dark as if it was midwinter. He didn't mind the dark. He rubbed his hand over the handle of the gun he was holding, the wood as warm beneath his touch as the glass was cold. The phone rang, jangling him out of his reverie. He had been expecting the call. It was time to go to work again. There were names on a list. Names that had to be crossed out. He cupped one hand instinctively on his crotch and felt his cock stiffen as he put down the gun and answered the phone with the other.

"It's me."

Delaney watched as Sally flashed the blinking cursor around the website. She clicked on a hyperlink titled "Double Dates" and read aloud.

"'For some of the more adventurous, or just plain greedy, amongst you I also offer a double-date service with one of my gorgeous girlfriends. Click on the links left to see just how gorgeous. Double the honey and double the fun.'"

Sally did as she was told, moving the cursor to a list of four names on the left-hand side of the screen. *Crystal, Amber, Melody* and *Rose*.

Crystal was a blonde, Amber was a brunette and Melody had black hair. Black skirt, top, and black make-up. Goth-style.

Bingo.

James Collins opened his locker door in the changing room and yawned as he changed out of his surgical scrubs. It had been a long and difficult day. He had had to perform an emergency C section on an illegal immigrant. A failed asylum seeker from some godforsaken country the government was keen to return her to. Back to poverty, malnutrition, all manner of abuse and, most likely, an early death. With a baby born in the UK, however, her status would be reconsidered. They had delivered the baby, but it was premature and struggling from the start. Two hours later and the baby died. The mother came through surgery fine, but he could see in her eyes, as she came round from the anaesthetic, that something else had died that afternoon for her. Hope.

James reached into the back of the locker and picked up a small teddy bear, dressed in surgical scrubs. His daughter, Amy, had given it to him as a good-luck gesture when he moved to the hospital, from the North Norfolk and Norwich, eighteen months ago. The surgical cap on the teddy bear's head was in Norwich City colours. He jiggled it in his hand.

"Come on, let's be having you!"

He smiled sadly and put it back in his locker. Took out his bright yellow duffel coat and closed the locker door. It was Amy's birthday in three days' time. Her twenty-first, and he had taken the rest of the week off to visit her. It'd give him a chance to get out to the shops and buy her something spectacular for it too. James Collins was a strict believer that special occasions should be marked appropriately. He had already made the call to his favourite jeweller in Piccadilly and he would visit there first thing in the morning before catching the train from Liverpool Street to Thorpe station in Norwich. The Canaries were playing at home at the weekend too, so he had, he sincerely hoped, double cause for celebration.

He sketched a wave at the receptionist as he strode through reception. The thunderstorm that had been raging only minutes before had stopped as suddenly as it began. He paused outside in the sheltered entrance and shivered suddenly, looking behind him. He thought he sensed someone watching him but there was no one there. Someone must have walked on his grave, he thought with a half-amused smile. He fastened the buttons of his coat and was glad to leave the hood of the duffel down as he strode across the car park. The cold air and the brisk walk would do him good, wake him up a bit.

Five minutes later and he was walking across the heath. Cutting through some trees on a little short cut that took a few minutes off his journey. He stopped abruptly. There was a sharp pain in his neck and he raised his hand to brush the stabbing branch away. But no branch was there and the muscles in his arm suddenly didn't seem to work. His knees buckled, toppling him to fall face up on the wet and muddy ground. A face he recognised was looking down at him.

A look of confusion passed momentarily across his face. If he could have articulated a question he would have done so. But the paralysis had spread to his face now. His eyes closed and the pump under his ribcage, made of tissue and muscle, spasmed.

A low sound of thunder rumbled overhead again and, as the wind picked up whistling wet leaves over his motionless form, the rain fell. Sending splashes of mud into the air and forming a channel of artificial tears from the surgeon's closed eyes.

265

★　★　★

Delaney pulled his jacket off the back of his chair and shrugged into it.

"Did you get that address?" he asked Sally Cartwright.

She picked up a piece of paper from her desk and handed it to him.

"Thanks." He stuffed the paper into his jacket pocket. "Get on to records. I want to know if any other crimes were reported in the neighbouring properties around the same time."

"Sir."

Kate stood up also and put on her coat, looking for her scarf for a moment and then grimacing as she remembered why she no longer had it.

"Where are you going, Kate?"

Kate turned round to Delaney, ready to say something flip, but when she saw the concern in his eyes the temptation vanished. "I need to go home."

"You're not staying at that house. You can stay with me."

Kate hesitated for a moment and then nodded, relief coursing through her blood. "I still need to go home, get some things."

Delaney picked up his car keys off his desk.

"And one other thing, Jack."

Delaney looked at her quizzically.

"We'll take my car."

"We have to make a slight detour first." Delaney turned back to Sally as they walked to the door. "Keep me in touch."

"Sir."

She stuck her thumb up in the air without looking at her boss, her attention focused on her computer screen, looking at the reports Kate Walker had printed out and the crime-scene photographs. She wondered whether she'd ever be able to look at photos like them and not feel physically sick. She fervently hoped not.

Sanjeev Singh was tall but as thin as a Lowry stick man. He wore large, black-framed glasses and was never dressed in anything other than a two-piece brown suit. He had always been of a nervous disposition and so why he had put a jangling bell over the entrance to his shop was a mystery to anyone who knew him.

He flinched as the door creaked open and the brass bell above it danced on its coiled brass spring, jangling his nerves once more.

"We're about to close," he called over his shoulder as he placed an art deco sugar sifter, conical-shaped and decorated in Spring Crocus pattern, carefully back in a display cabinet. He put the price page next to it: four hundred and fifty pounds.

"Nice piece."

He turned round and smiled at Kate, but his smile faded as Delaney stepped forward.

"We're not here for antiques."

Sanjeev Singh lifted his arms and made an expansive gesture with his shoulders, a gesture he had used many times to good effect in the amateur pantomimes he had appeared in. "I am sorry, but antiques is all I deal in."

Delaney showed him his warrant card. "It's information we need."

Singh frowned. "I don't understand."

"Four years ago you sold your petrol station in Pinner Green. We want to know why, and we want to know who to."

The antique dealer's shoulders slumped, and any pretence at good humour disappeared. "My lawyers handled the sale. It was to a development company. I wanted to get out of the trade. Buy an antiques shop. The timing was right. Now I am sorry, but I really have to close."

"It wasn't good timing for my wife, Mr Singh."

Sanjeev Singh looked at Delaney again, recognition dawning in his eyes. He gestured with his hands again, hands that were suddenly trembling even more than was usual.

"Look, I am sorry about what happened to your wife. The next day someone made me an offer for the place and I accepted it."

"Why?"

"Why do you think? I don't know who was behind it but their methods were pretty clear."

"Somebody wanted you out?"

"I'd had an offer before but I turned it down. I thought that if they were desperate for my property they could pay top dollar. But that same week the florists next door had an accidental fire. Their dog, a Labrador, died in the fire. They sold. And after what happened to me, I sold too."

"Who to?"

The man shrugged again, apologetically. "I don't know. It was all done through a lawyer."

"Okay." Delaney gestured to Kate. "Come on, let's get your things."

Kate held up her hand. "One minute." She turned to the trembling Indian. "One more thing."

Sanjeev clasped his hands together. "Please, I have told you everything I know."

"What's your best price on the sugar sifter?"

A smile almost came back on his face. "You have a remarkable eye, madam. This here is —"

"Yes, I know," Kate said, interrupting. "It's Clarice Cliff. What will you take for it?"

Some minutes after they had left, Sanjeev Singh finally brought his shaking hands under enough control to pick up a telephone.

Kate pulled her car to the side of the road with a practised spin of the wheel. She snapped her seat belt open and turned to Delaney. "I won't be long."

"I'm coming with you, Kate."

She turned the key to open the front door of her house and the first thing that struck her was the cold, the wind was blowing from the inside out. The second thing was the carnage.

Every room in the maisonette had been turned upside down. In the lounge bookcases had been toppled to the floor, sofas and chairs upended, CDs and records strewn as though a hurricane had blown through the place. Her bedroom was equally ravaged, and in the kitchen, plates and crockery had been smashed, the table legs snapped off, food scattered everywhere. Kate was too numb to cry out. She looked at Delaney, fury bubbling through her. She slammed the open back door shut. "We have to get him, Jack. We have to stop him."

She began to shake, willing herself to stop but unable to get her twitching muscles to comply.

Delaney took two quick steps to her side and enveloped her in a hug. "It's going to be all right, Kate. I swear it."

And Kate, feeling the strength in his arms, feeling the passion in his voice, believed him. For the first time in years she felt protected. She loved him, she knew that now more than ever. He was the first man she had ever truly let into her life. He had hurt her, but she realised that she had been hurt so deeply because she loved him so deeply. She held him as though she could bind him to her for ever. Jack Delaney was part of her now and she would never let him go.

Delaney pulled out his phone. "Dave, it's Delaney. I need to get a couple of units down here. Kate Walker's house has been trashed."

Ten minutes later, Kate put down the small suitcase that she had packed, and locked her front door. Delaney picked up her suitcase and walked towards her car as she fished in her pocket for her car keys. She was just thinking that at least the Clarice Cliff sugar sifter hadn't been in the house, when a shot rang out in the night air like a sudden crack of thunder. Kate instinctively looked up at the sky then screamed as Delaney rocked on his heels, a surprised look on his face, then stumbled and fell sideways to crumple on to the cold, wet pavement.

Kate rushed over to him, calling his name, begging him to speak. But Delaney was beyond speech; he was beyond comprehension. She tried to shield his body with her own as she fumbled in her pocket for her phone, looking about desperately to see where the shot had come from.

"Stay with me, Jack. Stay with me."

Her voice was no more than a whisper, but it echoed in her mind like a thunderous prayer. Before her trembling fingers could punch in 999 on her phone keypad, the sound of police sirens from the squad cars that Delaney had asked for came roaring into her street. And she prayed continually as she tried to find a pulse. "Stay with me, Jack. Please stay with me."

He rubbed the soft fabric over the gleaming grip of the gun. He had already anointed the wood with beeswax and polished it in with an old yellow duster. He was just giving the final finish with the superior cloth. He rubbed it some more, seeing his reflection looking back at him, distorted in the smooth surface of the wood. His eyes were widened and smiling.

He held the cloth to his nose and sniffed deeply as though it were an oxygen mask. Then he opened it out and lay it on the coffee table, like a trophy. It was a pair of plain, white cotton panties that he had stolen, like the scarf, from Dr Kate Walker's house.

Day Three

The rain had stopped sometime in the middle of the night. But the ground wasn't cold enough yet to freeze, and so the paths that ran through Hampstead Heath like veins through a body were slick with wet mud and leaves. Gillian Carter, a twenty-seven-year-old bookshop assistant, picked her way carefully down one of the paths. Not an easy task as the dog she had on the other end of the lead, a Briard, weighed nearly as much as she did and had the energy of a roomful of pre-school children on a diet of Red Bull. A bird clattered out of the trees ahead and the dog leapt after it. Gillian Carter, faced with the choice of losing control of the dog or herself on the slippery downward slope, chose the former and let the lead fly from her hand.

"Jake!" she called after the dog, but he was focused on the bird swirling upwards through the air and soon disappeared deep into the bracken. Gillian stopped to catch her breath and sighed. It wasn't even her dog. She was looking after him for some neighbours whilst they went for a holiday to Tenerife. Lucky buggers, she thought, as she skirted around a particularly large puddle on the path. She didn't envy them Tenerife, just the sun. Gillian would kill for a week of sunshine. She absolutely detested England in the winter, and even though every year she promised herself a trip to sunnier climes, she had yet to deliver on that promise.

"Jake!" she called again as she followed his trail through the bracken, more in hope than expectation, but was pleasantly surprised to see the frisky dog bounding up to her. There was some cloth in his mouth.

She bent down to take it from him and realised that it was a Burberry scarf. Some chav and his girlfriend getting jiggy with it on the heath, she speculated with a disapproving quirk of an eyebrow. Although, to be fair, in this weather she admired their resilience, if not their respect of urban social niceties.

She would have turned back to the path but the dog trotted into a small clearing ahead and barked at the prostrate and motionless figure of a small, bald man.

"My God!" Gillian gasped and ran over. She knelt and tried to find a pulse in his neck. She couldn't be sure but she thought she could feel the faintest of murmurs. She pulled out her phone and dialled emergency services. Slipping out of her Barbour jacket, she laid it under the man's head. Thank goodness that he was wearing such a thick coat, she thought, because even though it made him look like an ancient, hairless Paddington Bear, it had probably saved his life.

Kate Walker knew she shouldn't do it, but, as she sat at her friend's computer terminal, she couldn't help herself. She typed in the access code Jane Harrington had, under duress, given her, and typed in DELANEY to pull up his hospital records. She knew enough not to trust anything the staff at the hospital had told her. She wasn't a relative; she didn't know exactly what she was. Girlfriend didn't sound right. Partner was a bit formal for what they had had. Mother of his child, she decided, that was what she was, and that gave her rights.

The first hit came up with Siobhan Delaney.

Not the rights to look at confidential medical records, maybe, but the man she loved was recovering from an operation and she wanted to know how bad the damage was, she justified to herself.

But not the right to read his ex-wife's records. Kate found herself unable to click the screen away and carried on reading it instead. That night had defined Delaney, after all, for the last four years. It had certainly defined their relationship, if such it was. And so, moral qualms pushed aside, Kate read the report.

Everything was much as she knew it to be. His pregnant wife, suffering heavy blood loss, was rushed into theatre. They had performed an emergency C section. The baby, and subsequently the mother, had died. The procedures seemed in order, everything but the outcome was in order.

Apart from one thing.

She read the document again and wished she never had.

Kate closed down the computer screen. She'd read the reports on Jack's injury. He had been incredibly lucky.

274

The bullet had passed through the lower part of his left shoulder, it had broken no bones and was well clear of any organs. Had the police not arrived when they did, she reflected, it was quite likely that whoever had shot him would have crossed the road and finished the job. And her with him, likely as not. She shivered at the thought.

The door creaked open and Jane Harrington came back into her office, carrying a couple of mugs of coffee.

"Keep meaning to get some WD40 on that," she said.

"I'm sorry?" Kate looked back at her, not at all sure what she had said.

"The door. Needs some oil."

Kate took the coffee and took a sip. It was welcome. She had been up all night. Waiting for Delaney to go into surgery. Waiting by his bedside after the operation. At seven o'clock she had called her friend. She needed to do something, even it was just to see his records for herself. Things were spiralling out of control, that much was clear. And Kate needed to do something. She needed to try and take control. And the one thing she did know about was medicine.

Her friend observed the way she held both hands round the coffee mug, as if to warm more than her fingers. "How is he, Kate?"

"He's going to be okay. For now. The bullet did as little damage as possible under the circumstances. He must have an guardian angel looking over him."

"Or the other kind."

275

"What do you mean?"

"He's not had a lot of luck just lately, has he?"

Without being aware she was doing it, Kate ran a hand protectively over her stomach. "Maybe that's all about to change."

"What about you?"

"What about me?"

"With everything that's going on, Kate. Have you made any decisions?"

Kate took another sip of her coffee. "Yeah, I've decided I'm not going to take any more crap in my life."

He was at the bottom of a deep pool, but the light streaking down from the green disc ahead was bright and strong, the gravel and pebbles beneath his questing fingers were dappled with it. They shone like precious stones. Jack held his breath as he searched. He had to find it, that one special pebble. He had to find it and put it back in its rightful place and then everything would be all right. The world would be right again.

He didn't know how long he had been under but he felt the stale oxygen in his lungs swelling his chest painfully. He let a slow trickle of air bubble from his lips as he raked his fingers through the stones. He tried to fight back the rising panic as the carbon dioxide in his lungs now put a dull throbbing in his head. He let out another trickle of air and with one last scan of his straining eyes he realised he had failed in his mission, for now at least. He kicked his legs and swam up to the ovoid shape, the underside of his rowing boat. But as he neared it and tried to put his hand up to pull himself out, a thick arm descended, wrapping around his neck and keeping him beneath the water. His legs thrashed wildly as stars started exploding before his eyes, he knew he had to break free, he couldn't hold his breath any longer. He had to break free or drown. But he couldn't. He couldn't loosen the grip.

Delaney eyes flew open in panic, he tried to breathe but couldn't. Then the man standing over him, dressed in a white doctor's coat, released the grip on his throat slightly and Delaney gulped in hungry swallows of air.

The man grunted, letting Delaney breathe but keeping an iron grip on his throat, keeping him pinned to the hospital bed. "You got a good reason why I shouldn't kill you here and now?"

"No. But you have."

"That a fact?"

Delaney shrugged as calmly as he could under the circumstances. "Seems to be, Norrell."

Norrell glared at him and finally grunted again. "I'll make a deal with you."

"Go on."

"I'll let you live and I'll even tell you who was behind the petrol station job. Who it was that got your wife killed."

"The shooter."

Norrell shook his head. "The shooter was just a tool. You want the man who set the whole thing in motion."

"And in return?"

Norrell shook his head. "Nothing."

"Nothing?"

"You're a loaded gun, Delaney, I'm just pulling the trigger." Norrell took his hand off Delaney's throat. "It was Mickey Ryan."

Delaney rubbed his sore throat. The man really did have hands like hams. "How do you know?"

"He came to me first. I turned him down."

Delaney was impressed. People didn't turn Mickey Ryan down. He was as close to an organised crime godfather as west London had. From a small-time drug dealer, he had built his empire up over the years like a Richard Branson of sleaze. Serious crime had been after him for years, but he was clever, his money was invested offshore. Put into holding companies. Shells. It made sense he was behind the property deal in Pinner Green. Never mind the downturn, as far as Delaney was concerned property prices were still the crime of the century. No wonder scum like Mickey Ryan was involved.

"Why did you say no?"

Norrell shrugged. "My dad used to work for him when I was a kid. He treated my mother like a piece of shit."

"Right."

"I mean she *was* a piece of shit. But . . ." He shrugged again.

"So what do you expect me to do?" Delaney asked.

"Do what you do best."

"Which is?"

"Fuck people's lives up."

Norrell looked at his watch and winked at Delaney. "This place isn't good for my health. I'll see you around." He strode out of Delaney's private room.

Delaney thought about pushing the alarm button by the side of his bed, then discarded the notion. He knew why Norrell had just volunteered the information. He might just as well have put a gun to Mickey Ryan's head himself. There was a contract out on Norrell and if Delaney removed Ryan he also removed the contract. Delaney didn't like the idea of being used by Norrell, but in the end, in the grand scheme of things, he didn't much give a shite either. Mickey Ryan was a dead man walking. That was all that mattered. It was time to cut off his feet. Delaney lay his head back on the pillow and closed his eyes, strangely peaceful. The waiting was over.

He had taken the day off and so had plenty of time to prepare. His lizard-skin cowboy boots had been polished to a high shine. His black jeans had been neatly ironed, as had his white shirt. He held the shoestring tie in his hand and snapped it a couple of times. Form and functionality.

He had just had a long bath and was planning to have a nice relaxing morning. He was going to need plenty of energy tonight. He lay back naked on his bed and flicked the leather tie at his penis. He immediately started to stiffen and he flicked it again, harder this time. His hand moved down and he held himself for a moment, and then took his hand away. It was all about release. It was all about control.

Delaney groaned, his eyelids twitched and then fell still once more. He was in that halfway stage, not quite awake, not quite asleep, when you know your dreams have hold over you, but you are powerless to let them go.

The smell was universal. The noises in the dark. Hospital. Other hospitals.

Jack Delaney was nine years old. He was walking back from school alone. His best friend Rory had been off sick with measles and he was forbidden to visit him. Jack was okay with that. He had seen kids with the measles right enough and he could do without them. He'd catch up with Rory when he was well.

Like Jack, Rory was big for his age, bigger even than Jack. Everyone said when he grew up he'd either be a policeman or professional wrestler. It was their joke. What Rory wanted to do when he grew up was be a carpenter like his da. Heck, his ma always joked, sure enough he could just pick the trees out of the ground, he'd have no need for lumberjacks for his raw materials. Rory took it in good humour, you had to keep the women on your side.

Jack agreed with him on that one. He didn't know what he wanted to do when he grew up, though. They talked about it often enough but he couldn't fix himself on anything. Fireman one week. A soldier a few years back before the Troubles had flared up in earnest. Sometimes he secretly dreamed of being a priest. Jack could see himself standing up there in the pulpit, holding everybody in awe as he railed and castigated. He was not so hot at the academics, however, and he saw how the black crows knew everything about everything, and that must take an awful lot of book studying and the like.

He bent down to pick up a pebble form the path. He threw the stone high in the air to clatter down on the salt-crusted stones on the beach below, when he heard the cry. And he recognised the voice.

He rushed down the path and around the corner. And there, sure enough, was Liam Corrigan, his cousin. Liam was a couple of years younger than Jack, a few inches shorter, and was surrounded by four older boys with mischief on their faces and sticks in their hands. Jack could see that Liam had tears in his eyes and a small trickle of blood running down his nose.

Jack knew the other boys. All MacWhites. All trouble. Like the family had always been. Jack turned to the eldest. "Brave of you to be taking on the one boy."

Barry MacWhite looked at Jack and grinned, strolling over to him. "You want to join in, do you? Do you want some of —"

281

But he never finished the sentence as Jack had smashed his fist furiously and suddenly into the older boy's nose. The boy dropped squealing to his knees, Jack snatched the stick from his hand and turned to the three remaining MacWhites.

"Come on then, ya gobshites."

He waved the stick in front of him and pushed Liam towards the road. "Get out of here, Liam."

And as his young cousin ran off the road for help, Delaney turned and faced the others, an anger beyond his years burning in his eyes and the other youths circled him as warily as a pack of dogs would approach a wounded wolf.

Had help not arrived when it did, things might have gone a lot worse for Jack than it did. But that was just the first time he ended up in hospital because of his cousin Liam. On that occasion it was for a fractured wrist. On the second occasion it was for something far more serious.

"He's coming round."

Jack heard the voice and tried to open his eyes. He felt as if he had been run over by a herd of cattle. Every muscle in his body ached. But most of all there was a stabbing pain in his side.

"God bless you, Jack. You've done a marvellous thing."

Jack blinked his eyes and could just about make out his aunt looking down at him, smiling gratefully.

"Is he going to be all right?" he asked.

"Yes, Jack," his aunt said, taking his hand and patting it. "He's going to be just grand. You both are."

The fact that she crossed herself immediately after saying it might have given others cause for concern, but Jack Delaney was sixteen years old and invincible.

"You've saved his life, Jack. You've saved his life," cried his aunt, bursting into tears.

Jack shrugged. "Sure, it was only a kidney."

A hospital trolley laden with pills and syringes and God knows what else clattered past his bed and Delaney cursed silently. The thin tendrils of sleep that were clinging to him were severed by the sound. He was awake now, he was in pain, and he was going to have to deal with it.

He leaned his head further up the pillow and groaned, the last few images of his dreams lingering in his consciousness. Why had he been dreaming about his cousin Liam? Why had he been remembering those incidents? It wasn't just being in hospital. Delaney groaned again and raised himself to sit up in bed. He ran his good right hand over his bandaged shoulder and strapped-up left arm and grimaced. Who was he kidding? He knew exactly why he was thinking about Liam. He threw back the covers and slid his legs to the floor. Standing up and wincing at the pain in his shoulder, he looked at the clock. Way past time. The pain forgotten as he picked up his clothes from the chair beside his bed.

★ ★ ★

As an alarm bell sounded, Kate and Sally ran concerned down the corridor and into his room.

Kate couldn't believe her eyes. "Bloody, stupid, bloody man!"

"Where's he gone?"

"I don't know, Sally. You're the detective. Where do men with no brain cells go?" Kate snapped.

Sally shrugged. "Paddington Green?"

Kate glared at her. "Yeah, not funny."

They went back outside and Kate stopped one of two nurses who were hurrying down the corridor. "What's going on?"

"A prisoner's escaped from the secure room."

Kate sighed. "Don't tell me — Kevin Norrell."

The nurse nodded. "The officer who was guarding them is seriously hurt."

"And the other prisoner here? The one with the broken jaw?"

The nurse looked at Kate, shocked, as if she could hardly believe the words that were coming out of her mouth. "He's dead."

Sally took Kate's arm. "You don't think Jack's busted Norrell loose?"

Kate shook her head, her voice trembling with anger and fear. "I don't know, Sally. Let's find the stupid man."

Melanie Jones sat at her desk writing on her computer. She read what she had just written and then highlighted and deleted it. It was all garbage. This was supposed to be her big break and what did she have to show for it? They had a guy in custody who they figured was good for the murders, but she had listened to his voice at the police's request and she couldn't be sure it was the man who had telephoned her. She had no idea what Delaney had been doing with his comments about deformed genitalia in his press statement either. She had dealt with the police enough times to know that they didn't release that kind of detail. If she didn't know better, she would have said he was deliberately trying to rile the murderer. But if he was already in custody, what was the point? She thought ironically about the title of the book she had in mind. *Intimate Conversations With a Serial Killer*. Some intimacy! She'd exchanged about ten words with the man. And the main part of the book, looking at the investigation through the eyes of the lead detective, had gone tits up as well. The suspect had been arrested by plain clothes and not only had Jack Delaney been taken off the case it looked like he had been taken out for good. Some nutter, probably an ex-girlfriend and good luck to her, had shot him and left him in intensive care in South Hampstead Hospital. Be just her luck if he died on her as well. So much for the New York office and the dream job. She had seen herself as a modern-day Truman Capote; as it was she was turning into more of a Lois Lane. Everything happened when she wasn't there, and her Superman turned out to be an Irish drunk whose IQ was no higher than her shoe size.

"Shit," she said aloud, for the thirtieth time that day. And then the phone rang.

She picked it up, suppressing a yawn. "Melanie Jones, Sky News."

The lilting brogue on the other end of the line jolted the yawn into oblivion.

"Roses are crap, me darlin'. Violets are shit. Sit on me face, and wriggle a bit."

"Delaney?"

"Ah no, sad to hear he's not well."

"Who is this?"

There was laugher on the other end of the line and the accent changed to English. "Well now, it's not Santa's little helper. But I could be your lucky charm."

And Melanie recognised the voice, belatedly hitting the record button built into her digital phone system.

"I'm listening."

"www.truecrimeways.com."

"What's that?"

"The password is Whitechapel and your birthday."

"But what is it?"

The line went dead and Melanie was left listening to a single persistent tone. She blinked for a moment as though mesmerised and then hung up the phone, her fingers flashing across her keyboard with more enthusiasm than she had had all morning.

Delaney winced, held his side and leaned against the wall of the visitors' centre. He put a cigarette in his mouth and searched through his pockets for a box of matches. He twisted his hand to the other pocket and picked out the box with his fingertips. He pulled the box open with his teeth and managed to get a match out. But how he was going to strike it he had absolutely no idea.

"Jack Delaney!"

He looked across and cursed as he saw Kate Walker and Sally Cartwright bearing down on him. Great, he thought, double tagged.

"What the hell do you think you're doing?"

"I'm trying to have a cigarette, Kate."

Kate glared at him. "I thought you'd given up?"

"I did. I'm very good at giving up. I do it all the time."

"You should be in bed, boss," Sally said, taking the box of matches off him and lighting his cigarette.

Kate shook her head, resigned. "You realise Norrell has escaped."

"Yeah, I know."

"It's not safe for you, Jack."

"He's not going to do anything to me."

"How can you be so sure?"

"I just know." Delaney drew deep on his cigarette. "Sally, I need you to drive me."

Kate sneered. "Are you mad? You're not going anywhere."

"I have to."

"For God's sake, Sally, talk some sense into him."

"Where do you want to go?" Sally asked.

"I'll tell you in the car."

Kate stepped between them. "No, if anybody is driving you it will be me."

Delaney looked across at Sally, then shrugged with a little smile and kissed Kate full on the lips, who was too startled to back away. "No, I've got another job for you to do."

"What?"

"There's a man in intensive care. I saw him on my way out and recognised him. He was shot on Hampstead Heath last night. Near where we found the first victim."

"I thought the latest theory was it was a Jack the Ripper copycat, killing prostitutes."

"Maybe we were supposed to think that. He was shot in the same area with a tranquilliser rifle. I don't believe in coincidences, Kate. Check it out, find out if it's the same tranquillising drug."

"What does it mean if it is?"

Delaney ground his cigarette under his heel. "I have absolutely no idea."

He turned to Sally. "Come on, Constable, you can drive."

Sally shrugged helplessly at Kate and followed him to the car.

George Napier hung up the telephone. He was far from pleased. Serious crimes had just released Ashley Bradley on police bail. On top of that Kevin Norrell had escaped from the police guard at the South Hampstead Hospital. And if that wasn't enough, Delaney had gone walkabout too. Napier opened the bottom drawer of his desk cabinet and pulled out a bottle of milk of magnesia. He had just taken a healthy swig, when Diane Campbell walked into the room. Why couldn't she keep a damn leash on her Irish bloody inspector? he'd like to know. Was it too much to ask?

Diane read his expression and nodded, at the bottle. "Ulcer?"

Napier grimaced. "Indigestion."

"It's going to get a lot worse."

"What are you talking about?"

Diane picked up the TV remote control from Napier's desk, pointed it at the large television in the corner of the room and turned it on. Melanie Jones's picture-perfect face filled the screen.

"Sky News is now exclusively able to reveal a gruesome new development in the murders of two sex workers. One was found on Hampstead Heath three days ago and the second found murdered in a flat in Camden Town. Sky News understands that horrific details concerning the murders lead police to believe they are dealing with a Jack the Ripper copycat killer. Sky News has been given exclusive access to scene-of-the-crime photographs and forensic details that show that there is no coincidence. In a further development, the suspect the police were holding in connection with these killings has now been released."

Diane Campbell pushed the mute button cutting off the sound as the television now flashed up pictures of the two dead women.

"How the hell did they get hold of this, Diane?"

"The killer told them, sir."

"Why?"

"Clearly he didn't think he was getting the recognition he deserved."

"Get that reporter in here. And where the fuck is Delaney?"

It wasn't the first time Chief Inspector Diane Campbell had heard that question, but it was the first time she had ever heard George Napier swear.

Sally pulled the car to a stop outside a betting shop on the Kilburn High Road. It was called Right Bet and was either in danger of going bust or the owners felt it didn't do to advertise wealth.

Delaney struggled to get the seat belt out of its socket and Sally leaned across. "Let me."

She pushed the button and his seat belt snapped back. Delaney rubbed his sore shoulder. "It would be a lot easier if I didn't wear the fricking thing in the first place. I'm in enough pain as it is, you know."

Sally smiled at him. "Clunk click, every trip."

"Just wait here." Delaney opened the car door.

"You sure you don't want me with you?"

"Quite sure."

Delaney got out of the car and walked to the shop, kicking aside an empty tin of Special Brew as he entered. It was a small shop. No customers. Sheets of paper posted around the room with the various horse and dog race meets covered on them. In the corner was a small television showing dogs running at Brough Park in Newcastle. Behind the counter was a large, bored-looking, bald man in his forties with a barrel of a beer belly and, in defiance of the regulations, a lit fag dangling from his lips. He looked up from his copy of *Sunday Sport*.

"Help you?"

"Is Liam in?"

"And who wants him?"

Delaney looked over his shoulder at the empty shop behind him then back at the man again. "That would be me." The large man opened his mouth to say something but Delaney didn't have the energy for it. "Just tell him it's Jack Delaney."

The man grunted and disappeared through the door to his left.

Delaney looked up at the television screen. A brindled greyhound carrying the number seven won the race. Delaney's lucky number.

"Jack Delaney, you Irish motherfucker!"

Delaney turned round to see his cousin grinning at him. He may have been smaller than Delaney at age seven, now he was four inches taller and good few stones heavier. And all of it muscle. He threw open the hatch and grappled Delaney in a bear hug.

"Oi. Watch my fecking shoulders."

"Sorry, big man." Liam released him and gestured. "Come on back. I'll pull the ring on a cup of tea."

Delaney followed him through the counter and back into a medium-sized office. A desk, an armchair, a fridge, some filing cabinets. The dusty window at the back showed a yard with a skip, a shopping trolley and a couple of cars. One of them a brand new jag. Liam was doing okay for himself, Delaney reckoned, but then he already knew that.

Liam opened the fridge and pulled out a couple of tins of lager. Foster's, thankfully, not Special Brew, and handed one to his cousin.

Delaney awkwardly pulled the tab and took a couple of grateful swallows. He hadn't realised how thirsty he was.

"So, what can I do for you, big man?"

"I need a piece, Liam."

"I see." His cousin nodded seriously and gestured at his bandaged shoulder. "This got anything to do with the fancy dress outfit?"

"Yup. I want to repay the compliment."

"I'd advise you make a better job of it if you do."

"Count on that."

Liam smiled, not doubting it. "And what makes you think your law-abiding cousin would have access to unlicensed and unauthorised firearms?"

"Just get me a piece, Liam."

Liam considered for a moment and then stood up. "Anything for you, Jack. You know that."

He stood up and moved the fridge to one side, pulled up a loose floorboard, rummaged beneath and pulled out a cloth-wrapped package, which he handed to Delaney.

"Ammunition in there. You want to tell me what you need it for?"

"Nope."

"You want any help with it?"

Delaney held up the bundle. "Just this."

Liam laughed. "What are you going to do, stick it down your trousers? Jesus, man, you'll be back in casualty with your cock shot off, and what'll I tell your daughter then? Hang on. I'll get you a holster."

Delaney nodded gratefully. His cousin had a point.

★ ★ ★

Kate Walker tapped on Diane Campbell's office, walked in and shut the door behind her. She wasn't surprised to see the superintendent standing by the open window smoking a cigarette. Jack Delaney and Diane Campbell could support a tobacco plantation between them.

"Hi, Kate."

"Diane."

"Want to tell me where Jack Delaney is?"

"Believe me, if I knew I'd be more than happy to tell you."

"Why do we put up with him?"

"God's punishment for a previous life."

"Now I *do* believe you have spent too much time with him." She tossed her cigarette out of the window and walked across the room as Kate opened her shoulder bag. "What have you got for me?"

Kate pulled out two photos and a sheet of paper which she handed to the superintendent.

"Both female victims had the same puncture wound to the neck. A very forceful puncture wound made, I believe, by a tranquilliser gun or rifle."

Diane had picked up on what Kate had said. "What do you mean by 'the female victims'?"

Kate pointed at the paper she had given Diane. "Last night a man was shot on Hampstead Heath. Again it looks like with a tranquilliser dart. He had a near fatal dose of the stuff in him. He was lucky to survive the night."

"Does he have any idea who did it?"

"He's not speaking yet."

"But he's going to make it?"

293

"Yeah, he's going to make it."

Diane's forehead creased as she looked back at the photos. "So, you're saying this is the same killer. What's the connection? Mr James Collins the surgical registrar is not exactly a female prostitute, is he?"

"Not unless my seven years of medical training missed something very important."

"So what the hell is going on?"

But if Dr Walker had any answers to that they certainly weren't showing on her face.

Jimmy Skinner rubbed his eyes. He was used to staring at a computer monitor for hours, but that was playing poker. Wading through reports was a different matter. Plus, he reckoned he was wasting his time. Paddington Green were in charge of the case now. But the killer was still at large, the public were at risk, and at times like this all hands were called to the deck. It just wasn't the deck he would have preferred.

He flicked on and read the inventory of what had been found in the second victim's apartment. All the videos and DVDs were sex videos. As were the magazines. No *Home & Country*, no *Good Housekeeping*, not even a Delia Smith cookery book. He lived on his own and never ever cooked and even he had a copy of her summer cookery book. For this working girl the property was clearly just that: a workplace. She lived elsewhere, he'd bet on it like he was holding a royal flush.

He made himself a cup of coffee and went through the copies of the paperwork again. There were about twelve shoeboxes' worth of them, mostly receipts for items all paid for by cash, and letters from prospective or satisfied clients. There were no phone bills as there was no landline to the property, she obviously only took bookings on her mobile.

As he rubbed his tired eyes an hour later he realised one receipt didn't match all the others. A vet's bill. It was the one thing that didn't have a connection with anything in the flat. Suddenly energised he picked up the phone and got the directory service to connect him directly with the office named on the receipt.

A short while after that and Jimmy hung up the phone, picked up his coat and was hurrying out the door. The vet had confirmed the receipt was regarding surgical work done on a Siamese cat, but the name didn't match the one Jimmy had given him. The vet refused to give out the name and address unless he saw some identification. His premises were in Mornington Crescent off the Hampstead Road. Jimmy stood up and pulled his jacket off the back of the chair when Diane Campbell came in and leaned against the door frame.

"You got something?"

Skinner nodded. "Got a lead on the second victim."

"Good. Looks like we might have the name of the first, too."

"How come?"

"Her mother's made contact. At least she thinks it's her daughter."

"Thinks?"

"She hasn't seen her since she was fifteen years old."

"Family row?"

"The father was abusing her."

"What's her name?"

"When she left home she was called Maureen Carey. But no such name is flagging on our databases."

"Working girl?" Jimmy shrugged. "Likely not using her real name."

Campbell nodded in agreement and stood aside for Skinner to leave. "Keep me posted."

"You got it."

Sally pulled her car to a stop by the McDonald's on the corner of Shaftesbury Avenue and Dean Street, ignoring the angry honking from furious motorists behind her.

"Are you sure you don't want me to come with you, sir?"

"Quite sure, Sally, thanks."

"You going to be back in time for a drink tonight?"

"I thought you had a hot date?"

"Hardly that, sir. Just dinner with Michael Hill. But a few of us are going to the Pig first. You wouldn't be a gooseberry."

"I'll think about it."

Sally put her hand on his arm as he reached across for the door handle. "I want to help, sir. Whatever it is you know I've got your back."

Delaney nodded and quickly opened the door before she could press the matter. This was something he had to take care of himself and it was way past time.

It was a typically grey, wet and windy late-autumn day in Soho as Delaney walked up Dean Street, pulling his jacket as best he could around him. Since dislocating his shoulder and then being shot he was certainly feeling the cold a lot more. Christ, I'm getting old, he thought. Maybe he should do a Kate Walker, get out of the madness of it all while he still had a chance. The thought of Kate made him smile almost, took a little of the chill off his bones. To think he had almost let her get away again. And for what? For the fear he wouldn't be able to change? That he would carry the past around with him like a hunchback unable to straighten himself? Well, today was the day for all that to be put in the past once and for all. If Delaney was a sickness then Kate Walker was his cure. She would take the curve from his spine and make him walk tall again. But first he had business to attend to. The man who was responsible for his wife's death, who had put the weight on his back in the first place, the man who was responsible for Delaney being shot, for the murder of Derek Watters, for the attack on Kevin Norrell. The man responsible for all that was going to look in his eyes today. That man was going to look in his cold, brown eyes and regret he had ever heard the name Jack Delaney. Today was the day for drawing a line.

A crowd of loudly smug media types spilled out of the Groucho Club as he passed, knocking into him and making him wince as his shoulder jarred. Any other day he would have had words, but today he kept his head down. The pieces of the puzzle were finally coming together and Delaney had no time for petty distractions.

He looked at his watch. Two o'clock. He used his less damaged shoulder to push a door open and walked into one of the new breed of bars that had sprung up in the area. All polished wood and chrome and bright lights. Might as well be drinking in an IKEA store, he reckoned, but today he hardly registered it. He ordered a large whisky straight up and downed it one. He ordered another and held out his hand looking at the slight tremble in his fingers. He put it down to his injuries. His nervous system was shot to pieces, that's all it was.

He finished his second drink and left the pub, crossing over the street fifty yards further up the road and heading down a narrow cul-de-sac, at the end of which was a small club called Hot Totty. It didn't open until the late afternoon, but Delaney waited for a moment or two and then taking a deep breath he pulled a balaclava over his head, pushed the door open and went inside. A thin man in his mid-twenties was behind the counter of a small bar refilling the spirit optics. He called over his shoulder as he heard the door.

"We're not open."

"I've not come for a lap dance."

The man turned round and nearly dropped the bottle of whisky he was holding. Delaney was pointing a gun straight at him.

"Hey, I just work here."

"Is he in the back?"

The barman nodded nervously.

"You got a good memory, son?"

The barman considered it for a bit not sure what he was supposed to say. "No, sir."

Delaney jerked his thumb at the door behind him. "Get out then. You want to stay alive, keep it that way."

The man held his hands up, nodding and scuttling out of the door like a scorpion on a hot skillet.

Delaney thought about Mickey Ryan as he watched the barman scurry away. There wasn't a detective in the Met who hadn't come up against him in one way or another. But he was the original Teflon man, nothing stuck to him. Witnesses were silenced, detectives were bought off, blackmailed or terrorised. He was a brutal, vicious, successful, self-made man. A shining example of everything Thatcher's Britain had created.

Delaney took off the balaclava. He didn't care if Mickey Ryan saw him. In fact he wanted him to know who was putting him in the ground.

He walked to the back of the small auditorium, past the stage and the pole, not even registering the slightly sour smell of body oil that tainted the air like a cheap perfume.

It wasn't hard to find Ryan's office. He pushed the door open holding the gun forward and walked in. It was a windowless room, but glowed with opulence. Rich carpeting, Tiffany-style lamps, artwork on the walls. His dead wife's brother-in-law would fit right in here, Delaney thought. Mickey Ryan was sitting behind a large desk typing on a laptop. He looked up, bored.

"What do you want, Delaney?"

Delaney gestured at the cubic man who stood not far from his boss.

"Put your hands up, Nigel."

The man glared at him. "My name's not fucking Nigel."

"Just do what he says, Pete."

The man raised his hands, glaring venomously at Delaney.

Delaney turned back to the man behind the desk. "Tell him to stop staring at me, Mickey. I might just wet myself."

"What the fuck do you want, Delaney?"

"You know what I want."

"I'm the fucking oracle of Delphi, am I now?"

"No, you're a two-bit slag who has made good on other people's misery for far too long. And now it's time to pay the rent."

Ryan laughed out loud. "Do you hear this guy, Pete? He should be on the fucking telly." His smile died. "After what happened to Norrell and that prison guard, you should have taken the hint, Delaney. Nobody fucks with me and walks away."

"That a fact?" Delaney moved the gun forward aiming at his forehead.

"You had the balls, Irishman, you'd have done it already. Your wife was in the wrong place at the wrong time, that's all. If someone hadn't interfered she'd still be alive today, wouldn't she? That's down to you."

Delaney's finger tightened on the trigger as he put his left hand on his right shoulder. "You should have killed me when you had the chance."

300

"Yeah, well, can't get the staff, isn't that what they say? But I've got a better man on the case now."

Delaney smiled unimpressed. "Who, Nigel here?"

"No," said Mickey Ryan. "Him." And pointed behind Delaney.

Delaney couldn't stop himself from turning round as he felt a presence behind him, and reacted unable to conceal the surprise at who he saw.

"Liam?"

"Sorry, Jack." And his cousin hit Delaney on the side of the head with a narrow leather cosh.

He dropped to the floor like a hanged man with the noose cut.

Jimmy Skinner rang the bell for a third time. There was still no answer. He looked around him then picked up the door ram he had brought with him just in case, and smashed the door open. A Siamese cat screamed at him and went howling and hissing past his legs, nearly knocking him over. He guessed the operation it had had, whatever it was, had been a success.

Inside the maisonette the smell was pretty bad. The cat obviously hadn't been let out for a couple of days. He walked into the lounge and opened the windows. On the mantelpiece there was a photo of a woman. He picked it up and looked at it closely, he could see a slight resemblance to the woman he had seen on the website but he would have never recognised her. The woman in the photo had mousy hair and wore little make-up. She smiled shyly at the camera. No wonder nobody had phoned in after their televised appeals for information about her. In the kitchen the cat's litter tray needed to be cleaned out. Skinner crinkled his nose, picked up a black leather Filofax from the kitchen table and took it back into the lounge.

He flicked through the pages and turned to the diary section. She had kept a list of appointments with clients. One of the names, Paul Archer, jumped out at him, but he couldn't put his finger on why. Seemed he liked rough games and she had refused to see him any more, blacklisted him with her contacts too. He filed the name away. Somebody had a grudge with her, that much was obvious. Another part of the Filofax was day-to-day diary stuff. After half an hour he flicked back to the contacts section; he sighed and closed the Filofax and walked over to a table that had a collection of framed photographs on it and picked one up. It showed two women, one in her twenties and one in her thirties. Hands around each other's waists and smiling at the camera, as if they knew their profession was to be judged now by the quality of that smile as much as it was by the service and care they provided.

And he realised as he looked at the photograph that they had all got it completely wrong.

Delaney felt like someone had taken a heavy hammer and struck him on the head. It was definitely time for a new job, he thought. Somewhere warm. Somewhere quiet. But, as he cracked open his bloodshot eyes, he realised that new employment prospects were the least of his problems. His hands had been tied behind his back and he was sitting in a lock-up garage somewhere, propped uncomfortably on a wooden chair. The door opened and Mickey Ryan walked in, followed by his cubic minder and his traitorous fucking cousin. If Delaney could have worked up the saliva he would have spat at him.

There was a metallic clang. Delaney looked across to see the gorilla of a henchman putting a toolbox on the workbench that ran along the whole left-hand side of the garage. The man made Kevin Norrell look human, he realised with a shudder.

"You might wonder why you are still alive, Delaney."

"Must be my guardian angel."

Ryan laughed, his blue eyes sparkling with amusement. "I wonder if you'll still be laughing when my man here goes to work on you with a pair of needle-tooth pliers."

Liam stepped forward. "Nobody said anything about that."

"Nobody points a gun at me and gets away with it. You're going to learn that, Delaney. And that grassing tub of lard Norrell is going to be next." He turned to Liam. "Put one in his gut, give him something to think about."

Liam raised the pistol he had been holding in his right hand, a semi-automatic with a silencer. Delaney could see no mercy, no compassion in his eyes as he pulled the trigger.

The minder made a sound like a dog swallowing a fly and dropped to the floor, a hand fluttering towards his heart but not making it. Liam pointed the gun at Mickey Ryan.

"The fuck you think you're doing?"

"The fuck you think I'm doing?" Liam retorted.

Ryan shook his head. "We had a deal."

"I don't make deals with scum. Gut shot, wasn't it?" He pulled the trigger again, and Mickey Ryan dropped to his knees, squealing and holding his stomach. "Hurts, doesn't it?"

Ryan's face had gone purple and he hissed between his teeth, but if they were words they were not intelligible.

Liam grabbed a Stanley knife from the toolbox and slashed the ropes binding his cousin.

Delaney stood up and wobbled on his legs. He had to hold on to his cousin's arm before he could steady himself. "What's going on?"

Liam smiled. "I made some calls after you left. Figured out what was what and realised you'd be way out of your depth."

"I had it covered."

"Sure you did, cousin. But you weren't going to kill him, were you?"

Delaney didn't answer.

"Which means that one way or another he would have ended up killing you."

"Maybe."

"No maybe about it."

"What did you have to hit me for, then?"

"You might be ten kinds of death-wish on legs, Jack, but I still enjoy my life. I did what I had to do. And you should be grateful, so take a Panadol and shut the fuck up with the whining already."

Ryan gurgled again, hissing through wet lips, his face contorted with pain.

Liam turned to Delaney and held the gun out. "Do you want to do it?"

Delaney made no move to take the pistol. Liam nodded then fired two bullets into the kneeling man's head. He slumped sideways and the gurgling stopped.

Delaney looked at the dead body. He wasn't sure what to think any more. "What now?"

"Now, cousin, we walk away from here."

Delaney shook his head. "We can't. There's DNA all over the place. You go. Leave me the gun."

Liam reached into his overcoat and pulled out a large brown packet. "Did you know Mickey Ryan was in big with the old IRA? Back in the seventies?"

"No."

Liam nodded. "Back in the day he made a fair few bob out of it. Pissed a fair few people off too. People who didn't take the laying down of arms at all happily. Formed new groups."

"The Real IRA?"

Liam shrugged. "Amongst others. Either way, he's on a list. And this . . ." he tossed the packet on the workbench, "is the boys' old friend."

"Semtex?"

"There won't be enough left of Mickey Ryan, his sidekick, or this garage to fill a teaspoon."

Delaney nodded. It didn't feel like closure. He just felt empty.

"I guess that makes us even, Liam."

"Hardly." He handed back his mobile phone. "Thought you might like this back."

"Thanks." Delaney flipped it open and pushed the speed dial for Kate Walker.

"Jack, where the hell have you been?"

Liam smiled, he could hear every word. "What is it with you and feisty women?"

"Are you still at the station?" Delaney asked Kate.

"Yes, I'm still here."

"Good, stay there. I'm on my way in."

Sally Cartwright looked at her watch for the fifth time.

"Has he stood you up, Sally?"

"Yeah, funny, Danny." Sally flashed a none too amused smile at her colleague at the other end of the table. There were a few of them there, having a drink or two and, as yet, Michael Hill hadn't shown up. Danny, jealous that she was going out for a curry with him, had been making snide little remarks, doing himself no favours in her book at all. But she wasn't worried about Michael, she'd seen the eagerness in his puppy-dog eyes. He was probably nervous. No, it wasn't Michael Hill who had her looking at her watch, it was Jack Delaney she was concerned about. There was a darkness is his eyes when he had left her on Shaftesbury Avenue. Something darker than she had ever seen before.

A cheer went up from Danny and a couple of his mates as Michael Hill eventually came in and walked over to join them. Sally thought he looked nice. Black jeans, a nicely ironed white shirt and a black jacket.

"It's Rhydian!" Danny called out. "Go on, sing us a song."

"Ignore him," Sally said. "He's an idiot."

"I will."

He sat down beside her.

"Actually, I'm glad you're here," said Sally.

"Of course. We're going for a curry, aren't we?"

"Yes. Later. But I meant I'm glad you're here because I want to talk to you. About work. About the crime-scene photos of the second victim that were posted on the Net. There's something a little wrong with them."

Michael Hill stood up. "Well, if we're going to talk shop, there's a little bar I found. I thought we could go there for a drink first, before the ruby? Bit quieter than here."

Sally looked down at his feet as she stood up. "New boots?"

Michael Hill looked down at his snakeskin cowboy boots, polished to a gleam, and smiled as he admired them, stroking his black shoestring tie as he did so. "Fairly new, yes."

Sally looked at her watch again and then shrugged; if anybody could take care of himself, Jack Delaney certainly could. Besides, she had earned herself a bit of fun.

She stood up and gave Michael a quick kiss on the cheek. "Come on then. Let's leave the peanut gallery to it."

Sally headed for the door, Michael Hill put his hand to his cheek where Sally had brushed her lips, and then followed her, desire dancing in his eyes and the faintest of smiles quirking the corners of his mouth.

★   ★   ★

Diane Campbell was leaning against Jack Delaney's desk. Looking through the Filofax that Jimmy Skinner had just brought back from the flat in Mornington Crescent. Kate Walker, meanwhile, was working at Sally's computer going over the forensics reports on both the dead women. "So Jennifer Cole's real name is Katherine Wingrove."

Jimmy Skinner nodded, a gesture on his tall thin body somewhat akin to an albatross dipping for food. "She was a midwife at the South Hampstead Hospital, and did escorting work on the side. The first victim, Maureen Casey but calling herself Janet Barnes, was a student nurse, also at the South Hampstead, about eighteen months ago. According to Katherine Wingrove's diary, she had been working in prostitution since she was fifteen years old and had come to London as a runaway from domestic abuse. She wanted to qualify as a nurse, put that life behind her, but found she couldn't. Student bills to pay, debt mounting up. Katherine Wingrove helped her out, showed her the classier end of the trade. She gave up the nursing and took up escorting full-time."

"Why did nobody recognise them at the hospital?"

"They look completely different, with the make-up and clothes on. Katherine Wingrove was on scheduled holiday this week so no one was expecting to see her anyway. And Maureen's own mother took some time to come forward she looked so different."

"Either way it's not about prostitution, it's about the hospital. All three of his victims have worked there at some time."

Kate typed in the address that Melanie Jones had given the police, truecrimeways.com. It opened on to a general site detailing true crimes, murders of a particularly brutal and violent nature. On the sixth page was a picture of a gravestone, at the bottom of a long article about Fred West. Following the instructions they had been given, Kate clicked on the cross at the top of the gravestone. A box appeared requesting a password.

Skinner watched what she was doing. "It's just like the paedophiles, hiding hyperlinks within a seemingly legal site. You need to know where it is and a password to get into the specialised area." He said the word "specialised" with a definite curl to his lip.

"And people actually pay money to look at these pictures?" Kate asked the room in general as crime-scene photos of the mutilated women appeared on the computer screen.

Diane shrugged. "Kate, people pay a licence fee to watch *Holby City* at dinner time."

Kate nodded, she had a good point. How close-ups of heart surgery, ribcages being cracked open and worse, had become evening family viewing on the BBC she had absolutely no idea.

"Can they be traced, whoever's putting up these pictures?"

Diane shrugged again. "Paddington Green has their best technical people on it but they don't hold out much hope. Not of finding the guy who posted these pictures. Anyone can set up a bogus account, from an Internet cafe or a library. Hack into our systems, download the photos and put them up where they like. It can be impossible to trace."

"Why lead us to it then?"

Diane rummaged in her handbag. "Because we hadn't mentioned it to the press. These sad fucks need an audience, Kate. Pardon my fucking French."

Kate sensed that Diane Campbell was hanging out for a cigarette. She was proved right as Diane found what she was looking for in her handbag, opened the window in front of Delaney's desk and lit one up.

Kate looked at the photos on the screen, pausing at one and then flicking through her files to look at the same photo in hard copy. She leaned in and peered at the computer screen when a voice behind her made her heart leap into her throat.

"You better have one of those for me, Diane."

Kate spun round and jumped out of her chair. She didn't know whether to kiss him or slap him.

"Where have you been, Jack?"

"Christ, Delaney. You look like you've been run over by a combine harvester," Diane Campbell added.

Delaney ran a hand over the rough stubble of his chin and nodded. "I've had better days."

Diane Campbell threw him a cigarette which he just about managed to catch with one hand. He leaned in for her to light it for him. "Jimmy has identified the first two victims," she told him. "They both worked at the South Hampstead as did the third. The escorting isn't the link, it's the hospital itself."

Kate pointed at the computer monitor. "And there's something else. Look at this picture that was posted on the web. Sally Cartwright left me a note, something she'd picked up on. Asking me to check our forensic records."

Diane walked round. "What is it?"

"Look closely at this picture of the second victim. You can just about see the foot of the photographer reflected in the bit of mirror that the killer left."

"And?"

Kate held up the photo from her file. "And in this one you can't see anything. The mirror is clear, no reflection. No foot."

Delaney shrugged. "So? What does that mean?"

"The second is from our files and the first isn't. We don't have it. It means that whoever it was who put these pictures up on the Internet in the first place hasn't hacked into our files. Because that photo wasn't in our files in the first place."

Diane nodded, taking it in. "So that means —"

"Christ!" Delaney interrupted her as the implications hit him. "Where's Sally Cartwright?"

Skinner ran a hand over his head. "She said she had a hot date tonight."

"Michael Hill."

"That's right," Skinner answered him. "Danny Vine wasn't too happy about it, been moaning all afternoon."

"Who's Michael Hill?" Kate asked, puzzled by their tone.

"He's the scene-of-crime photographer, Kate. He took those pictures and if there is one on that site that

311

isn't on our files then he took that one too, and made a mistake when he was putting them up on the Net."

Diane stabbed her cigarette in the air. "We've got the bastard then."

Delaney shook his head angrily. "Not yet we haven't."

Kate Walker stood up. "For Christ's sake, Jack. Are you telling me he's got Sally?"

"He doesn't know we're on to him. There's no need to panic."

Diane Campbell shook her head. "He's been playing games with you all along."

"It doesn't fit the pattern, Diane. She never worked at the hospital."

"And what if she mentions what she asked Kate to look into?"

Delaney didn't answer her, what colour left in it was draining from his face.

Jessica Tam smiled at the sour-faced receptionist as she headed for the exit but, as usual, got nothing in response. The woman had been working there long enough to recognise most people by now, but there was no sign of it on her stony face. Maybe she reserved the smiles for the doctors and consultants, in that regard she wouldn't be unlike many others that worked at the South Hampstead. Seemed to her that if you didn't like people, being a receptionist wasn't exactly the best job in the world. Jessica loved people, loved helping people in need, and for her nursing wasn't just a job, it truly was a vocation. Shame it didn't pay any better, though, she couldn't help thinking as she stepped out into the cold car park not at all surprised to see it was raining again. Be nice to be able to save up enough to buy a better car. One that had heating that worked properly, that didn't steam up every time in wet weather. One that would start first time in the winter. She looked up at the sky above her, far too dark for this time of year. It was nights like these she wished her paternal grandfather hadn't come all that way and fallen in love with an English barmaid. Mind you, if he hadn't come to England, she thought with a little wry smile, she wouldn't have been born.

She slipped her handbag off her shoulder and fumbled for her car keys, thinking to herself that her car might be a bit of a heap, but at least she didn't have to walk across the common and through the heath. She shuddered thinking of the poor woman who had been found there and said a silent prayer for her colleague Mr Collins who was probably one of the nicest registrars she had ever worked with. A loving father, a kind and generous man. She couldn't even begin to imagine why anyone would want to hurt him. Her hands shook slightly as she tried to fit the key in the car door and fumbling she dropped them to the ground. She bent over and startled slightly as a man stepped up from behind her and snatched them up from the ground. She looked up a little scared, but then smiled, relieved, as she saw who it was.

"Dr Archer. You startled me."

Paul Archer smiled back at her, his brown eyes almost black in the gloom of the poorly lit car park.

313

"Then for that I do apologise. I really must make it up to you in some way."

Jessica Tam held her hand out for her keys and Paul Archer smiled once more.

Some pleasures are to be savoured. Michael Hill thought. Some to be played out over time, like a symphony. But some morsels you want to rush at, devour and move on to the next.

He looked at the blonde woman, dressed only in her underwear, one hand hanging from a manacle. At the moment she was unconscious, but she would be awake soon enough. Would he do her quickly like the others, or would he leave her for a while? She wasn't part of the original plan but then she had made herself part of it, wrote herself into a leading role when she was only supposed to be a supporting extra. Jack Delaney's eager-eyed sidekick, lusting after the Irishman like the rest of them. Asking questions, beavering away, keen to get on the arrogant prick's good side. She had asked one question too many, however, and the thought of how Delaney was going to react to what was going to happen to her . . . well, that was just going to make it all the more enjoyable. He smiled at the prospect and then collected himself, he needed to focus, there was other work to do first. He went to the side table and picked up a dark, curly-haired wig and put it on. Looking at himself in the mirror on the wall he smiled again. The perfect disguise. Jack Delaney, eat your heart out. "Hey, cowboy. Time to ride," he said out loud.

A coughed laugh behind him made him spin round.

"You're really pathetic, you know that? You're not a tenth the man he is."

Michael Hill spun round and shook his head angrily. "The way I see it, one of us looks pathetic, but it isn't me."

Sally grimaced as she tried to loosen the manacle on her wrist.

"Hurts, doesn't it?" He held up his right wrist. "I should know. My aunt used to hang me from the manacle and beat me when I was a child."

"That's a tattoo, Michael."

"Shut up!" he barked angrily at her and slapped her.

"And you never lived with your aunt as a child."

"You don't know anything about me."

Sally fought to keep her voice level, she had read the books at college. She knew that people like him got off on fear. It was all about power and control. The moment she showed herself as weak, the moment he smelled her fear, was the moment she was lost. "I'm a detective, dickhead. I don't just go out on dates with men without finding out about them first. Your parents died when you were ten years old and your twenty-one-year-old sister took custody of you because your aunt was registered blind."

"I told you to shut up!" He raised his hand as if to slap her again but then dropped it, his voice almost a whisper. "You don't know anything about me."

Sally softened her own voice. "I know that you're scared, Michael. But it's not too late. You can put a stop to this. You can get help." Her eyes pleaded with him. "Let me help you."

315

Hill walked across to the table again and picked up a length of cloth, then stepped forward and tied the cloth round her mouth. He leaned in and whispered in her ear. "I've someone to take care of first. But I'll be back for you. Then we'll see who's scared."

Sally twisted her head away, the feel of his moist breath in her ear far worse than the slap he had given her.

He headed to the corner of the cellar and up the steps. Sally stared at him defiantly until the small square of light disappeared as he closed the hatch above.

Sally howled with rage as best she could through the tight gag, then slumped against the wall. Her eyes scared now, filling with tears as fought to keep control of her bladder. She wasn't sure she had done the right thing provoking him, but she knew one thing: if she was going to die it wasn't going to be without a fight. After a few minutes working her jaw she managed to loosen the gag, enough to shout for help, but as her voice echoed in the thick walls of the cellar she realised it was a futile exercise. No one was ever going to hear her. She twisted her wrist once more, grunting with pain and desperation as she tried to slide her hand through the manacle.

And failed.

Delaney hung up the phone and shook his head. "He's not at home." An army of flak-jacketed officers had descended on Michael Hill's flat. But there was no sign either of him or Sally Cartwright.

316

Diane lit up another cigarette. "He may not be meaning to hurt her." But her voice betrayed her true feelings.

Kate walked across from the printer. "This is a list of everyone working at the South Hampstead over the last year. And the smaller list is ones who have all at one time worked with the three victims so far."

Delaney scanned the small list — names, addresses and phone numbers — and two of the names jumped out at him straight away: Paul Archer and Jessica Tam. Jessica had been one of the team who had fought so desperately to save his wife's life. He remembered her genuine grief that they hadn't been able to save either of them. He remembered her kind words, her genuine solicitude. He remembered her small, delicate body, her almost oriental features. Most of all he remembered her gentle smile and her humanity. And then he remembered what had been done to the other two women.

He snatched up the phone, looked at the list and punched in a number. It rang for a while before it was answered.

"South Hampstead Hospital."

"Can I speak to Jessica Tam please?"

"She's off shift, I'm sorry. You've missed her." The voice at the other end of the line was curt.

Delaney hung up and looked at the list again. She didn't live far from the hospital. He dialled her home number, it rang for a while but there was no answer. He stood up and hunched as best he could into his jacket.

"Come on, Kate. You can drive."

"Let uniform deal, Jack," Diane Campbell said, a warning tone in her voice. "You are in no fit condition to do anything."

"I can't just sit here, boss. By the time we get there she'll be home."

"He's right, Diane," Kate said as she stood up and put her own coat on.

Campbell sighed and lit another cigarette, calling out from her perch by the window as they walked to the door. "Jack . . ."

"Yes."

"Just be fucking careful."

Jessica Tam fought desperately to stay awake as the man above looked down at her with the cold smile of an executioner.

It had all happened so quickly: she had opened her door, hardly registering the dark-haired man standing there before he had moved quickly forward, there was a sharp prick in her neck and her legs had gone rubbery beneath her. Unable even to speak she had been bustled back into her house, the door kicked closed behind them, and she was laid on her couch. As the man looked at his watch, like an anaesthetist waiting for a sedative to take hold, she knew all too well what was going to happen next if she lost consciousness; she could see it in the absolute chill of his eyes. If she could just fight it. Keep awake, then there was hope. But she could almost feel the rhythm of her heart slowing. She tried to lift her head, but it felt as if a sandbag had been placed over it. Maybe it had. Her eyes flickered open very slightly, she tried to seize the light, draw herself up along it. But she just felt so tired. So very, very tired. Her eyes closed again and she half formed the thought to fight it, to open them again, and then the thought died.

Kate pulled her car behind a Land Rover parked on pavement outside the nurse's house, and cut the engine.

"You wait here, Kate," Delaney said.

"I'm coming with you. No arguments."

Delaney shrugged and regretted it immediately as spikes of pain shot through his battered shoulders. They got out of the car and walked towards the house. Delaney looked through the back windows of a blue Transit van that was parked outside, but he couldn't make anything out, the windows were too deeply tinted.

Inside, Michael Hill couldn't believe his eyes as he crouched low and looked through the window. Jack Delaney and his bitch of a girlfriend walking towards the door. How the hell had he tracked him down? The man had the detecting skills of a blind goose. So far everything had had to be laid out on a plate for him. He hefted Jessica Tam under one arm and lifted the tranquilliser gun, which he had reloaded, in the other. There was nowhere to go. He pointed the gun at the door and waited.

The doorbell rang. He stayed motionless. It rang again. He could hear Delaney move around the side of

319

the house, peering in the windows, but he wasn't visible in the hall. The bell rang a third time. He held the nurse tighter to him, grateful that she was so small.

After another couple of minutes he heard footsteps moving away. Then a car engine starting up and the car pulling away. He let out the breath he had unconsciously been holding and propped his arm under Jessica Tam and around her waist. Walking her to the door as if she had had too much too drink.

He opened the door and manoeuvred her clumsily towards his vehicle. He was halfway there when Delaney stepped around from the side of the van and pointed a pistol at him.

"Your exhaust pipe is still hot."

Michael Hill stiffened, holding the gun against the petite nurse's head.

"I'll kill her."

Delaney looked at the man's curly brown wig. Could see the madness dancing in his dark eyes. He had no doubt at all that he meant what he said.

"You pull that trigger and you're a dead man."

"Maybe I'm a dead man anyway. But we're not finished here yet. I'm a force of nature, Delaney."

Delaney looked at him and wondered at his own hesitation. Earlier that day he had been unable to kill a man responsible for the death of his wife and the death of his unborn baby. Something in him had changed, that much was clear. A couple of months ago he wouldn't have hesitated. He'd have put a bullet in each of Mickey Ryan's kneecaps first and then put one in his head. He looked at the frail woman who had tried so hard to help him all those years ago. He was powerless. He looked at the expression in the man's eyes facing him. He took a step closer, saw the pupils grow wider as though the man had come to some kind of decision. He moved slowly towards the man, positioning the barrel of the gun in the centre of his forehead.

"Drop the gun, Michael."

"Look into my eyes, Delaney. You know I'll do it."

Delaney looked in his eyes and then pulled the trigger. Michael Hill's head snapped back in a way the spine wasn't designed for. His dark brown wig fell off and as he crashed to the floor with his arms held out, his head landed with a wet, slapping thud, jolting one of the brown contact lenses he was wearing loose. He now had one brown eye and one blue and looked, Delaney thought, with his blond hair and white face exactly as David Bowie might have looked if he had carried on with the heroin.

The nurse, Jessica Tam, had fallen from his lifeless arms and was now laid across his body in an unnaturally intimate manner.

Delaney barely registered the sound of car tyres as Kate pulled back into the driveway. He picked the nurse up in his arms and carried her over to the car. Kate opened the door for him to lay her on the back seat and then leaned over her to check her vital signs. She put a finger on her carotid artery and then bent over to listen to her breathing.

"She's got a strong, steady rhythm, Jack. She's going to be fine. Just drugged, that's all." She looked over at

321

the dead figure of Michael Hill and shuddered. "Are you okay?"

Delaney looked down at his hand, which was trembling now and nodded. "I'm fine."

He pulled out his phone, and turned his back to shield himself from the wind as he made a call.

"Jimmy, it's Jack. I've got Michael Hill. He's dead. He had a gun. We struggled. He lost."

"Glad to hear it."

"Don't be too glad. He didn't tell me where Sally Cartwright is."

"I've got another address, Jack. One from his original application. His aunt's. She died recently."

"Where is it?"

"About a quarter of a mile from where you are. Priory Road. Number thirty-two."

"Put it out. I'll make my way there. And get an ambulance sent over here."

"You reckon he needs it?"

"It's for the nurse. At least we saved one of them."

Delaney walked over to Michael Hill's supine body. He took the tranquilliser gun off him and put it in his pocket. Then wiped his own gun and put the dead man's hand over the grip of the gun, fitting his finger in the trigger guard. He squeezed the dead man's hand a couple of times and then used it to throw the gun on the floor about three feet away.

He walked back to Kate. "You didn't see any of that. We struggled. His gun went off." He ran his fingers through his hair, realising his hands were still trembling and there was nothing he could do to stop it.

Kate stepped forward and hugged him. "You can't save everyone, Jack."

Delaney kissed the top of her head. "I can try."

Kate looked up at him and ran her hand over his unshaven face. "What am I going to do with you?"

"I've got to go. The ambulance and the others won't be long. Will you be all right waiting here?"

"Just find Sally, Jack." She kissed him. "And be careful."

Delaney nodded at the body. "He's dead, Kate."

They're both dead, he thought, as he walked off into the wind and rain not daring to let himself believe that Sally Cartwright was still alive.

Michael Hill's aunt may have only been dead a short while but her house had already been stripped of furniture; a painted dresser in the kitchen, a bed in one of the upstairs bedrooms, some old clothes hanging in a musty wardrobe. But nothing apart from that. Just dust and damp.

Delaney toured the rooms once again to see if he had missed anything. But he hadn't. The house was empty.

He pushed the front door shut and leaned against the porch wall; using his body to shield against the wind, he lit a cigarette. He took a deep drag and played back in his mind what Michael Hill had said before he shot him. He was a force of nature, he'd said. And before that he said he wasn't finished. No. He hadn't. His exact words were "We're not finished". The women being mutilated, the man not. The whole Jack the Ripper nonsense. "We." He cursed as he fumbled for his phone.

We. There were two of them.

"Shit!"

Detective Inspector Robert Duncton of the serious crimes unit thundered up the stairs, the men behind running to keep up. Half of them were in flak jackets and armed. He got to the top of the stairs and walked along the external corridor. He was not in a good mood. White City had been pissing all over his investigation again. Little men trying to play with the big boys. One of them, Jack Delaney, had just shot dead the prime suspect and was now claiming that Michael Hill was acting with a partner. That there were two of them. If they had made a mistake in letting the first one go it was the sort of thing that could wreck a promising career. And Robert Duncton's career was very promising indeed. At least it had been up until today.

He waited for two of the armed officers to position themselves either side of the door and hammered on it with a fist as heavy as his heart.

Ashley Bradley's grandmother peered out. "Can I help you?"

Duncton took her by the arms and moved her outside. "Is he here?"

"Ashley?"

"Yes, Mrs Bradley. Is your son here?"

"No, he's not in right now. And he's my grandson."

Duncton gestured and the armed men piled into the house. A few seconds later they emerged shaking their heads.

"I told you," said Mrs Bradley.

Duncton sighed. "Where is he, then?"

"He's gone to the cinema. Some film he wanted to see. He loves romantic films."

Delaney jogged painfully back the way he had come and had to stop by a bus shelter to catch his breath. He leaned against it as he pulled out his packet of cigarettes, cursing at the awkwardness of only having one arm to use as he fumbled one into his mouth. A handsomely dressed middle-aged couple walked past, putting as much room between him and them as possible. Delaney didn't blame them. He used the flat of his hand to brush some of the dust from his trousers. He sneezed. He lit his cigarette and sneezed again. And then he realised, the cigarette almost falling from his mouth, but not quite. "Idiot!" He almost shouted it.

The middle-aged couple ahead looked back, but Delaney didn't even register them. He began running back towards the house he had left just five minutes previously. Running in real earnest now.

Ashley did like romantic films. Quite often in the early screenings it meant there was a fair scattering of women in the audience. Single women who didn't want to come later and feel jealous of the happy couples sitting all around them. Ashley could relate to that. He settled back and enjoyed the trailers. His overcoat was pulled lightly together, his jeans were unbuttoned beneath it and with a hole already cut in his right-hand pocket he was good to go.

325

While he had been sat there she had already eaten a hot dog and was now munching her way through a bin-sized bucket of popcorn. Not that he was objecting, he liked to hear women eat. He enjoyed listening to the wet sounds her lips made as they slapped together, the little, almost inaudible groans of pleasure as she swallowed.

He gave himself a little preparatory stroke. The next trailer was for a Sandra Bullock film. Ashley Bradley was a big fan of Sandra Bullock. Had been ever since *Demolition Man*, when she ran around in her tight black pants and futuristic cop outfit. Ashley had had a really bad couple of days and he figured he deserved a treat. And treats didn't come much better than Sandra Bullock in tight clothing. He closed his eyes for a moment, picturing her in her uniform, when the sound of men running loudly down the gently sloping aisle made him snap them open again.

Robert Duncton and four of his men stopped opposite Bradley's seat, fanning out, two of them training semi-automatic pistols at him.

"Get him."

The other two leaned in and yanked him up. His coat flew open, his jeans dropped, and his penis, semi-priapic, twisted and scarred, wagged in the direction of the woman sitting next to him.

She looked at it, screamed and promptly threw up.

Ashley's day wasn't getting any better.

Nor was Detective Inspector Robert Duncton from Paddington Green's. "Get him out of here," he shouted, stepping back and wiping some of the splatter from his once immaculate trousers.

Delaney pushed open the front door that he had earlier forced and walked in again, listening for any sounds, but there were none. He flicked the light on and walked down to the kitchen. He turned the light on in the kitchen and looked at the floor. It was as clean as he remembered it. Too clean. There was no dust on it. He walked across to the dresser that was positioned in the far corner opposite the sink and leaned against the wall at a diagonal. He put his hands either side of the base unit and pulled. It was sitting on a rug and came away surprisingly easy. He pulled it a little further out and looked behind it. There was a trap door.

Bingo.

He bent down, put his finger through the ring and pulled it open and called out.

"Sally."

"Sir, you can't come down here."

"It's all right, Sally, it's just me."

Delaney took off his jacket and walked down the stairs.

"You can't see me like this."

"I can't see a thing," said Delaney. "It's like the black hole of Calcutta down here."

"Don't mention Indian restaurants."

Delaney could hear the fragility behind her laugh, he reached out with his jacket and she managed to drape it around her shoulders. Delaney went back to the bottom of the stairs and fumbled for the light switch.

He found and turned it on; a bare bulb flared up overhead. It was a small wine cellar. Empty apart from a side table, a mirror and his young assistant who was manacled to the wall, her arm raised like an Overeager child with the answer to a difficult question in class.

"Did he hurt you, Sally?"

She shook her head. "He took me to another bar for a drink. He must have slipped something in it, because I remember feeling suddenly woozy and I hadn't drunk that much. He said he'd drive me home. The last thing I can remember is getting into his car. And then I passed out."

Delaney took a hold of the ring set into the wall with his one good hand and tried pulling it. It wouldn't budge. He managed to loosen the manacle a little, but not enough for Sally to free her hand.

"Don't worry, Sally, we'll get you out."

"Michael Hill, sir. Did he hurt anyone else?"

"No, and he's not going to hurt anyone again. He's dead."

"Good!"

Delaney nodded. She was right. He headed back to the steps. "I'm going upstairs to find something to get you free with."

Delaney walked up the stairs and into the kitchen and stopped dead as he saw the rifle pointing at him.

He looked at the person holding it and held his hands up. She looked familiar to him but he couldn't place her at first. And then he did. She was the receptionist at the South Hampstead Hospital. She wasn't smiling.

"Put the rifle down," he said.

The woman smiled and there was poison in it. "I don't think so."

"Who are you?"

"Not that it's going to matter to you, but my name is Audrey Hill."

Delaney nodded. "Michael Hill, he's your husband?"

"No, Detective Delaney. He's my baby brother. I brought him up."

"You know who I am then?"

"I know exactly who you are."

"And you knew what your brother was doing?"

"He didn't do anything, Detective. He never does without my permission . . ." She looked at Delaney with flat eyes, and he felt a chill run up his spine. "Not any more."

Delaney swallowed drily, his mind racing, running through the options. He wasn't thinking so much about himself, he was thinking about the young, near-naked detective constable chained to the wall in the cellar beneath them. He had to keep her talking, he had to keep this madwoman away from her. He didn't know what he was going to do but he knew this much, she stopped talking and it was over for him. Over for both of them.

"Why then, Audrey?"

She moved closer to Delaney, her unblinking eyes staring at him like a entomologist might examine a newly discovered specimen. "Neither of them suffered. They were all painless deaths. Anaesthetised and then a simple cut to the jugular. They died in their sleep."

329

"And the surgeon?"

The woman shrugged. "We were disturbed. I'll get back to him later."

"What had they done to you?"

Delaney tried to edge closer to her but she raised the rifle and shook her head very slightly. "This is a tranquilliser rifle, but it's loaded for very large animals. It's hard to describe the damage it would do to a human central nervous system."

Delaney held up his hands, calming. "Why did you kill them, Audrey?"

"Because of what they did to me."

"What?"

"Were you aware that one in seven hundred people wake up during an operation under general anaesthetic, Detective?" she said.

Delaney wasn't. "No," he replied.

"You're paralysed, immobile, you can't move. Not even an eyelid. But you can feel. Feel the cold steel of the scalpel slicing into you. Feel your flesh parting as they open you up."

Delaney didn't respond, it was putting it mildly to say that he already had a very bad feeling about this woman, he knew what she was capable of, after all. He could feel the anger and sickness radiating off her like the shimmering haze of a tarmac road in a heatwave.

Audrey Hill took another step closer to him. "You can hear too, Detective Inspector. And that's the worst part of it. They were talking, the two sluts whispering to each other about clients they'd fucked. The surgeon talking about football to the vapid nurse. Talk, talk talk,

When they should have been concentrating on what they were doing. The anaesthetist spotted something was wrong and put me under again, but by then it was too late."

"I can understand it must have been a terrible experience —"

"You understand nothing!" She spat the words at him, the rifle shaking in her hands for the first time as her hands shook with fury."

"They killed our baby."

"What do you mean?"

"What do you think I mean? Our baby died!"

"Yours and Michael's?"

"We were a family. We were supposed to be a family. They took that away from us."

Delaney looked at the rifle trembling in her hands, and held his hand up again, trying to keep the disgust from his face and voice. "It's okay."

"Nothing is okay. It was supposed to be routine but they made a mistake with the anaesthetic and had to deliver my baby by Caesarean section. I heard them!"

Delaney could see the madness and rage still dancing in her eyes. "That must have been terrible for you."

"He died because of their butchery. Then they performed a hysterectomy. Performed it without my consent."

"They were trying to help you."

"No." Her voice was quiet now and Delaney didn't feel more reassured by it, in fact he felt the opposite. "I am a trained veterinary nurse by trade, not a receptionist. I took that job just to get close to them,

Detective. So I understand surgery. I heard them admit their mistakes. They murdered my baby and then they cut out my womb. So that's why, Detective. A life for a life."

"And the mutilations? Did they deserve that?"

She smiled joylessly again. "It's what they did to me." Her eyes dropped to her stomach and the smile fell from her lips. "They mutilated me."

Delaney could hear the change in the tone of her voice. As if their conversation was at an end. He had to say something. Do something.

Audrey Hill raised the rifle a fraction, pointing at his heart now, as if she had come to a decision. "Do you believe in God, Inspector?"

Delaney shrugged. "Yeah I do. Someone has to be responsible for all this shite."

She didn't smile this time. "Now that we know how big the universe really is . . ." She shook her head puzzled. "How can you believe in God? We're not ants. Were not even germs. So if there is no justice from God, we have to make our own, don't we?"

"It doesn't have to be like this."

"It already is, Detective Inspector Delaney."

Delaney heart thudded in his chest as he heard a familiar voice shout out.

"Jack," Kate called from the front door. "Are you in there?"

"Stay back!" Delaney shouted, almost screamed it. "Just stay where you are."

"Jack!"

Kate walked into the room and as Audrey Hill spun round and pointed the rifle at her, she froze in place.

"Maybe I'll just shoot her then."

Delaney saw her hand trembling on the trigger, the madness in her eyes and stepped forward. Kate Walker was the woman he loved. He knew that now more than ever. He loved her and she was carrying his child. He wasn't going to lose another one. "Jessica Tam isn't dead and Michael isn't bringing her here," he said.

"What are you talking about?"

"I killed him. Michael's dead."

The woman shook her head, shocked, as she spun round and trained the rifle back on him. "You're lying!"

Delaney took another step towards her. "I put a bullet in his diseased brain, Audrey. He's dead, it's over. Now put down the rifle."

Delaney watched her hands tremble. He didn't know if it was a deliberate tightening of her finger on the trigger as the rifle fired, or if it was accidental. He didn't register the sound of Kate screaming, he didn't know that Sally Cartwright had come charging into the room and was throwing herself at Audrey Hill.

Falling to the floor, he didn't know anything at all.

He was already dead.

Epilogue

When she was seven years old Kate Walker had attended her grandmother's funeral. It was a bitterly cold day in October, and, as she had stood in the rain in her black coat and her black skirt with a black hat on her head that did nothing to stop the swirling bite of the wind, she had decided she didn't like funerals or cemeteries. Why couldn't people live for ever? Why couldn't she be seven for ever? Why do people have to grow up and die?

Maybe, at heart, that was why she had become a pathologist. Maybe she chose her career to answer that question. As a young boy will break apart a favourite toy to try and see how it works, maybe she had been breaking apart human bodies. Dissecting and disassembling them to their component parts, flesh, tissue, sinew and blood, to answer the question that, outside religion, had no answer. She had learned that as a child Michael Hill had killed and tortured animals, for the same reason, before his sickness had been identified and he had been put on medication. Medication his abusive sister had later withheld from him. Had she, herself, been doing the same thing all this time, Kate wondered, only with dead human bodies? Maybe she was a lot more like him than she realised. She shivered. She was nothing like Michael Hill. She was alive, for one thing.

She shivered because it was cold that day as well. Not as bitterly cold as the day of her grandmother's funeral, but the wind had an edge like a scalpel and Kate put her right hand around the folds of her scarf and pulled it tight to her throat. It was a cashmere scarf, white, and she found comfort in the warmth of its touch. She never thought she would buy a coloured scarf ever again.

She looked down at the gravestones. At the surname DELANEY carved twice in bold chisel strokes.

She still didn't know why people had to die. In all her years of medical training she hadn't even come close to knowing. She only knew that people did. The important thing to do, she had decided, if you were living, was to live.

Jack Delaney had come back to life in more ways than one. She took her hand from her scarf, took his hand in her own and squeezed it.

He looked at her and smiled sadly and she had never felt more alive. She remembered the confusion of that evening. Delaney collapsing to the floor. His body in such a bad state, after the battering he had taken over the previous few days, that his heart had literally given out at the massive dose of tranquilliser shot into him. He claimed that he knew that Kate would have her medical bag with her in the car, and, moreover, as he knew that the surgical registrar James Collins had survived over night, after being shot with the same drug, he was going to be fine. But Kate didn't believe him. He knew the risk he had been taking, but he took it anyway. He deliberately goaded the woman into shooting him because she was threatening me, Kate thought, and threatening the life of our unborn baby. Kate couldn't remember the words she mumbled as she stabbed the adrenalin shot into his lifeless heart, but it was a prayer of some kind. And in those few moments between life and death her own heart almost stopped itself as the world tilted on its axis once more for Delaney and he breathed again. Opening his eyes and smiling with them at her as though reborn.

She looked back down at the gravestones of his wife and son and realised she could never tell Jack the terrible truth about the boy. That when the baby had been born it had needed blood; the surgical team had checked automatically but Jack Delaney was not a match.

He wasn't a match because he hadn't been the father.

Jack knelt down on one knee, laid some flowers on his wife's grave, stayed there for a moment, then stood up and put his arm around Kate's waist. "Let's go."

They walked back towards the cemetery gates. Jack had told her that the man responsible for his wife's death was dead. He didn't provide any more details, nor yet did she ask for them. What she knew was that Jack Delaney was a new man. There was still a darkness at the heart of him but he had closed a chapter on his life and was ready to start a new one. A new one with her.

For the first time in her life she truly felt protected and she truly felt loved, the barriers she had fought so long to build were coming down.

That night they made love for the first time. It seemed.

It was three o'clock in the morning. Kate murmured drowsily, half awake, half asleep. She settled into her pillow and put her arm around Delaney's waist and then started, flashing to the morning she woke up with Paul Archer in her bed. But as she lay back on her pillow she remembered more; lowering her barriers had let Delaney truly into her life, but it also brought back memories, as though it was only now that she was strong enough to deal with them.

She was quite drunk. Goodness knows how many vodkas she had had. She was dancing to another female singer now. She sang along and wobbled a bit. She sat down on the sofa.

"Ooops."

Paul Archer stood up and reached for his jacket. "I'd better be getting home."

"Where do you live?"

"Finchley. I used to live down the road. My soon-to-be ex-wife has the house." He shrugged with a smile. "The bitch."

She looked at her watch. "It's too late. You'll never catch a taxi. Not at this time of night."

"Then I'll walk."

"To Finchley?! No!" She wagged a finger and was aware her words were slurred. And the more she tried to concentrate, the more slurred they seemed to become. "You'll stay here. No funny business. But you might as well stay."

Paul Archer smiled. He was a good-looking man, and she reckoned that smile had charmed the pants off plenty of women in the past. But all she wanted to do was go to bed and sleep for a week. She stood up and stumbled her way to the hall closet where she pulled out a duvet and handed it to him. "The sofa is large enough to sleep on." She knew that, because the last man she had given the duvet to was Jack bloody Delaney. "You sleep here and I'll see you in the morning."

She went to her own bedroom, left her pile of clothes on the floor and climbed into bed. She looked at the ceiling for a moment or two, at least the room wasn't spinning. She turned off the light and a short while later she heard Paul Archer come into the room.

"It's cold out there. Can't I sleep with you? Like you say, no funny business, I promise."

She couldn't remember speaking but she remembered shaking her head. And she remembered the sound of him taking off his clothes and climbing into bed and thinking what the hell, as long as he just went to sleep.

"You try anything," she said, "and you're out the door." She remembered him leaning over her.

338

Showing his left wrist which had a Celtic tattoo of a chain. He turned it around so she could see the chain was broken. "See this. I had it done the day after my wife made me leave my house. It's a symbol of freedom. I used to have a watch on this wrist which she bought me. I sold that the same day as well. Ten thousand pounds. She was a passive bitch as well, but she warmed up when I taught her how."

Kate's eyelids drooped. "What are you saying?"

His voice was hard now. "I'm saying it would be no fun fucking you like this. Like a drunken slut. But I want you to know that when I am ready . . . I will fuck you. And what you want will have nothing to do with it."

She struggled, trying to tell him to get out, but she couldn't seem to speak and his voice became soft and soothing like melted molasses as he stroked her forehead.

He spoke some more but she couldn't remember the words, she couldn't make them out. It was like nonsense he was speaking. And she couldn't keep her eyes open. She felt herself falling as if into a deep chasm of sleep and then she remembered no more.

Kate sat bolt upright in bed and reached for the telephone on the bedside cabinet, hurriedly dialling a number.

Delaney stirred and rubbed his eyes. "What's going on?"

"Shush."

The phone rang a few times and was picked up. The voice on the other end of the line far from pleased.

"This had better be good. Have you any idea what bloody time it is?"

"Jane, it's Kate."

"Kate." The sleepy voice on the other end of the line became more alert. "What the hell's going on? Are you all right?"

"I'm fine. Just tell me . . . Paul Archer. He worked with children, you said?"

"Yes."

"What specialty?"

"Paediatric psychology. Mainly in the area of trauma counselling."

"Does he use hypnosis?"

"Yes, I think he does."

"Son of a bitch."

"Has something happened?"

Kate smiled. "No. Nothing happened. That's exactly the point. I'll speak to you later." She hung up the phone and smiled broadly at Jack. Then she realised something else.

"Oh, shit." She almost whispered it.

Helen Archer looked up a little startled as Kate came into one of the rooms for witnesses at the courthouse. Her hand flew involuntarily to her mouth like a wounded bird as she bit on a fingernail. She willed her hand down. "Sorry, I'm a bundle of nerves today."

"I can understand," said Kate.

"I nearly felt like not turning up. I'm not sure, when I see him, how I'm going to react. I'm not sure I can do it."

"He's a forceful man. I don't blame you, Helen."

"But he deserves to pay for what he's done, doesn't he?"

Kate looked at the woman, could see the nerves running through her body like electricity, making her twitch and fidget. "When we talked earlier this week, you said he was wearing a watch. That night, when he attacked you . . . you said he was wearing the watch you bought him as an anniversary present?"

Helen Archer nodded, a little puzzled by the question. "That's right. He always wore it. He didn't care about scratching me. About hurting me."

"That was the same night?"

"What same night?"

"As the rape?"

Helen stood up and gestured with her trembling hands, agitated now. "Yes, of course it was the same night! Why are you asking me that?"

"He told me he sold the watch, Helen."

"When?"

"The day after he moved out of the house."

"He's a liar. He's always been a liar. When did he tell you this?"

"The night he stayed at my place. I am getting some of the memory back. Flashes of it."

"Are you saying you don't believe me?"

"What about his wrist, Helen? What can you tell me about his wrist?"

"There's nothing to tell. He had his watch on." She shook her head angrily. "I don't understand why you are talking like this."

"Because he had his wrist tattooed, Helen. The day after he moved out of the house."

"He's lying."

"To me? At that time, why would he? You made no mention about his watch in your police statement. It was only to me you mentioned it and that was after he told me about the watch. Only I didn't remember at the time."

Helen Archer seemed to slump, she sat back on the chair and looked up at Kate, pleading with her sad eyes. "What if it didn't happen that night? Not that one time. But what if it happened a lot before, when we were married? Does that make him any less guilty?"

Kate sighed. "I don't know, Helen."

"What if he made my life a living hell?" Her voice was more strident now and she stood up again. "What if he phoned every day after he moved out? What if he kept leaving messages on the answer-phone? Not threatening messages. Not anything you could take to the police. But I understood what he meant. I understood the subtext. With Paul it was his way, always. You didn't tell him it was over."

Kate remembered the whispered words Paul Archer had said to her.

"So you set him up, you invited him over and let him have sex with you?" she asked.

342

Helen tore at her thumbnail. Her voice on the edge of manic. "What are you going to do?"

"That was why there was no evidence of drugs," said Kate. "There never were any, were there?"

Helen looked at her, the desperation naked in her eyes. "What are you going to do?" she said again.

But Kate couldn't answer her.

Back in the entrance foyer of the courthouse, Delaney stood up gratefully from the long wooden bench he had been sitting on as Kate approached. He could see how tense she was.

"What did she say?"

"She lied to me, Jack. She lied to everyone."

"What are you going to do?"

"I have to do what's right. I'm going to have to testify. I'm an officer of the court."

Kate Walker felt a tickle in the back of her throat. She coughed into her hand a little and realised she was sweating. She had been in court many times before, but this time felt different. She looked across, reassured to see Jack sitting in the public gallery. He gave her a smile. But she couldn't get the muscles in her face to smile back. She placed her hand on the Bible and promised to tell the truth, the whole truth and nothing but the truth.

"Can you tell us in your own words what happened that night?"

Kate blinked, she had been lost in thought and had missed most of what the barrister had been asking her.

She looked across at Paul Archer. He was sat with his arms folded, looking at her with a calm, self-assured expression.

"We had been drinking. I had been drinking quite a lot, in fact. It was late. It was cold and I thought it unlikely Dr Archer would flag down a cab easily."

"And so?"

"And so I offered him the use of my sofa."

"Your sofa?"

"Yes. Nothing else. Dr Archer took advantage of my hospitality by coming unbidden to my bedroom and climbing naked into my bed."

"Are you saying he assaulted you?"

"He assaulted my hospitality. He assaulted all acceptable norms of behaviour."

"But did he touch you?"

"Not then, but he made it very clear that he intended to . . ." she gestured apologetically to the jury, ". . . in his own words 'fuck me' at a later stage and what I wanted would have nothing to do with it."

She looked at the jury and back at Paul Archer before he had a chance to wipe that smug smile off his lips and she knew the jury had seen it too. "He made it clear he liked his women to resist him, Your Honour. He left me in no doubt as to his intentions towards me."

Archer's brief stood up. "My client is not on trial for things he may be imagined to do in the future."

Kate pointed at Helen Archer. "He raped that poor woman." She turned again to the jury. "And he should be made to pay."

344

Archer's barrister leapt to his feet again, summoning some outrage. "I object, Your Honour."

"Sustained," said the judge. "The jury will disregard that last remark."

Which was like telling a drowning man not to breathe in.

Delaney leaned against a lamp post. He lit a cigarette and wondered how long it would be before smoking was banned in all outdoor public places too. As it was you could be fined fifty pounds for flicking a fag end into a drain. But the law was the law, you had to respect it.

The sky overhead for once had a remarkable amount of blue in it, the soft white clouds that dotted here and there were motionless and the sun was actually shining. It was a bright, crisp, chill autumn day. An autumn day like it should be. As it was in his childhood, when the seasons knew how to behave themselves.

It was a day for new beginnings.

Kate came out of the courthouse, her smile, the epicentre now of Delaney's solar system, as bright as the sun itself.

"What happened?"

"He got seven years and four months."

"You don't feel guilty?"

"Not a bit of it."

Delaney nodded. "A certain degree of moral flexibility allows us to do what we do." He grinned and flicked his cigarette into the drain at his feet watching it spark as it hit the grating below.

"I didn't perjure myself, Jack, I just didn't tell them I knew Helen Archer was lying."

At that moment the woman in question came out of the courthouse, she was surrounded by friends and family. She looked across at Kate and gave her a small, quick smile.

Delaney pointed at the statue adorning the roof of the court building. "Audrey Hill told me that there is no God and we all know that Justice is blind, so we just have to look out for each other, don't we?"

Kate linked her arm in his as they walked away. "Seems to me that looking after you is going to be a full-time job."

Delaney dropped his voice to the rich burr of his childhood tongue. "That's because I'm all man, sweetheart."

Kate laughed. "All ego maybe."

Delaney's phone trilled in his pocket and he flicked it out to answer it. "Delaney."

The voice on the other end of the line took him straight back to that childhood, almost as if he had summoned it. Took him back to a day of sunshine and wonders and joy at the world.

"Jack, it's Mary, your cousin Mary. I need your help," she said.

And at that moment a crow took off from the roof of the court building behind them, its dusty wings flapping like shook canvas in the bright, still air, and its caw like the mockery of God.

346

Also available in ISIS Large Print:

The Fate of Katherine Carr

Thomas H. Cook

An intriguing cold-case mystery **Guardian**

George Gates is a former travel writer. He used to specialise in writing about places where people disappeared, sometimes individuals, sometimes whole societies. Now, since the murder of his eight-year-old son, Gates writes for the town paper about flower festivals and local celebrities.

Enter Arlo McBride, a retired missing persons detective. Knowing Gates' past, he mentions the case of Katherine Carr, a woman who vanished 20 years before, leaving nothing behind but a few poems and a strange story. It is this story that spurs Gates to inquire into its missing author's brief life and dire fate, an exploration that leads him to discoveries about life and death, mystery and resolution.

ISBN 978-0-7531-8556-8 (hb)
ISBN 978-0-7531-8557-5 (pb)

Dying of the Light

Gillian Galbraith

. . . winning combination of character development and crime . . . **thebookbag**

Midwinter, a freezing night in Leith, near Edinburgh's red light district. A policewoman's flashlight stabs the darkness in a snow-covered cemetery. The circle of light stops on a colourless, dead face.

So begins the hint for a serial murderer of prostitutes in the capital city, and Detective Sergeant Alice Rice is assigned to the case. It takes more than the death of one of their number to keep the working girls off the streets, and DS Rice joins them in the back lanes and waste ground, searching for evidence from the girls themselves. But, as she discovers, it is dangerous for any female to get too close to a killer who has nothing to lose.

ISBN 978-0-7531-8452-3 (hb)
ISBN 978-0-7531-8453-0 (pb)

Snatched

Mandasue Heller

Can she save both her children? A single mother faces down a ruthless killer on a Manchester estate in Mandasue Heller's thrilling new bestseller.

Her schoolgirl daughter disappears, her little boy nearly dies in a fire — single mother Sue Day thinks things can't get worse. But Sue's troubles are just beginning. As neighbours, social services and the police turn the spotlight on Sue and her ex-husband, someone is making sure that her luck stays bad. The only person Sue trusts is using her — and won't stop until someone dies.

ISBN 978-0-7531-8484-4 (hb)
ISBN 978-0-7531-8485-1 (pb)

The Mind's Eye

Håkan Nesser

Most engaging **Telegraph**

Janek Mitter stumbles into his bathroom one morning after a night of heavy drinking to find his beautiful young wife, Eva, floating dead in the bath. She has been brutally murdered. Yet even during his trial Mitter cannot summon a single memory of attacking Eva, nor a clue as to who could have killed her if he did not. Only once he has been convicted and locked away in an asylum does he have a snatch of insight — but is it too late?

Drawing a blank after exhaustive interviews, Chief Inspector Van Veeteren remains convinced that something, or someone, in the dead woman's life has caused these tragic events. But the reasons for her speedy remarriage have died with her. And as he delves even deeper, Van Veeteren realises that the past never stops haunting the present . . .

ISBN 978-0-7531-8376-2 (hb)
ISBN 978-0-7531-8377-9 (pb)